PRAISE FOR LOST C

"You will cherish this story for its lush description, engaging characters, gasp-worthy twists, and touch of magic. Lost Coast Literary is a heartwarming reminder of life's mystery and a must-read for book lovers."

— ANGELA M. SANDERS, *AUTHOR OF THE WITCH WAY LIBRARIAN MYSTERIES*

"I absolutely could not put this book down. The descriptions of everything from the bookish decor of "The Ballad" to the wonderful people of the town and their many activities had my nose stuck in this book from cover to cover...*Lost Coast Literary* is the perfect book for any bibliophile who is ready to get lost in their next favorite read."

— KRISTI ELIZABETH, *SAN FRANCISCO BOOK REVIEW*

"Ellie Alexander is a book lover's book lover, and her passion shines out through every page of her latest novel, *Lost Coast Literary*."

— JENNIFER DEBIE, *ROSIE'S BOOK REVIEW*

"It's a grown-up fairy tale, with a touch of classic iterate vibe, like Jane Eyre or The Secret Garden, only lighter...it will wrap you up in a world that feels both comfortably familiar and completely original."

— K.B. WILSON, *GENERAL FICTION REVIEWS*

LOST COAST LITERARY

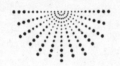

ELLIE ALEXANDER

Published by
Sweet Lemon Press LLC

LOST COAST LITERARY
Copyright © 2022 by Katherine Dyer-Seeley
All rights reserved.

Library of Congress Control Number: 2022900070

This is a work of fiction. All of the characters, organizations, and events portrayed in this novel are either products of the author's imagination or are used fictitiously.

Cover illustration by Jennifer Anne Nelson
Cover design by Gordy Seeley

For every reader who has found themselves transported to magical places through the pages of a book and in the process discovered who they were always meant to be.

CHAPTER ONE

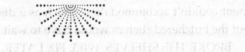

*J*ane Eyre? Jane Austen? Eyre or Austen? I picked up the matte cerulean phone case with a slate gray silhouette of Jane Eyre on the front, her bustled skirts and narrowed waist filling the soft leather cover, along with what was arguably one of the most recognized quotes from Brontë's classic: There is no happiness like that of being loved by your fellow-creatures. You can't go wrong with Brontë but then again, my *Emma* phone case was more traditionally bookish with its vintage watercolor design in romantic pink. Blushing rose vines, pastel butterflies, and pretty ribbons in a filigree pattern gave the *Emma* phone case the upper hand. Plus today, I was totally vibing on Austen. It had to be Austen.

That's the one. Don't overthink it.

I grabbed the case from the incurably tippy IKEA bookshelves my roommates and I had assembled while drinking not one, but three bottles of cheap Layer Cake red wine. Because twenty-four pages of instructions translated from Swedish to build a basic bookshelf called for more than one bottle of wine. As I removed the case from the top shelf, the entire rickety structure came crashing down. My most beloved possessions, hardcover collections of Sir Arthur Conan Doyle, *Anne of Green Gables*, and both Brontë sisters thudded to the floor.

Damn. I don't have time for this.

I can't be late. Not today.

I shoved the phone case, now with my phone in it, into my bag, ignoring the multiple missed calls and voicemails from my estranged uncle. At barely four hundred square feet my apartment couldn't accommodate so much as a dishtowel out of place, but the butchered shelves would have to wait.

BROKE THE SHELVES. WILL FIX LATER. SORRY.

I shot off a text to my roommates, grabbed a copy of the most recent book I'd been working on, a stack of reader's reports, and two prick-your-finger sharp purple pencils, and stepped over the carnage.

You can deal with that later, I reminded myself as I checked my appearance in the hallway mirror one last time. A single strand of my penny-colored hair had escaped from my ponytail. I tucked it in place and readjusted my olive glasses. I'd found the funky style at the California Antiquarian Book Fair. They were the perfect talisman for today.

I locked the door and hurried to the elevator. Fortunately, in the five months that I'd been in New York the one thing I had gotten used to was the subway system. I raced to catch my train, ending up breathless and starting to sweat as I ducked into the cramped compartment just before the doors closed. I rushed to grab the last empty seat on a hard, red plastic bench. A trickle of sweat dripped down the base of my neck. Great. The last thing I needed was a sweat-stained blouse.

The sweltering humidity and sulfur aroma of warm eggs made my nerves even more frayed. I glanced around trying to trace the source of the eggy smell. It didn't take long to discover that the woman seated next to me was making quick work of an egg salad sandwich. People who eat anything involving hard-boiled eggs on the subway should not be trusted. I inched away, sucked in a breath, and rummaged through my bag for a tissue to dab my neck.

The woman finished her smelly sandwich. She wadded plastic wrap into a ball and turned toward me. "You look nervous, hon."

"Yeah?" I chomped on my bottom lip. A hint of waxy coconut lingered on my tongue. There went my lip-gloss. "I have a big meeting at work."

"Ah. I see." She tossed the plastic wrap in her oversized bag and pulled out a carton of knock-off Oreos. "Want one?"

I shook my head.

She ripped the package open and devoured a cookie. "You have the greenest eyes I've ever seen and you look very professional. I'm sure you'll do great."

"Thanks." I bit my lip harder, raking my lip-gloss with my teeth. Why did strangers feel the need to chat? Small talk had never been my forte, as the honorable Miss Austen would say. With one exception. Books. If anyone brought up the topic of books or asked me my favorite read, I gushed like a thirteen-year-old girl. It was a serious problem. Ironically, my tendency to blabber over my latest book crush failed me in the dating department. The mere mention of Margaret Atwood or Amy Tan always sent dates scrambling for an excuse to make a quick exit.

"Where do you work?" she asked in a raspy voice. Given the stink of cigarettes lingering in the crowded compartment, I guessed my seat mate's throaty quality was due to years of smoking. No one in Silicon Valley smoked. Well, that's not true. No one *admitted* to it. That was one of the things I appreciated most about the city. Not the smoking, but the fact that no one seemed to care about what other people thought. And the smell. New York had a fragrance of stale cigarettes, street-side pretzels, and gritty hope. Silicon Valley smelled like the desperation of start-ups clinging to the last of their venture capital, smartcars, and aquamarine swimming pools that went unused.

"Publishing." I pressed my hands on my tailored black slacks, trying to force my leg to stop shaking. "I'm pitching a novel that I totally fell in love with at our sales meeting this morning. I'm going to absolutely die if I don't get to acquire this manuscript."

"Speaking of dying, I thought publishing was dead. Amazon and all that." She glanced to an advertisement for Amazon Prime above the handrails.

"Hopefully not. Otherwise I picked the wrong time to change careers." I scooted to my left to make room for a family moving toward the exit doors. I didn't bother to provide the woman seated next to me with a dissertation as to why publishing was thriving.

It was hard to imagine that a little over five months ago, I'd been living in Silicon Valley working at a soulless startup as a technical writer. The money was good, but editing pages and pages of mind-numbing, tech-heavy language and processing it into digestible, user-friendly content did nothing for my bookish tendencies. I'd minored in creative writing in college, but had followed Dad's advice to get a steady well-paying job. Look how well that had turned out.

No salary was worth the utter burnout I felt at twenty-nine. That's why one day last spring after eight hours in a windowless conference room hearing phrases like "let's circle back on that" or "I don't have the bandwidth" uttered at least a dozen times, I did something rash. Something slightly out of character. Something I had dreamt about, but never actually imagined following through on. I cashed in my savings and signed up for the Columbia Publishing Program. It wasn't cheap. The six-week intensive and move to New York had basically depleted my bank account, but I didn't care.

Honestly, even if I hadn't landed my dream job of being an assistant editor, I would have been fine working in the mailroom. Just the thought of being surrounded by books and people who love them made me smile. I still couldn't believe I was here. I, Emily Bryant, was in New York and about to pitch my first book at a major publishing house. Someone pinch me, please.

I was nervous about the meeting, but I didn't have a shred of doubt that I'd made the right choice. The only thing that made me worry was the fact that I was almost a decade older than most of my peers. My classmates at Columbia had gone straight from undergrad through the program and were launching their publishing careers in their early twenties. I hadn't envisioned living in a minuscule apartment with two roommates at almost thirty or basically starting over, but if I had stayed in Silicon Valley, I never could have lived with myself.

Don't go there, Emily. I reached for my bag and pulled out my worn copy of *Bridge to Terabithia* and one of my favorite purple pencils. I felt a familiar calm return to my body as I crossed out a line and made a new note in the margin. Editing centered me. I had re-edited this copy many times, but it didn't stop me from trying to find new ways to manipulate the story.

"You can't do that." The egg salad woman peered over my shoulder, invading my personal space. She looked as if she were ready to swipe the pencil out of my hand. "You can't write in a book."

"Yes, I can. It's my book." What I didn't tell her was that I had been re-writing book endings for as long as I could remember. It had become a hobby of sorts, or depending on interpretation, an obsession. Mom used to say that there was no reason to settle for an ending you didn't like. After she died, creating new endings had become my last point of connection with her. She would have agreed that there was no reason for Leslie Burke to die in *Bridge to Terabithia*. Instead of drowning in the creek, she could have swum to safety or been rescued. I refused to accept that books, even the most revered literary works, couldn't be altered and improved upon.

My phone buzzed. I inched away from the woman, who swapped her crumbly cookies for a pack of Marlboro lights. She clutched them tight as the train rumbled toward the next stop.

I glanced at my screen. The text was from the same number I'd been ignoring for a week. Last year, I'd made the mistake of not only following my uncle's Instagram account, but giving him my cell.

HI EMILY. IT'S UNCLE DANNY. SORRY TO DO THIS IN TEXT. HAVE LEFT DOZENS OF MESSAGES BUT HAVEN'T HEARD BACK. I HAVE SOME BAD NEWS. GRANDMA HAS PASSED. NEED YOU AND YOUR DAD TO COME TO CASCATA ASAP. SHE LEFT YOU THE BALLAD.

"What?" I gasped out loud. My neck prickled cold with damp sweat. My grandmother was dead, and she had left me a poem, a stanza?

The train lurched as it screeched to a hard stop. Another text bubble appeared on my screen.

THERE ARE SOME STIPULATIONS IN HER WILL— INCLUDING YOU COMING TO CASCATA IN ORDER TO INHERIT THE BALLAD.

That's right. The Ballad. I hadn't heard that name for years. Her estate, like every grand house, had its own unique identity.

"Hope they don't see you destroying books in your meeting," cigarette woman said in a warning tone, as she tucked a cigarette between her teeth and hurried off the train.

I stared at the gray text bubble on my screen. Gertrude was dead? And, even more surprising, she had left something— anything—to *me*?

Why?

The trickle of sweat transformed into a pool as if someone had just pushed me into the deep end. It was all too much. Gertrude. The heat. Humidity. Too many bodies packed together. The lingering reek of egg salad. A kid two seats away blaring K-pop on his phone.

I wanted off the train.

I needed off the train—now.

My stop was still five stations away.

Another text dinged.

HAVE TRIED TEXTING AND CALLING YOUR DAD TOO, BUT NO RESPONSE. KNOW THIS IS TERRIBLE TO

TELL YOU IN TEXT BUT WE NEED A FACE-TO-FACE. CAN YOU TALK TO YOUR DAD?

Yeah, like that would happen. I breathed in short bursts, sucking in air like it was about to run out.

I stared at Danny's text, trying to stop my fingers from trembling.

Dad hadn't spoken to Uncle Danny, Gertrude, or anyone else on his side of the family since I was eight years old. Neither had I. My memories of leaving Cascata were fuzzy at best.

The last time I'd been in Cascata was over twenty years ago. To this day, even a mention of Humboldt Bay or the beach made the veins in Dad's forehead bulge to the point of nearly bursting.

The origin of my family's falling-out had always been a mystery. A mystery that only revealed itself in snippets of untrustworthy memories. My therapist had once tried to reassure me that my spotty memories of my early childhood were normal. "A coping mechanism," she had called it. My brain's way of protecting me from the trauma of grief. Of course, in the same sentence, she had shared her concerns about my tendency to blur fiction and reality. Followed by a kind, yet firm, reminder that spending less time inside the pages of books and more connecting with the people around me might serve me better.

I hadn't heeded her advice, but I had learned that it was better to pretend like my family simply didn't exist. And, really, they didn't. Gertrude hadn't bothered to show up for Mom's funeral. That had been the turning point for me. Who doesn't come to her daughter-in-law's funeral? Who leaves her young granddaughter alone to grieve?

We might have shared the same DNA, but that was the extent of our relationship. In fairness I was probably tainted by Dad's perspective, but I didn't want to go to Cascata, and I certainly didn't want any part of an estate.

CAN'T TALK. ON MY WAY TO WORK. CAN I CALL YOU LATER? I'M SURE WE CAN SETTLE THE ESTATE REMOTELY.

Three animated dots appeared as Danny typed his response.

NOT REALLY A CHOICE. YOU HAVE TO COME. THE WILL SPELLS EVERYTHING OUT. THERE ARE SOME SPECIFIC REQUIREMENTS FOR YOU TO INHERIT THE PROPERTY. NEED YOU TO COME IN PERSON.

Crap. I let out a long sigh, barely noticing the overhead speaker announcing my stop. I gathered my things and held on while the train slowed.

Why now? This was a plot twist I would have loved in fiction. Not in real life.

I didn't have time to stress about this. This pitch meeting could mean the difference between being stuck writing reader's reports and rejection letters for another year or working on my own book for the first time.

Thanks a lot, Universe, I thought as I stepped off the train and turned toward uptown. The air was burdened with late August heat. Warm, ripe garbage piled along the sidewalk waiting to be collected and whisked away to a rotting piece of land on the outskirts of the city. Tourists queued for drippy ice cream cones and snapped endless selfies.

I power walked through the crowds. I had two blocks to pull myself together and make sure I didn't completely sweat through my new blouse.

You can do this, Emily. I breathed deeply and squared my shoulders.

The publishing house was located in an old Art-Deco building adjacent to the park. Every time I stepped into the lobby, my knees went weak. It was a thing of bookish beauty. An arched open stairwell cut from Italian marble led to an atrium on the second story where books stretched as far as my eye could see. A mosaic tile waterfall in cascading shades of blues cut through the marble floor. I wanted to break out in a happy dance as I scanned framed first edition copies and current bestsellers on display in clear, curved glass cases backlit with halo-like golden lights. The reception desk was flanked by towering vases filled with fragrant white lilies and gardenias.

I drank it in. I was here, actually here, following my dream. Sure, maybe it hadn't been quite as glamorous as I had imagined. I wasn't doing the serious editing work I had envisioned yet, but I was here and that had to count for something.

I paced around the marble lobby waiting for the elevator, as my mind drifted between rehearsing my pitch and panicking about how the hell I was going to explain that I desperately wanted to work on this book, but was potentially going to have to fly to California soon.

I blew out a long breath and ogled a leather bound first edition of *A Christmas Carol* behind the glass. If I had called Danny back earlier, would it have changed anything? Probably not. I'd been pulling all-nighters writing dozens of rejection letters. Getting in touch with an uncle I hadn't spoken to in years had been low on my priority list. I had figured that he wanted to try and use me as a way into contacting Dad, and I had no interest in getting in the middle of that.

The elevator dinged, shaking me into the moment. When I stepped out onto the tenth floor, I started toward the large conference room where the senior editors were already beginning to gather. An intern stopped me. "Hey, Emily. Piper needs to see you in her office."

"Now?" I adjusted the stack of reader's reports and the manuscript I was about to pitch.

"Yep. She said you can wait in her office. She'll be in soon."

My heart flopped. What did that mean? Had I done something wrong?

I stole a glance at the conference room and then headed the opposite direction to Piper's office.

In an attempt to shut out the anxious voice in my head, I tried to focus on the small room. It smelled like new books and something minty. The mint was from the trio of ceramic pots resting on the windowsill and the book aroma was due to the pale blue spines of trade paperbacks, hearty Army-green hardcovers, and blood-red mysteries, each of which had been arranged by color on a midcentury bookcase behind Piper's desk. Cover art framed the walls. Book bunting in rainbow tones stretched across the front of her tidy workspace, which was also occupied by organized pencil holders, bright colored paperclips, and a Jane Austen coffee mug. Stickers in the shape of a retro typewriter, a heart made from book stacks, and clever book words like bibliophile, book nerd, and #feels were stuck on the back of her laptop.

This was what I wanted. This is what I aspired to. Not that my cubicle was the worst. Piper had warned me when she hired me that the job was going to be a lot of grunt work, but that while I was stuck in cube world, crushing the dreams of aspiring writers with kind rejection letters, I would at least get to have a say in what books we published.

The meeting this morning was my first chance at that. The book I was pitching, *I Find You Tolerable,* was good. Like, stay up all night to binge-read it good. It was a re-telling of Jane Austen's life story. This time with a happy ending, an ending that I knew would resonate with readers. Jane doesn't write about love in the book, she finds her own love. Historical fiction, especially historical romcoms, were my sweet spot for genre. I had a solid feeling about this one.

But in the next moment doubt seeped in.

Was I wrong about that? Did I know what I was doing? My co-workers, other editorial assistants, seemed so self-assured and knowledgeable when they championed books at pitch meetings. Maybe I wasn't ready. Maybe that's why Piper had called me in.

A few minutes later Piper came in. She was in her mid-thirties with kind eyes and a literary scarf that I'd been coveting on Etsy for weeks. She greeted me with a wide smile. "Sorry to keep you waiting, Emily." She glanced at the stack of reader's reports I had placed on her desk. "You got them all finished? Nice work."

"No problem." I readjusted my glasses. They had a tendency to slip down my nose and give off an irritated librarian vibe.

She leaned back in a swivel chair and rotated from side to side, loosening her silky scarf. "How are you liking it here so far? You haven't had any regrets about giving up that tech salary, have you?"

I managed a laugh, feeling panic rise in my throat. Was Piper hinting that I had made a mistake leaving a good high-paying job at my age to make less money? "No, not at all," I managed to mumble.

"Okay, as long we get that out of the way first." She completely removed the scarf, folded it in a square and placed it on the edge of her desk.

I smoothed the sleeves of my shirt and concentrated on Piper's next question.

"Look, I got your email about *I Find You Tolerable*. It sounds like you really liked the book."

I smiled again. My knee finally stopped bouncing. "I didn't like it. I loved it. In fact, before you came in, I was admiring your Jane Austen coffee mug." I reached into my bag to show her my phone. "I had to swap out my phone case with this because it's perfect for today's pitch."

Piper gave me a probing glance. "Let's talk about your pitch."

I inched forward in my chair and launched into the speech I had stayed up late practicing. "My mom is the reason I love books. The story my dad likes to tell is that when I was younger, I would be completely devastated over any book that didn't end the way I imagined it should, so my mom encouraged me to re-write my own endings. That's what readers are going to get in *I Find You Tolerable*. A love story for the ages, an Austen re-write. In this book Jane finally gets to find real love, instead of dying a spinster who only wrote about love. I'm convinced this manuscript is going to be a bestseller."

Piper pressed her fingers together. "I love your enthusiasm, Emily, I really do." She paused and exhaled. "I'm sorry, but I'm afraid it's going to be a pass."

"A pass?"

"I ran it up the chain and the powers that be think Austen is overdone."

"Overdone? Austen—never." My voice cracked slightly. "I mean, this is a super-fresh take. It's giving Jane her own love story. I thought I was going to get to pitch this morning."

"I know, sorry. Time is tight, so unfortunately my bosses had to make some cuts." She gave me an apologetic smile. "It happens. It's the business. They feel like the market is saturated with Austen at the moment."

"So that's it? I don't even get to pitch it?" I bit the side of my cheek.

Piper gave me a pained smile. "No, sorry."

What a terrible day. First Gertrude. Now this.

Gertrude.

I clutched my silver locket, feeling it burn on my skin, as a memory of me clinging to Gertrude's legs, threatened to suck me under.

No. Not now.

Focus, Emily.

I released the locket and clamped my hands in my lap. I didn't have to open its brushed silver clasp to visualize Mom's face inside. I had memorized every subtle wrinkle on her skin and the way her lips curved into a permanent smile.

Piper appraised me. "Don't let this get under your skin. There will be other books."

"Yeah, I get it." Did I sound breathless? My cheeks began to burn.

She sat up straighter and set her feet on the floor to stop the chair from swiveling. "Look, I get it. I've been in your position. I know it's disappointing, but there will be other books. I want you in the meeting. You still get a say on the other pitches, okay?"

I nodded.

She tapped a silver smartwatch on her wrist. "We should get moving. Again, I'm sorry to be the bearer of bad news, but publishing is a long game. Put in the time. You'll have your own list in a couple years."

"Yeah, it's fine." I trailed off. *Please stay in control*, I said in a silent prayer to no one in particular. "It's just that I have a bit of an issue."

Piper's smile shifted. "What's the issue?"

My glasses began to fog. "A death in the family. I got a text on the way here, actually."

Piper sighed. "That's terrible. I'm so sorry."

"It was my grandmother. I didn't know her, really, but it sounds like I might need to fly out to California for a week or two. It's complicated. I don't want to go, but I'm not sure if I have much of a choice." I didn't want to come across as callous, but it was the truth.

I couldn't read her expression as she made a note on a sticky pad.

"No problem. How long do you need?"

"I'm not sure. Maybe a week." It couldn't take that long, could it?

"Whatever works for you and your family. You don't need to rush, but if you're up for it, I can send you with some reader's reports for the plane ride."

"Sure." My hands instinctively went to the silver locket hanging around my neck. It was the last gift Mom had given me before she died. Now Gertrude, whom I barely knew, was dead, too.

The rest of the day passed in a blur. I would have liked to take myself out for a strong gin martini with a twist of lemon. Instead I took the next train back to my apartment, where broken shelves and piles of books awaited me.

On the way, I texted Danny.

WHEN WOULD I NEED TO COME AND HOW LONG WOULD I NEED TO STAY?

He responded right away. THE SOONER THE BETTER. THE ESTATE REQUIRES LOTS OF MAINTENANCE AND THE WILL

STIPULATES THAT YOU NEED TO BE HERE IN PERSON BEFORE ANY OTHER PROCEEDINGS CAN OCCUR.

I wanted to shoot back a poetic slew of profanity. He hadn't shown up for Mom's service. I was supposed to drop everything and fly across the country for him? For a grandmother who had abandoned me?

YOU'RE SURE WE CAN'T DO THIS REMOTELY?

SORRY. NO. NEED YOU TO COME TO GET PROCESS STARTED. PROBABLY WILL TAKE A COUPLE WEEKS. ANY CHANCE YOU CAN TALK TO YOUR DAD?

I didn't bother to reply to that.

If possible, my shoebox of an apartment was even stickier than when I'd left. I cranked the window AC unit to high, not that I had faith it would do more than push sweaty stale air around the room. I ignored the mangled shelves and the whiny whistle of the AC for a minute in favor of making a pot of French press. The galley kitchen I shared with my roommates was more like a dark, neglected hallway crammed with miniature appliances better suited for a doll house. I turned on the kettle and scooped aromatic Ethiopian coffee into the French press. Orange blossom with a candy sweetness from the rich blend helped mask the lack of ventilation.

While the coffee steeped, I peeled off my interview attire and splashed my face with cold tap water. Then I gathered my hair into a ponytail, changed into a pair of shorts and the thinnest v-neck T-shirt I owned. I poured myself a cup of the strong brew, adding a splash of cream, and momentarily toasted my new career. Then I attempted to resurrect the shelves.

To call my effort to re-attach the shelves a success would be a stretch, but I managed to fake some semblance of construction. However, I didn't trust the shelves to support my collection of first edition hardcovers so I opted to stack them on the floor. With that task complete, I went to assess the state of my bedroom. It was already tight with boxes of my stuff. I had been planning to start organizing my things but there hadn't been time. If I was going to Cascata it would have to wait a bit longer.

While I remembered very little about my early childhood on Northern California's Lost Coast, the one thing I did remember was that it was cold and drizzly basically year-round. Did I even have any warm things to bring with me? August in New York hardly called for wool sweaters or rain boots.

I began the arduous task of packing my clothes while sipping more French press when my ringtone sounded and Dad's face flashed on my phone screen.

Shit.

I pushed my pile of tank dresses and cardigans to the far side of the bed before answering the FaceTime call.

"Hi, Dad, what's going on?" I tried to sound casual.

His whiskey-colored eyes pierced through me. "So, how did it go, Em? Did you sell your first book? You were supposed to call me as soon your meeting was done. I've been waiting by the phone."

"Right. Sorry. Something came up." I hesitated. If I told him about Uncle Danny's news that Gertrude had left me part of her estate, I knew he would freak out, but I couldn't lie to him either. "Dad, you haven't talked to Danny by chance, have you?" I clutched the phone tighter in anticipation of his reaction.

He scratched his cheek, and then gave his head a slight shake of confusion. "Danny? No. Why?"

"Nothing." My throat tightened. The walls of the tiny bedroom felt like they were closing in on me. "I didn't even get to pitch."

"I'm sorry to hear that, Em." His response was measured. Was that because I'd brought up Danny? "You pitch the next one, right?"

I inhaled as much courage as I could muster. "Yeah, I guess. That's the thing though, I'm not going to have a chance to do much work if I have to fly out to Cascata in the next couple of days."

"What?" A pained gaze crossed his face. "Oh, Em, don't go down that road with Danny. I don't want to see you hurt."

I repositioned the phone. "Listen, I don't think Danny's trying to hurt me." I tried to soften my tone. Had he listened to the messages Danny had left for him? Did he already know that Gertrude was dead?

I studied his aging face. The years had been kind to him. At sixty-three he could pass for someone much younger with his strong, stubborn jawline and copper skin, naturally tanned from working outdoors beneath the golden California sun. He raised me after Mom died. It had been him and me against the world since I was nine years old. Well, that's not entirely fair. Mom's parents were there, too. They let me spend countless hours swimming in their saltwater pool in the backyard and picked me up after school when Dad was busy digging irrigation trenches or planting native California black walnut trees.

I used to love tagging along with him on job sites. While he reviewed blueprints and soil samples, I would doodle in my sketchbook or find a shady spot to curl up with a well-worn copy of *Ella Enchanted* or *A Wrinkle in Time*. He wasn't a man of many words, but he appreciated words and that was all that mattered to me. He smelled like compost and pasty sunscreen, the old-school kind that came in a tube and left a thick white residue on the bridge of your nose no matter how much you worked to rub it into your skin. He loved nature and if you caught him in the right mood, he could talk for hours about migration patterns of butterflies and why it was critical to maintain patches of wildflowers and milkweed. What he refused to speak of was anything involving his family or our past.

"Dad, did you get Danny's messages?"

He gave his head a slight shake.

"Grandma Gertrude is dead," I blurted out.

A stranger might not have noticed the subtle shift in his posture. His callused hand absently massaged the base of his neck. "Yeah, I know."

"Dad, are you okay? Danny texted me on my way to work. He said she left me part of the estate, but her will says I have to be there. Why would she do that?"

"I wish I could tell you." He massaged the back of his neck with his free hand. "If you want my advice, Em, I would leave it alone. I don't want to see you getting sucked into their drama. I left that behind years ago."

"I know, but what do I do about the estate?"

"Let Danny figure it out. He's a smart guy." He cleared his throat and changed the conversation. "Tell me more about what your boss said."

I gave him the recap before we hung up.

Once our conversation ended, I exhaled slowly and set my phone next to the bed. Great. Now he was shutting down again, and I needed to try and organize my stuff.

Frustration threatened to overwhelm me.

I folded soft peachy and cream cardigans and my book-themed socks into tidy stacks, hoping that packing might help soothe my exasperation.

It didn't.

If I were being honest with myself, there was more. A longing took hold, manifesting itself like a physical ache in my body. Cascata. Grandma Gertrude. Memories that had haunted me for years. I sank onto the bed, letting them consume me. My fingers fiddled with the clasp on my locket until it fell open on my neck. I ran my thumb along the picture of Mom. Then I carefully pried her photograph out of the silver frame and set it on my bedside table. Beneath her picture was another. I removed the locket and stared at Gertrude's face. Her short graying hair and pixie like eyes had been ingrained in my memory, and yet I knew so little about her. I didn't even know who had put Gertrude's photo in my locket. Had it been Mom? Had she and Gertrude been closer than I thought?

Could Cascata hold the answers to my past? Maybe it was finally time to confront the family who had deserted me.

CHAPTER TWO

Two days later, after multiple attempts to fix the IKEA shelves and a long cross-country flight with a short layover in San Francisco, I found myself on a tiny plane bouncing up the jagged California coastline toward Humboldt County. The last time I'd been in Cascata felt like a lifetime ago. In all honesty, it was.

I pressed my forehead against the cold window, taking in the endless expanse of the Pacific Ocean. The sinking purple sun reflected on cresting waves. Wide banks of clouds hugged the shore. A flood of memories made my head feel fuzzy. Or maybe it was just the turbulence.

My most vivid memory of Cascata was from the summer I turned eight. Mom had taken me to Redwood Park, with its ancient forest in the heart of the small collegiate town, to break the news that we were leaving. She packed a picnic with our favorite bacon, guacamole, and slug slime spicy seasoning bagel sandwiches. Slugs played a predominant role in temperate rainforests. I remember it being nearly impossible to walk anywhere without passing a trail of slimy slug residue. Local merchants capitalized on the theme with creative bagel and pizza toppings, none of which actually contained slug slime. Thank goodness.

The sun made a rare appearance, cutting through the tallest trees on the planet and warming the damp grass, the day that Mom forever altered the course of my life. A group of college students in bikinis were spread out nearby, laughing and playing frisbee golf.

Mom leaned close and whispered in my ear. "Emily, that's Cascata. When the sun comes out, everyone is practically naked." She smelled of lemon and honey. "I'm going to miss the marsh and the way the clouds hang low on the horizon, but I'm not going to miss battling the mold and the slug slime on our front porch."

She went on to explain that we were moving farther south to Santa Clara where Dad would be starting a landscape architecture firm, we'd have my maternal grandparents and their dreamy swimming pool, and we'd be close to a research hospital.

At the time, I didn't understand that we'd never come back. Or why we needed to be close to a research hospital.

The pilot interrupted my thoughts with his announcement that we were making our final descent into Humboldt and to prepare for a bumpy landing. Charcoal clouds heavy with rain replaced the calming waves of the ocean as the plane banked toward the shore. Unlike the dazzling lights of New York, a pervasive mass of gray filled the skyline.

After a relatively uneventful landing, I made my exit, deboarding the plane on a set of stairs that descended into the cool evening air. Cascata's proximity to the coast meant that during the peak heat of summer, natural air conditioning in the form of cool ocean breezes blew into town. The paper-thin mist dripping from above made me glad I had packed a coat in my carry-on. I tugged it on and went into the terminal to retrieve my bag. A far cry from LaGuardia, the Humboldt airport consisted of a small baggage claim, coffee cart, and one gate for the single airline that flew in and out of the remote coastal community.

My bag was already waiting for me, as was Uncle Danny. I spotted him immediately. He looked like a slightly younger clone of Dad with a shaggy beard and black-rimmed glasses. They also shared a similar outdoorsy style. Danny wore a pair of jeans, ankle-high boots, a long-sleeved shirt, and a puffy black vest.

"Emily, over here!" He waved, holding a handwritten sign with my name.

"Hey." I greeted him with an awkward hug.

"How was the flight?" He took my bag and motioned to the exit. "The car is out front. I didn't bring the rest of the family. I thought it might be better if we had a chance to talk, just the two of us."

I followed him outside to his convertible Jeep. He opened the passenger door for me and put my suitcase in the back.

"You hungry? I thought we could get a bite and catch up." He slid into the driver's seat and studied me for a moment before turning on the car. "Wow, how long has it been? Twenty years?" He answered his own question. "I've thought this from your pictures online, but seeing you here, wow—you sure look like your mom."

The tender quality of his words made my throat constrict. "I could eat."

"Great. I'll take you to the pub." He pulled away from the curb. "So, tell me, how's the big city? New York, huh? That's a far cry from out here behind the Redwood Curtain."

"Yeah." Why was he talking like I had recently left?

"How do you like it there? People probably don't smile and say hi much."

"They didn't in Santa Clara either." I focused my gaze out the window as he drove along the winding Redwood Highway. Cascata was well off the beaten path, nestled on a remote stretch of coastline between the redwood forest and marshy lowlands. We zoomed on the two-lane road past mud flats and cow pastures that paralleled the sea, up into the tree line where giant redwoods reached out to greet each other, their limbs creating an impenetrable brilliant green canopy that would shroud the sun even on a clear day.

"Did you talk to your dad? Is he coming?" Danny kept his eyes on the road. Did he feel as uncomfortable as I did? We rose out of the tsunami zone, trailing a camper van packed for summer vacation. Its wheel wells scraped the pavement under the weight of bikes, coolers, tents, and inflatable rafts. Mist collected on the tops of the mighty trees dripping with moss and sparkling with dew. Everything was bathed in a hundred shades of green. If these ancient beauties could talk, what stories would they tell?

"No, he's not. Why would he come?" I took off my glasses and wiped a smudge off the lens with the edge of my jacket. "Listen, this is super weird for me. I don't really know what to say or why I'm even here. You know as well as I do that Grandma Gertrude and I never spoke. I don't remember much about her."

He kept his focus on the road. "I'm sorry that he's not coming, but Mom would have been so happy to know that you're here." He steered the conversation to news of my cousins, Arty and Shay, who were basically strangers to me, as was my aunt Keeshawna. I had a visual of his family in my head only due to the fact that he had tracked me down on Instagram a few years ago. Otherwise, I wouldn't have been able to pick any of them out of a police lineup.

The stunning scenery made for a gorgeous backdrop as Danny expertly navigated precarious drop-offs and tight turns. Not an inch of the forest floor was visible beneath the deep layer of glossy ferns and thick chunks of bark. The trunks of the imposing redwoods were nothing short of jaw-dropping. I felt as if I had been transported into their mystical, indigenous kingdom. They dwarfed Danny's Jeep and vanished into the cloud cover above.

Everything smelled of the wet and cool ancient earth, mingled with sappy pine and damp leaves. Once we began our descent out of the vast forest, glimpses of the ocean came in and out of my view. Fog clung above and below the cliffsides, like a slice of a fractured geode. The landscape shifted, showcasing swaths of purple and yellow wildflowers, spindly trees bending from the coastal winds, and herds of elk bedded down for the evening in grassy meadows.

Flashes of memories as ominous as a tidal wave triggered on a distant shore flooded my body. My toes in the wet surf. Women laughing. Books. Story time. Hot chocolate.

I clutched the hand rest and pressed my eyes shut as tightly as they would go.

A tiny voice in the recess of my brain whispered calming words. *It's okay. You're home.*

Home?

I opened my eyes a crack as a small sign pointing to Cascata came into view. Danny turned off the highway and steered into the sleepy town which was cut off from anything resembling a modern city. There were no big box chains, no fast-food restaurants, Starbucks, blow-dry bars, or high-end grocery stores. A tile mosaic lookout toward the northern coastline greeted visitors who made the trek to the often forgotten seaside town known for its craftspeople—artists, singers, poets, sculptors, and dancers who called quirky Cascata home.

"Here we are." He pulled into an angled empty parking space in front of a three-story butterscotch-yellow Victorian in the center of the palm-lined plaza in the heart of the city. Two bright blue surfboards were strapped down on the roof of the car next to us. The breezy plaza was enveloped by historic buildings restored to their original glory in varying shades of lapis, eggplant, pistachio, hickory, and graphite. Timeworn bricks carved a pathway around and through the plaza, dotted with eucalyptus trees and fragrant bunches of lavender.

I got out of the Jeep and took in the pub. The first floor and trim were painted in a contrasting dark green with funky lettering and artwork. Colorful glass balls had been strung along the peaked roofline, along with random decorations from every holiday, including a massive fake spider nearly as large as Danny's Jeep that hung above the sign on the door reading: *CASCATA PUB & CAFÉ*.

"This is your place?" I recognized the café from Danny's Instagram feed.

"Don't you remember it? Hasn't changed much. A fresh coat of paint every now and then. The coastal winds give the place a constant bashing, but otherwise we keep things the same. People seem to like it that way." He moved to hold the door open for me.

Inside, the funky décor continued with a cedar bar and colorful ceramic tap handles. Surfboards hung from the walls and ceilings along with inflatable palm trees and strings of chili pepper lights and pink Valentine hearts. The smell of hops and grilling burgers made me aware that I hadn't eaten anything since leaving New York and that with the time change, it was past ten for me.

"Grab a seat." Danny nodded to a table tucked into the far corner. "I'll get us drinks."

Jack Johnson played on the speakers. An eclectic mix of families and college students crammed into the pub, making the windows steam up and my head hum.

As I took a seat, the weight of the day crashed down on me. What was I doing? This was a mistake. I never should have come. Was it too late to run? If I could find an Uber, I could be back in New York tomorrow.

Did Cascata even have Uber?

Doubtful, I thought as I ran my hands over the laminated menu, noting the bony skeleton mounted above the booth next to a plump stuffed Santa. An open balcony with more seating upstairs continued the all-embracing theme. Intricately painted Day of the Dead skulls and retro travel posters of the redwoods and north coast made for a strange collection of décor, and yet somehow it worked.

Danny returned with two beers and a platter of fish tacos and toppings. "Make sure you douse those with the cilantro lime sour cream and pico de gallo. I made them fresh myself."

"Thanks." I reached for a taco and the beer, wishing I could stop the uncomfortable churning in my stomach. Dad was right. I should not have gotten on the plane. This was a mistake.

I took a sip of the beer and was struck by the barrage of flavors which were as unusual as the pub's oddly mismatched furnishings. Peppery spice mingled with sweet citrus and hops. It was like nothing I'd ever tasted.

"That's our Shark's Tooth," Danny commented with an approving smile. "It made us famous here on the Lost Coast twenty years ago when no one was brewing craft beer. Belgian white with coriander and orange. It never gets old. Been on the menu as long as I've owned the place. Speaking of that, do you remember how you used to hide out in the balcony upstairs? Your parents would bring you with a stack of books and pencils when we were renovating the building. You would spend the whole day with your books and pencils, coloring and reading."

I peered upstairs at the four-foot-high railing that enclosed the balcony. "No. I don't remember much." Weird fragments of half-formed memories flickered in my head, like light glinting on shattered glass.

He scooped shredded cabbage onto a taco. "Yeah. That makes sense. You were just a kid." We ate in an awkward silence until I decided to just go for it.

"What happened? Dad never talks about it. What is it that I don't know?" If I had come all this way, I might as well try to get some answers.

He puffed out his cheeks. "Emily, this whole thing is a mess. I made a promise to Mom on her deathbed that I would do everything in my power to get you and Stephen here and figure out a solution for the estate. But there's more. Her will, which I'll give you a copy of, explicitly spells out that I'm not at liberty to share any more with you. If I do, we lose the pub. You see, she bought this building for Keeshawna and me as a wedding gift. It's our primary source of income." He paused and studied my reaction for a minute.

Could he sense my frustration? That wasn't my question. Before I could respond, he continued.

"I can tell by your face that you're confused. Honestly, I am too. Mom was an amazing woman, but her putting our financial security at risk doesn't feel right. It's not like her. Her will makes all of us, you included, jump through a bunch of strange hoops. I know she must have had her reasons, but I'm just as dumbfounded as you."

The sick feeling returned to my stomach. I should have listened to Dad's advice and stayed in New York. "How did she die?" I drizzled sauce on a taco.

"Heart. She'd had trouble for years."

"I'm sorry." I bit into the juicy taco. Like the beer, an array of flavors and textures mingled together in an ambrosial balance—crunchy tangy slaw and Danny's melodic sauce. This was a seriously good taco.

He took a long, slow sip of beer. "She lived a good life."

Did she? I wouldn't know. Part of me wanted to scream. How was it that Danny's perspective of Grandma Gertrude was completely different than mine? Even if she and Dad had had a blowup, why had she abandoned me? When no one from the family bothered to acknowledge Mom's passing, I had known then that these weren't my people. A bitter taste lingered on my tongue, and not from the beer.

I decided to get pragmatic. "Can you suggest a good place for me to stay in town?"

Danny reached into his pocket and handed me a keyring with two keys, a utilitarian key and an old-fashioned brass key.

"What's this?"

"The keys to The Ballad. She left it to you. The house, the property, everything in it. There are some stipulations, like I said. You can review the will when we get to the house. It explains everything."

I picked up the keyring. It was warm from being in Danny's

pocket, and my first tangible connection to a woman who was nothing more to me than a faded memory that flickered in and out of focus like a failing light bulb. The absurdity of the moment hit me. "I don't want this, Danny. I don't want anything. Like I said, this is super weird for me. I don't really know you. I didn't know Gertrude. I used to be sorry about that, but I'm not anymore. I was just a kid. That was on her. And I know that you were close to her, and this must be weird for you too, but just tell me what I need to do to close out the estate, and I'll be on the next plane back to New York." I tried to hand the keys back to him, but he pressed my fingers closed.

The story I'd written about my past in my head to make sense of being abandoned was that the fallout between my parents and Gertrude must have been so brutal that they all decided it was better to sever ties for good. The only thing that made sense was that Gertrude must have hated that my parents had decided to leave Cascata. Maybe she felt betrayed by their leaving. Maybe she had begged them to stay, and when they'd refused, she held a grudge that she couldn't let go even with the passing years.

"Emily, it's out of my control. This is what she wanted. It's all spelled out in her will."

"No, sorry, I don't mean to be rude or ungrateful, but I don't need a house in Cascata. I live in New York. Plus, like I've said at least a dozen times, I didn't even know her."

But you want to know her, a voice in my head nudged. I forced it away and focused on Danny.

"I understand, but you have a legal obligation to fulfill, and then there's the fact that you're the only other editor in the family." The faintest glimpse of a smile that reminded me exactly of Dad tugged on Danny's lips.

"Editor? What's that have to do with it?"

Danny polished off his taco. "Finish your beer and I'll show you."

I wondered if the shock tingling through my body was evident on my face. The only other editor in the family? What did Danny mean by that?

CHAPTER THREE

$\mathcal{D}$anny's cryptic response made me chug the rest of my beer. We stepped outside where dusk filled the skyline with a marmalade sheen. People mingled in the center plaza with its leafy palms, flowerbeds, benches, and center fountain. A red brick sidewalk cut diagonally through the park, surrounded by colorful Victorians smashed together like Boston brownstones. We passed a surf shop with teal and pineapple sea and river kayaks, surf and stand-up paddle boards, diving equipment, and any other gear a newbie or intrepid adventurer might need for a day on the water.

"I take it water sports are big here?"

"When you live on the coast, you better love the water."

The plaza was oddly familiar. I found myself recognizing storefronts and replaying memories of eating pink doughnuts and drippy ice cream cones in the center park.

A toy shop, Tongue & Cheek Toys, caught my eye. The exterior of the building had been painted like the carousel scene from *Mary Poppins*. Sidewalk chalk, games, and kites in the shape of whales, flying dragons, and princesses had been strategically displayed in the front windows to draw in Cascata's youngest shoppers.

Next we passed Oceanic Coffee & Tea. I almost begged Danny to stop because the aroma of fresh-brewed coffee was so intense that I could barely resist. My stomach reminded me that two tacos and a beer were enough for the night.

The last shop on the far edge of the plaza made me stop in mid-stride. Letter Press was the stuff of my every childhood dream. An original letter press, assortment of vintage typewriters, and library card catalogues called to me from the large bay windows. The shop was closed for the evening, but I vowed to come back after peering in the windows to see rows and rows of leather and soft-bound notebooks, wax seals, Italian notecards, Montblanc pens, literary candles, and more.

This is my kind of shop, I thought to myself as we continued.

"Letter Press was Mom's favorite store. She would spend hours in there," Danny said with a satisfied smile, as if he had read my mind.

The boutiques, bookstores, and coffeehouses shifted to neighborhoods as we turned onto Grammar Street. White picket fences and gardens with flowering artichoke thistles in striking blues and mimosa trees with spindly pink blooms reminded me of something out of the pages of Dr. Seuss.

The houses appeared to get bigger and bigger as we approached the end of the street where a stately Victorian mansion situated on a hillside cliff stood like a towering fortress—The Ballad.

My breath caught as I gaped at the house that looked as if it had been plucked from the pages of a storybook. Painted in a delicate cream with bright white trim, the house exuded an angelic glow. Its patterned roofline, gingerbread shingles, ornate gables, and corner tower made me want to pinch myself.

This? Grandma Gertrude had left me this?

A copper weathervane in the shape of a rooster spun with the wind on the turret on the third floor as a memory of a grand literary party came rushing forward. Guests in costumes. A Sherlock complete with a deerstalker cap and magnifying glass.

Gandalf with his flowing robes. Hester Prynne's scarlet letter fashioned from a deep red silk ribbon. The scent of grilled salmon and roasted corn. Fairy lights. Music. Me as Pippi Longstocking. My naturally reddish hair sticking out in two wiry braids, and mismatched knee-high socks. Was it real, or a story I'd made up in my head?

"I think I remember this." A tingly sensation ran up my arms.

"It's hard to forget, isn't it? It's quite a house. Did I mention that it's on the National Register of Historic Places?" He motioned to a plaque posted on the black wrought iron fence that enclosed the enormous property. "It was built in 1884 and Mom was a stickler for making sure any updates were done to period."

He moved onto the wraparound porch where there were four green rocking chairs, potted plants, and strings of Tibetan prayer flags. "Why don't you go inside and spend some time looking around? I have to finish a few things at the pub. I can come back for you if you want to stay at the hotel, or you can stay here. It's up to you."

"Okay." I wondered if he could sense the trepidation in my voice. The house belonged on the pages of an F. Scott Fitzgerald novel. Not to me.

"Keeshawna got the guest room ready, but we also reserved a room at the hotel just in case." Danny looked like he was trying to gauge my comfort level.

"I think I'll stay and explore more." The thought of staying in the strange, sprawling mansion by myself sent a shiver up my spine, but I couldn't contain my curiosity either. I had been given a rare opportunity to learn about a grandmother who had only inhabited cobwebbed corners of my brain.

"Great. Make yourself at home. I'll bring your luggage in." He reached into the interior pocket of his vest and handed me a rolled-up file folder. "Here's the will. Go ahead and review it and let's plan to meet at Oceanic Coffee & Tea tomorrow morning." He gave me another awkward hug and left.

I unlocked The Ballad's front door and took a slow, steady

breath before stepping inside. The foyer was dark. I fumbled around for a light switch. When my hand finally connected with the switch, light flooded into the room, revealing exquisitely restored walnut hardwood floors. Stained glass windows in the curved entryway reflected twinkling butterscotch, plum, and sapphire beams onto the far wall. Two rooms adjoined the entrance hall. To my left was a parlor painted in muted beach tones with a built-in fireplace and bookcases filled with spines arranged by height and held together with chunky driftwood bookends.

Books. Oh, my God, so many books. I let out an audible gasp, unable to tear my gaze from the parlor, where an abundance of titles that rivaled that of any small library called to me. I could spend an entire day admiring Grandma Gertrude's enchanting collection of books. Books were my addictive craze. Forget about ice cream, chocolate, pot, your drug of preference. Give me a stack of books any day.

I felt like an over-enthusiastic puppy let outside for the first time.

Bone.

Squirrel.

Fire hydrant.

Books. Books. Books.

They aren't going anywhere, Emily, and you have a five thousand square foot mansion to explore. I tugged my attention away from the captivating shelves for the moment.

An intricately carved circular staircase sat in front of me. The ceiling stretched at least twelve feet above me. Period details were evident in the weighty carved moldings and brass hardware. A sign hanging from the newel post at the base of the steps read: PRIVATE.

Odd. The upstairs was private?

A cream-colored hallway lined with framed watercolor paintings and floral geometric handwoven area rugs led to the back of the mansion. The entire house had a cohesive natural ocean color palette in milky greens, harbor blues, and soft grays and creams.

But it was the room to my right that caught my eye. The hand-carved door was shut. Another sign hung from it: LOST COAST LITERARY.

"Lost Coast Literary," I repeated out loud. There was something oddly familiar about the name. Was it a memory? Something else?

I turned the handle, but the door was locked. Maybe one of the keys would open it. I tried the basic house key first with no success. The antique key didn't work either.

There must be a key somewhere else, I thought, as I ventured upstairs. The serene, soft lighting and gleaming redwood accents continued on the second floor. Ornate millwork, jeweled windows, and knotted spindles gave the space a spellbinding aura. I was completely caught up in its trance.

The house creaked and sighed as if readying itself for sleep as I wandered into a study with yet another fireplace and a bathroom with patterned tile floors and an attached sitting room. Farther down the hall there were five spacious bedrooms with carved oak fireplaces and three more bathrooms.

I fought back cloudy memories of running through the long hallway and pretending to put on lipstick in front of the antique mirror. Were they real or was I grasping?

The weight of the last few days and heaviness of the situation felt like they were collapsing in upon me. After checking each of the bedrooms, I decided that the last one on the left must have been the room Keeshawna had intended for me. A pretty ceramic vase with purple hydrangeas had been placed on the bedside table. The shutter style windows had been left slightly open to allow the Pacific breeze inside. A London mantel which had once burned with sooty coal had been converted to gas. I flipped a switch, sending orange flames flickering in the fireplace.

A four poster bed beckoned me in the center of the room with its butter-yellow down comforter. The sounds of chimes outside the windows brought another round of memories to the surface. Had Gertrude read to me here? Nestled somewhere in the recesses of my brain was the sound of her voice lulling me to sleep with passages from *The Secret Garden.*

"Do you hear those garden chimes, my sweet Emily? We have our own secret garden here, just like Archibald Craven's Misselthwaite Manor." Her silky hands had caressed illustrations of topiaries and creeping ivy as she turned the pages, waiting for me to soak up the pictures that accompanied the magical words.

Was it true? My hand went to my locket where the photos of her and Mom hung around my neck.

I couldn't trust my memories. They blurred together with the stories I had told myself about my family growing up and butted against Dad's narrow, unyielding perspective on the Bryant family. Being here was different than I had imagined, like The Ballad was welcoming me in with its sentimental melody.

I pushed thoughts of my cloudy past away and unpacked, placing my clothes in the vintage wardrobe and my toiletries in the adjoining bathroom with a clawfoot tub and a view of the sea.

Somehow, after unpacking I never made it back downstairs. Instead I curled up on the bed to review the will. I was the sole heir to The Ballad and Lost Coast Literary. However, in order to secure my inheritance, I was required to edit Gertrude's forsaken manuscripts.

Forsaken? The word girl in me was intrigued. Why were the manuscripts forsaken? And why did I need to edit them?

As I read on, the will spelled out that I could not list, sell, or make any changes or improvements to the property until the entire stack of manuscripts had been edited.

How bizarre.

A tingly sensation pulsed through my skin as I read and re-read the will. In order to inherit her property I had to edit old manuscripts? It didn't make sense.

Additionally the will noted that Danny and his family inherited the pub, the building, and all of its contents. Some of

Gertrude's specific personal items had been bequeathed to my cousins Shay and Arty, but otherwise we were to divide everything else amongst the family and split any remaining profits equally from an estate sale.

After spending an hour reviewing the legalese, I closed my eyes and drank in the sound of the ringing chimes and the faint hint of seaweed in the air. I felt oddly out of place and yet accepted by Gertrude's house. Maybe it was the lulling rhythm of the distant waves crashing on the shoreline, the tinge of salt, or the gentle, calming whistling of the wind, but before I knew it, my head fell heavy on the pillowy mattress, and I fell asleep dreaming about lost manuscripts and long-forgotten memories.

CHAPTER FOUR

$\mathscr{I}$ woke the next morning feeling surprisingly rested and eager to find the strange stack of manuscripts Gertrude had insisted I edit in her will. I dressed in layers, unsure what sort of weather was on the horizon for Cascata, and if I were being honest with myself, looking put together was like a form of armor as I prepared to step into unfamiliar family territory. My hair was tousled from a good night's sleep, so I pulled it into a messy bun, dabbed my cheeks with sunscreen, lined my eyes with a touch of chocolate liner and mascara, and finished the look with a nude lip gloss. I opted for a pair of moss-green glasses, skinny jeans, a lightweight hoodie, and my favorite pair of laser-cut bookish earrings. *Not bad, Emily, especially after a night alone in the cavernous mansion*, I thought, appraising myself in the mirror before heading downstairs to the office.

I stopped at the base of the stairs and studied the intricately carved office door. Morning light flooded into the arched entryway. To my surprise, a rusted key hung on a small hook next to the sign that read LOST COAST LITERARY.

How had I missed that last night?

That hadn't been there? Had it?

It was almost as if The Ballad were teasing me, offering me fleeting glimpses into the secrets contained within her walls.

Without hesitating, I stood on my tiptoes, took the key off the hook, and opened the door. I held my breath as I turned the handle and stepped inside. The office was as big as my entire New York apartment. Walnut hardwood floors and thick rugs gave the room a gentle feel, as did the Edison style lamps flanking a large desk. Period bookshelves with an intentionally distressed ladder ran the length of one wall. Every shelf was filled with titles in every format—hardcover, trade, mass market—and labeled by genre. There was upmarket fiction, assorted collections of the classics, shelves upon shelves of historical fiction, poetry, and thrillers. One entire bookcase contained nearly every editing manual I'd studied during my time at Columbia, along with some of my favorite writing self-help books like *The Artist's Way* and *Bird by Bird*, but no sign of forsaken manuscripts.

A butterfly print featuring the native butterflies of California and a hand-drawn map of Cascata hung behind Gertrude's desk. There were peace plants and succulents in glazed ceramic vases catching the light from the curved bay windows.

I caught a faint whiff of lavender essential oil as I moved closer to the desk, which was situated in front of a large bay window. The desk was tidy, with neat stacks of manuscripts, colored pencils in mason jars, sticky notes, and rubber bands. I flipped through the manuscripts to see if I recognized any author names. There were two non-fiction manuscripts that had recently been published, but again nothing labeled "forsaken," which only heightened my curiosity.

Had she simply been eccentric?

Was it a joke?

The one thing I was able to glean from her office was that she had been a tea drinker. That was obvious from the teacup and tins of assorted book teas, shiny canisters shaped to resemble hardbound books with punny names like Matcha Do About Nothing, War and Peach, and Oliver Lemon Twist.

I picked up a creamy embossed business card from a holder.

"Gertrude Bryant, book editor," I blinked and read the card aloud before adjusting my glasses to see if I had read it incorrectly.

Gertrude had been an editor? That's what Danny had meant? Why had Dad never mentioned that she was an editor, too? What was the connection to me?

I sat in her plush velvet chair, trying to gain control of my emotions.

Did I know that about her? Had I forgotten?

Did she know about me? Is that why she left the house to me?

"Gertrude Bryant, book editor," I read again, hoping that if I repeated it aloud something might click.

It didn't. I leaned against the high-back desk chair. A framed black and white photo in the center of the desk caught my eye. I picked it up for a closer look and allowed my body to sag against the chair as tears welled. The photo must have been taken not long before we left. In the grainy picture taken at the beach, my parents were grinning with their arms wrapped around each other. Mom's long, silky ginger hair caught the wind and brushed in front of Gertrude's face, who was laughing and kissing the top of my head. We all looked so happy. What had gone wrong? What could have been so terrible to tear us apart? And why was I here now?

I choked back tears, put the photo down, and opened the top drawer of her desk. Everything an editor of her generation might need was contained within the desk—notebooks, paper, paper, and more paper, and a variety of pretty notecards. I was struck at the contrast between the digital editing world I'd left in New York and Gertrude's office, which as far as I could see didn't contain a laptop or even a desktop computer. Time appeared to have stopped in her office sometime in the late 1980s. Her desk, while organized and tidy, was stuck in a time warp. There were memo pads, a fax machine, typewriter, and bottle of whiteout. I scanned the Rolodex on the desk and discovered names and numbers for agents, editors, and other professionals in the industry. I had so much to learn about her. Who were her clients? Did she freelance or do contract work for publishing houses?

Projects in production and those awaiting edits rested on the edge of her desk. I flipped through some of her most recent work, feeling the eager hum of anticipation that always came with diving into a new project.

Did Grandma Gertrude feel the same? Did the thought of wordsmithing someone's work entice her? I let my fingers linger on the pages as I leafed through the manuscripts, feeling a flash of connection.

It seemed like she had edited the gamut, everything from non-fiction to sci-fi. Her editorial feedback letters were thorough. I smiled to myself as I read familiar sentences that I could have written.

"One small suggestion you might take a moment to consider is your protagonist's motivation in this scene. What is her internal need and how are her choices reflections of that motivation?"

How strange to read Gertrude's comments and share a connection with her. And how weird to go through her things. Even though I knew she was dead, it felt like I was violating her privacy somehow. I hesitated.

Was this really what she wanted?

All of this was going to belong to me now?

As I returned her client files to their original spots, I noticed a small two-toned leather trunk with brass straps near the foot of the desk. I unbuckled the straps. An intense smell of mothballs hit my nose. I waved the scent away with my hand and investigated the trunk. A stack of manuscripts bound with large rubber bands sat on the bottom with a blue sticky note on the top. One word was written on the note in Gertrude's handwriting, which I recognized from her letters: FORSAKEN.

Forsaken. This was it. I'd found the forsaken manuscripts.

My hands felt clammy as I leafed through the stack, hoping to glean a clue as to what I was supposed to do with them. The will stipulated that I was to edit each of them. But how?

Did she want me to copy edit them? Give them a full editorial review?

There had to be dozens in the stack. Unlike Gertrude's other work, the forsaken manuscripts were completely unmarked. Not a single manuscript contained an author's name or contact information. Some of them didn't even have titles.

This was getting stranger by the minute.

A few days ago in Piper's office I would have relished the opportunity to put my touch on the page, but here in Gertrude's estate I found myself frozen. Editing could run the gamut of so many things. What did she want from me? Was this a test?

Tiny beads of sweat formed on my forehead. My glasses started to fog up.

You're just going to have to do it, Emily.

I picked up the top manuscript in the stack, which was untitled, and made some simple notes on the first page, noting a few grammatical errors and that the author referenced dialing a friend on her cell phone before the blaring ring of the phone interrupted her work.

If I had to guess, I figured the author was likely older than her protagonist, which was fine, but I cautioned the author to build authenticity by ensuring her cultural references matched the age of her main character.

As I was about to look at the next manuscript in the stack to try and get a sense if there were any common themes or issues amongst the forsaken pile, the phone on Gertrude's desk blared.

I startled, then dropped my pencil.

Geez, Emily, jumpy much?

Before I could answer the phone, it stopped ringing.

I looked from the manuscript to the phone and shook my head.

Okay, that was weird timing.

I moved on to the next section. The protagonist faced an inner conflict as she prepared to conquer a childhood fear. The setup was believable. A work-sponsored surfing event forced the character to confront her longstanding phobia of open water, but the author had missed a chance to share that struggle with readers. I made some suggestions about allowing the protagonist to take a beat, to even consider walking away and *not* facing her fear regardless of the consequences, before finally pushing herself outside of her comfort zone.

Is this what Gertrude intended? Was I on the right track?

I set the manuscript aside and flipped through the rest of the stack.

Were they all like this?

I had to be missing something. If Gertrude was giving me the house and her literary agency, why hadn't she left more details about her intentions for these manuscripts?

I massaged my jaw as I unbound the next manuscript. This one was titled *The Egyptian and the Alabaster*.

For starters, that title had to go. Anything that reduced characters to their skin color or ethnicity was a no in my book.

I gave the first few pages a skim. Then I moved to Gertrude's couch and read a while. It was a romcom in the style of a Jasmine Guillory novel about a young college student, Tamir, who worked at his family's bubble tea shop where he spent most of his time crushing on his classmate Kenzie, who had no idea he was even on the same planet. It was clear from the first few pages that Kenzie was a classic villain and completely wrong for Tamir, even though he didn't realize it. I was familiar with that romcom problem. Boy loves girl (or boy) who doesn't love him back, while his true love waits in the wings.

Gertrude was editing a diverse, contemporary romcom? Not exactly what I had expected to find in the stack, but then again I had no idea what I should be expecting.

The writing was solid, but the plot was in desperate need of work. Maybe that's why Gertrude had labeled it as forsaken. I skimmed the final pages to see if she had notes for the author, but there was nothing beyond the final chapter. Like the rest in the stack, no author was listed anywhere on the manuscript.

Was I supposed to suggest more extensive revisions? Or should I entirely re-work the scene for the author, being prescriptive in my feedback?

I removed a red pencil from Gertrude's collections of pencils, Sharpies, and ballpoint pens and made a few edits and notes.

In the first scene, Tamir works up the courage to finally talk to Kenzie when he delivers bubble teas to her and her friends. He overhears them planning an upcoming podcast for Cascata College radio about race relations on the Lost Coast.

It sounded like a good premise however, Tamir is Egyptian and Kenzie and her friends are all white. The scene as it was written was problematic on many levels.

~

"What do you think, girls? Are we agreed? Next hot topic is race." Kenzie twirled her honey-blonde curls.

Tamir cleared his throat, carefully balancing a tray of mango tea with blueberry bobas. "Here's your order." His face flushed with color. "You guys are going to do a podcast on race? That's cool."

"Right?" Kenzie turned to take her tea. "It's super timely and such an important issue. I think we have the perfect voice and platform for sharing how hard it is to be a person of color in Cascata."

Tamir tried not to fumble his words. He was talking to her. He was actually talking to Kenzie. Not just taking her order but having a real conversation. "That's such an awesome idea."

~

I stopped reading and rolled my eyes. *Come on, Tamir. Crush or no crush, you're going to pass the mic to four white women to talk about race? I don't think so. I can fix this.*

I redlined the section and re-wrote the scene. Instead of encouraging his crush to go ahead and expound on her thoughts on race, Tamir confronted her. *No girl is worth sacrificing your values,* I noted in the margin.

Before I could read on, my phone buzzed with a text from Dad. DID YOU MAKE IT SAFELY?

I set the manuscripts aside to text him back. YES, GOT IN LATE LAST NIGHT. HOW ARE YOU?

FINE. His single word response told me everything I needed to know.

CAN I CALL YOU LATER? WE NEED TO TALK. I hoped that would appease him, as I returned the bundle of manuscripts to the trunk and locked the office door. I wanted to explore more, to ferret out the truth of my memories and my past. Already, after one night, I was opening my eyes to the possibility that Gertrude had been as complex as any character on the page.

But for the moment, I was due to meet Danny. The house would have to wait.

Outside, the musk and sandalwood scent of the Pacific and a cool morning breeze greeted me. By morning's light, the Queen Annes in the neighborhood were even more impressive. So were the brightly colored Victorians converted into shops and boutiques that surrounded the plaza. The beach motif—seashell wreaths, wooden crabs, aqua waves—ran through most of the buildings. I admired ceramic pottery and blown glass ornaments at the gallery before making my way to Oceanic, a popular hangout for college students and locals alike. That was true for most of the Lost Coast. Not many tourists ventured this far off the beaten path, unless they were dropping students off at Cascata College, the small liberal arts college nestled at the edge of the redwood forest.

A group had gathered in front of the surf shop that Danny and

I had passed by last night. I froze in mid-stride as I overheard a staff member trying to console a woman who had her wetsuit half zipped. She was using her surfboard like a barricade as she rocked back and forth on her ankles, repeating, "I don't think I can do this. I don't want to do this."

Her words had an uncanny familiarity, like the passage I had just edited.

What was wrong with me?

I scouted the area around us.

My adrenaline must be running on high.

I was imagining this, right?

I stole one last glance at the woman, shook my head and moved on to the coffeeshop.

The smell of strong coffee and cinnamon rolls made my stomach grumble as I walked inside. Retro couches in tangerine and teal sat in the center of the coffee shop. Smaller two and four-person tables were scattered throughout the rest of the cozy space. Vinyl records and old album covers in silver atomic-style frames blended with lobster and octopus throw pillows and acrylic paintings of the sea.

At the coffee counter I studied the chalkboard menu. One side of the menu listed classic lattes, mochas, pour-overs, and the other had an extensive list of bubble teas.

Bubble tea, really?

It's just another coincidence, Emily, I told myself, not fully believing it.

I needed to pull it together if I were going to have a coherent conversation with Danny.

I touched my throat and studied the assorted coffee mugs resting on shelves next to the menu. None of them were uniform. Not like the classic Italian white mugs found at most New York coffeehouses. Oceanic's coffee mugs shared one similar theme—the sea. There was a turquoise turtle mug, an ocean-hued glass mug, and mugs with funny sayings like Life's a Beach and Resting Beach Face crowding the counter.

I decided on a latte and breakfast burrito with hash browns, eggs, and veggies.

The young college student behind the counter with dark skin, even darker hair, and a welcoming grin waited to take my order. My eyes were drawn to the chalkboard name tag pinned to his apron.

"What can I get you?" he asked.

"Uh, um, I, um." I was having a hard time finding words as I stared at the name embroidered on his brown apron. "Sorry, is your name Tamir?"

"Yeah." He tapped his chest. "I'm Tamir."

"Weird. Sorry." I pushed my glasses up the bridge of my nose and studied his apron, unable to pull my eyes away from his name tag. "Not that your name is weird. I happened to be reading a manuscript earlier, and the protagonist is named Tamir. It's not a name I've heard much."

"Yeah, tell me about it. I've said that to my parents for years. You know how much easier it would have been if they had named me Ryan or Brady or something all-American?" He motioned behind him where a couple prepared food in the open-concept kitchen. "Nope. They had to go for a family name. They claim the name came to them like a sign from Allah during Ramadan the first year they were married. Tamir was my dad's great-uncle's name, but really, I think they were just lightheaded from the fasting."

I chuckled. "It's a great name." And I'm totally losing it, I thought as I paid for my order.

A guy in line behind me stepped up to put in his order, while I waited for my latte. I couldn't help but eavesdrop.

"Hey, Tamir, how's it going?" the guy asked.

I stole a glance at him. He was dressed in a faded flannel and jeans. He reminded me of a rugged Hugh Jackman.

"Not bad." Tamir switched on the espresso machine.

"I haven't seen you around the pub. I thought you were going to come to our storytelling night."

Tamir kept his focus on pulling shots of coffee. "Yeah, I've been pretty busy."

"You should come by, man."

"I don't know," Tamir made himself smaller by curling his shoulders over as he topped my latte off with foam and handed it to me.

"Listen, no pressure," the guy in flannel said. "I'd love to see you do your thing, that's all."

I took my drink and went to find a seat.

Tamir returned a few minutes later with my breakfast burrito, a side of guacamole, and a ramekin with fruit salad. I sipped my coffee and waited for Danny to show up. I was going to have to find a way to tell him I planned to sell The Ballad. I couldn't get a read on what his angle was, but I didn't have time to waste. My new life was waiting for me in New York. According to the will I had to stay in Cascata until I finished editing the forsaken manuscripts. If I were here and putting my dream job on hold, I intended to do everything I could to understand why Gertrude had left me all those years ago, only to now give me the most valued piece of her life.

A group of college students squeezed into the table next to mine. They were clad in Cascata gear with matching ponytails, fleece leggings, and Birkenstocks.

I would have to bet that studying in Cascata was a very different experience than studying at Columbia. Grecian architecture and Harry Potter-style buildings in the heart of New York were about as far apart from Cascata's dense redwood forests and laid-back beachy atmosphere as they could be. The students' conversation mingled with the background noise as the coffee shop grew busier.

I checked my phone. Danny was running late, and I felt anxious to get things rolling. I was nearly finished with my latte when Tamir approached the table next to me, balancing a tray of creamy orange drinks with blue bobas floating at the bottom of the clear glasses like bubbly gems. "Here's your order. Did I hear you say that you guys were going to do a podcast on race?"

The dregs of my latte caught in my throat. I coughed. Did he just say podcast?

No, I had to be imagining things again. Maybe I was slipping into a fictional world.

One of the young women turned to face him. She had a heart-shaped face, light blue eyes, and curly blonde hair twisted into a ponytail. "That's us." She took her tea. "It's super timely and such an important issue. I think we have the perfect voice and platform for sharing how hard it is to be a person of color in Cascata."

What was happening? Was I dreaming?

I coughed hard, nearly spraying coffee across the table. Then I pinched my forearm—hard—trying to make sure I wasn't asleep. Pain radiated up my arm, and a small red circle formed on my skin.

Tamir finished passing out the drinks and tucked the tray under his arm. His voice quivered a bit as he spoke. "Uh, don't you think that it's ironic that the four of *you* are going to talk about race?"

The young woman scowled. "No, why?"

"Because none of you have skin like this." He tapped his forearm.

I was afraid he was going to drop the empty tray from the way his body visibly quaked.

The pages that I had re-worked played out in front of me word for word. Everything around me faded while Tamir and the students he was arguing with came into crystal clear focus like a cut scene before a commercial.

Was this stress? Was I hallucinating? I pinched myself. Twice. This wasn't real. I must be having a mini breakdown. After all, I had just flown across the country, learned that Gertrude was dead, that she too had been a book editor, and that I had inherited her house and business. That was breakdown worthy, wasn't it?

I listened as more of my edits came out of Tamir's mouth.

Maybe this was another coping mechanism, blurring fiction and reality like my therapist had said. A way to push out the pain and confusion of being in Cascata again. I rubbed my sweaty palms on the top of my jeans, otherwise remaining perfectly still as I tried to take in every word Tamir said.

Or was it jet lag? Yes! I'd heard that people had strange reactions to lack of sleep and time zone changes.

Tamir continued to push his point as the young woman and her friends fumed.

"I don't think you get it," she tried to clarify in a huff. "We're trying to use our voices to help put an end to white privilege."

"But isn't that white privilege?" Tamir blinked rapidly, shielding his body with the empty tray as he echoed what I'd penciled on the manuscript.

The room began to spin. My breath felt shallow. I tried to drink more of the latte, but my stomach bottomed out like a plane ride from hell where the captain reminds everyone to buckle their seatbelts for some "bumpy" air ahead just as the plane plummets a hundred feet in the sky.

Either I was losing it, or my edits had just happened in real life.

CHAPTER FIVE

"*A*re you giving me the side eye?" Kenzie stared Tamir down.

He took a step backward.

"You should be grateful. We're trying to help you." She flipped her hair.

Her friend, with a matching blonde ponytail, leaned in. "Drop it, Kenz."

Tamir reeled backwards as if physically assaulted by the impact of her words. He tucked the empty tray under his arm without saying more and returned to the coffee counter.

Kenzie stared him down. "This is the problem with race." She spoke loud enough for everyone to hear her. "You can't say anything if you're white."

Her friends encouraged her to sit down, but she shot Tamir a nasty glare and stomped toward the door. As she tried to yank the front door open, her Birkenstock wedged in the threshold, causing her to nearly smack her face into the glass.

"God!" She tugged her sandal free and slammed the door.

The coffee shop had gone quiet. Chatter amongst customers, the whir of the blender, and hum of the espresso machine had ceased with her outburst. Kenzie's friends gathered their things.

They reminded me of the troupe of self-absorbed characters from *Mean Girls*.

I drank the last drops of my latte, taking sidelong glances at Tamir to make sure he was still here. My scalp prickled like my brain cells were working overtime, trying to process what I'd just seen. This was more than a coincidence. I wasn't imagining this— my edits were actually happening in front of me.

Oh, God.

One cup wasn't going to suffice after what I'd just witnessed. I stood to get a refill, placing my hand on the center of my stomach, and forcing myself to breathe.

Kenzie's friend who had tried to calm her down apologized profusely to Tamir. "I'm so sorry about that. We'll get out of here if you don't mind giving me some cups to go."

Tamir handed her four cups.

"She didn't mean it. She's just on edge because our Poly Sci prof has been all over us to examine our roles in race and Kenzie has always thought of herself as super progressive, so I think the conversations we've been having on the quad are getting to her, you know? She thought this podcast would make a big statement."

"Yeah, yeah. I get it." Tamir stuffed his hands into his apron pockets. "It's cool."

"I know, that was bad but she's usually pretty cool."

Why was she defending her horrible friend? And why was he saying it was "cool"?

"You need straws and lids?" Tamir asked, reaching for a stack of recycled plastic straws.

"Yeah, thanks." She secured lids onto the drinks. "I've seen you around campus. You're an English major, right? Didn't I hear that you were going to do a podcast too?"

Tamir turned away from her to grab two breakfast scrambles from the kitchen window. "Uh, that fell through."

"Oh, right. Sorry, and sorry about Kenzie. Maybe I'll see you on campus?" She stalled for a second as if trying to find a way to salvage the conversation.

"Yeah, sure." Tamir looked to me. "Did you need a refill?"

Kenzie's friend balanced the bubble teas and ducked away.

Someone must have turned up the music because a reggae beat and customer chatter returned to the crowded shop. I handed Tamir my mug. "A black coffee would be great."

He deftly filled my cup while passing plates laden with thick-cut bacon and sourdough toast to another customer. "Room for cream?"

"Sure. Thanks." Still dazed, I took the coffee from him and found myself trying to take in every detail about him. His thin, yet muscular arms. A misshapen mole on the top of his cheekbone. His enviable black lashes which practically touched his thick eyebrows. Who was the real Tamir? What was his motivation? Did he have a quest other than pining over the wrong girl?

My mouth felt like parchment paper as I tried to think of something to say to him. "Do you know those women?"

"Not really." He wiped down the counter. "I mean, I kind of know them."

I momentarily considered telling him about the forsaken manuscript. I could feel the words welling up in my throat. Did I owe him an apology? An explanation? Had my edits crushed his dreams? But no, Kenzie was clearly the wrong girl for him. "I wouldn't worry about her. She doesn't seem worth it."

"Huh?" His eyebrows squished together.

I fumbled over what to say next. Instead of coming up with a platitude about love, I just stood there staring at him.

"Are you okay?" Tamir tilted his head and looked at me with concern.

"Yeah, sorry."

A man behind me cleared his throat to signal me there was a line waiting.

"Sorry. I'm just cold. I'm not used to rain and sixty degrees in August." I cradled the mug in my hands and went back to my table. At my seat, I glanced around the shop, not really able to take anything in. I half noticed a Fleetwood Mac original album cover mounted on the wall near my table and that the light wood floors had been buffed and painted in three shades of blue.

Was this in my head? Had I made it up? Dad had always claimed that my voracious approach to reading meant that I spent more time in fictional worlds than this one. It's not that I didn't have friends. I got invited to my fair share of birthday parties as a kid. It was more that I was most comfortable with my books. For sleepovers I would pack pajamas, a toothbrush, and at least three titles in case I got into a particular book mood. Even now as an adult I enjoyed happy hour with my roommates, but I was usually the first one to call it a night and sneak off to the comfort of my bedroom, seeking solace in the pages of my favorite reads.

I removed my glasses, rubbed my eyes, and blinked about a dozen times, hoping that I might wake up from a strange dream.

"Emily?" Danny's voice cut through the fog. "Hey, how's it going?" He waved his hand in front of my face, trying to get my attention.

I sat up straighter and put my glasses on. "Oh, hi. How are you?" My voice sounded robotic.

"I could ask you the same. Rough night?" He straddled his chair and rested his elbows on the table. "You look kind of groggy."

I shook my head a bit. "No, believe it or not, I slept great."

"The Ballad sings everyone to sleep with the sweetest of dreams," he replied with confidence. "Must be a touch of jet lag."

Yes, jet lag. That had to be it. There was no other logical explanation. It was a quirky moment. A crazy coincidence. Nothing more. I'd embellished the experience, making it seem weirder thanks to jet lag.

Only I'd slept better than I had in years last night.

"Sorry I'm late." Danny pushed back his chair. "Let me grab a coffee and we can chat."

While I waited, I massaged my temples and reminded myself

to breathe. I didn't know Danny well enough to tell him what had happened. It was probably a random coincidence that I had spun into something more. Right? It had to be.

I scanned Oceanic. No one else in the busy shop appeared fazed by Tamir and Kenzie's encounter. It had already been replaced by talk of tide tables and fishing forecasts.

"So, you had a good night's sleep and now you're ready to face the day." Danny raised his ceramic mug to me. "Where should we start?"

That was a loaded question. If it were up to me, I would start twenty years ago when my parents took off and never looked back. Somehow, I didn't think that's what Danny meant.

"Why didn't you tell me that Gertrude was an editor?"

He shrugged. "I thought it would be better for you to see her office in person. That's part of your inheritance, too. Lost Coast Literary goes to you."

"But I don't get it. She didn't even know me, and why am I supposed to edit old manuscripts? It doesn't make sense."

"No idea on that, really." The same ambiguous smile crossed his face. "I know it must feel like that, but hopefully the longer you're here, the more you'll be able to see how much she cared."

"I'm not staying. I have to get back to New York. This is my dream job. I gave up everything to make it happen—a huge salary, my family in Santa Clara. I need to get back to New York as soon as possible."

"Yeah. If it's really your dream job." He didn't sound convinced.

His doubt triggered something in me. I thought about Tamir's story and the forsaken manuscripts. How was I editing my own story? If books had taught me anything, it was that the easiest path rarely led to happiness. But my dream was in New York, not here. Was I intentionally trying to sabotage my own chance at happiness in order to understand our family rupture? Was it worth it? Dad's concern rang in my head.

I kept tight hold of my coffee cup in hopes that it might steady me. Confrontation has never been my strength, but I needed answers. "Like I said last night, I'm confused about what I'm doing here. Danny, I'm confused about what Grandma Gertrude wanted with me. I'm confused about everything, The Ballad, Cascata, all of it. And you should know that on top of that, Dad is really worried that I came."

Danny cleared his throat. "Whoa, slow down. It's eleven, the slow brunch hour." He tried to smile but it fell short when he saw my face. "Look, I get it. Like I said last night, this has to be a lot for you. It's a lot for me, too, but I'm trying to trust that Mom had her reasons. Maybe you can try to trust that."

"That's a big ask. I barely know you."

"You're a Bryant. You're family. That's what counts." He stirred his coffee with a small spoon.

I decided to cut to the chase. "Can we talk about what happened with my parents, then? I'm going to try to talk Dad into coming out here, but I have no idea how to make that happen when I have no idea what went wrong." I wondered if Danny picked up on the fact that I was on the verge of losing it. My head pulsed with pent-up frustration and confusion. I took off my glasses and wiped them on my sweatshirt again. Had the temp risen or was it me?

Dad had refused to divulge a single detail about his family. A family that had basically abandoned me from my pre-teen years through adulthood and I was supposed to simply embrace and be grateful that I had inherited a house and business I didn't want? No thanks.

Danny fiddled with the zipper on his vest. It reminded me of something a sailor might wear, dark navy blue with bright orange trim. "What has your dad said?"

"Nothing. Never. No matter how many times I've asked, so I just decided eventually to stop asking."

He tapped his knuckles on the table. The way he drew in a long, methodical breath reminded me of a lawyer carefully considering how their words might impact a client before speaking. "If your dad hasn't told you anything, I just don't think it's my place to say." Danny unclenched his fist. "I do believe that you're supposed to be here, though. Mom might have used unconventional tactics to get you here, but nothing she did was ever malicious."

"Danny, I don't think I'm *supposed* to be here. I really don't." I fiddled with my glasses. "I think the best idea is for me to forfeit the property—either to you or whoever—and take the next plane to New York. I don't have any attachment to Cascata or Gertrude. I'm sorry that you think I'm meant to be here, but I'm not."

"Don't do that, Emily." His voice got louder. "Give it—us—a few days? I'll keep trying to get in touch with Stephen, too. Okay?" It wasn't really a question. More like he was clinging to hope. His shoulders curled over as he waited for me to respond.

I pushed up my glasses. "Are you sure I have to edit the manuscripts?"

He nodded twice. "Yeah, the property is yours to do what you will after you fulfill your editing requirements."

My coffee had gone cold. Not that it mattered. I already had the jitters without another dose of caffeine.

He sounded resigned. "Let me introduce you to a friend who's a real estate agent. He should be able to at least start the process of figuring out an estimate on the property for you."

"Okay, thanks. What else?"

He reached for a packet of sugar, ripped it open, and sprinkled it into his coffee. "Your cousins and aunt are looking forward to seeing you. Are you up for a late lunch at the pub? I figured you'd want to spend some more time this morning going through the house."

Were my cousins eager to see me? Again, Danny's strange insistence that we were one big happy family made no sense.

"Sure."

"Good. You want to say one o'clock? We'll meet you there." He left his coffee untouched. "I'll make a call to Cameron, my friend in real estate. You're probably going to need to arrange an estate sale as well. I can put you in touch with another friend for that."

"Wait. Don't you want to go through the house, too? There must be things you and your family want as mementos."

Danny stood. "We can talk about that at lunch."

"Okay." I grabbed my purse and followed him outside, giving Tamir one last parting glance. I wasn't one for pity, but this felt so unfair. Why did I feel like a villain in this narrative? Danny was clearly upset about my decision to sell the house, and I had a sinking feeling that our lunch date later wasn't going to be the happy reunion he envisioned.

I needed to get back to The Ballad and check the forsaken manuscripts again. Had Tamir and Kenzie really just said the words that I'd written, or was it a random coincidence?

CHAPTER SIX

$\mathcal{I}$ left the coffee shop and sprinted down the brick path through the plaza, straight to The Ballad.

The minute I unlocked the front door, I dropped my bag in the foyer and made a beeline to the trunk of forsaken manuscripts. I had to know more about Tamir's story. I had to figure out how Tamir and Kenzie's scene had ended up playing out right in front of me. Not to mention where the manuscripts came from. How did they end up in Gertrude's office? Why did she want me to edit them? And if I edited another one, would it happen again?

I kicked myself for not asking Danny more about Gertrude's professional life. If I hadn't been reeling from witnessing my edits leap from the page, I might have had the wherewithal to probe deeper.

There was one place to start—the forsaken manuscripts. An equal sense of dread and excitement filled me as I lifted the creaky lid on the trunk and was met with the same musty aroma of mothballs.

I handled the stack gingerly as if they were fragile and might vanish upon contact with the air. Tamir's story was on the top. After another review there was nothing that pointed to who had penned the story. Not an author name. Or a return address. Nothing. I re-read through my suggestions, trying not to hyper-ventilate.

I pressed two fingers to the side of my neck to check my pulse. Heat rushed to my face, and my fingertips left sweaty marks on the pages. I wasn't imagining this. Tamir and Kenzie had acted out what I had scripted like a scene from the stage word for word.

OMG.

I sucked in short breaths.

This is really happening.

I set the manuscript aside and picked up the next manuscript, *Dashwood Toad.*

Yet again, no author name appeared anywhere on the page. Where had these come from and why had Gertrude insisted that I be the person to edit them?

My hands trembled. There was only one solution. I was going to have to edit again in order to prove or disprove my theory.

Your theory.

That sounds crazy.

I skimmed the first page of the next forsaken manuscript. It was easy to assume from the title that *Dashwood Toad* would be a regency romance in the style of my beloved Jane Austen, but after reading the opening scene I realized I was mistaken. The book began with a meet-cute on the beach. Sienna, a woman in her mid-thirties, is out for her afternoon run on the beach when a fluffy goldendoodle chases after her. The dog's owner tries to get the dog back but leaves without introducing himself.

"Dashwood! Dashwood Toad, get back here!" the man hollered as he sprinted through the hard-packed sand.

Sienna slowed her pace to let him catch up, feeling the wet tongue of his furry friend on her exposed leg.

"Dashwood Toad—knock it off!" the man yelled louder.

Sienna chuckled and reached down to pet the dog. Its fur was a mix of soft fluff and wiry curls.

The man raced closer, panting for breath. He caught the dog's tie-dyed collar. Then he clutched his taut stomach. Exhaling with force, he took a good minute to catch his breath. "Sorry about that. He thinks that anyone who happens to run by him is his new running partner. Obviously, I'm nowhere near fast enough. This is one of those 'who's running who' situations."

"No worries." Sienna brushed her hands on her Lycra jogging skirt, trying not to look obvious as she stole a glance at his athletic hippy style. "Is his name really Dashwood Toad?"

"Yes. This is the extraordinary Dashwood Toad, named after two of my favorite literary characters."

Sienna jogged in place to keep her heart rate up. "Dashwood, as in the Dashwood from *Sense and Sensibility*?"

"You got it." The man's breathing had returned to normal.

"I'm stumped on Toad, though."

"*Frog and Toad*. Classic children's lit."

"I completely forgot about those books. I loved Frog and Toad. The one where they make cookies, but Frog eats them all? I felt him on that, because how can you resist hot-from-the-oven chocolate chip cookies?"

"You can't." The man's arm jerked as Dashwood Toad caught sight of a beagle farther down the beach and bounded away, dragging the man with him.

The scene ended without the characters swapping names or contact information. How could a romance develop without a way to connect? I made notes in the margin, trying to ignore the nagging voice taking over space in my head as I penned a new direction for Sienna.

Was this a mistake?

Was I twisting fate? Playing God?

But I had to know whether there was something special about Gertrude's forsaken manuscripts. There had to be a reason she had insisted that I edit them.

Rather than having the man run off with his dog, I re-wrote the scene with Sienna introducing herself and inviting him out for cookies. Why not? A cookie date was syrupy sweet which is what romcom readers expected, and a slightly unique spin on the usual trope. Plus if my changes played out in real life again, a cookie date couldn't hurt could it?

I had to get to the bottom of what had happened earlier this morning. I returned the beach romance to the stack. There had to be twenty, maybe thirty manuscripts, of varying lengths in the trunk. My thumb skidded over the edges of each bundle like a magician shuffling cards, unencumbered with any worry of getting a paper cut. I studied individual pages, examining every manuscript like a coroner performing a detailed autopsy, hoping that the weight of the paper, the author's font choice, or the layout of the margins might provide some insight into the manuscripts' mysterious origins.

Nothing stood out. Most had been printed on recycled white paper in standard format accepted at any publishing house. They were boring. Common. Like every other manuscript I'd edited at Columbia. If I hadn't lived through this morning myself, I wouldn't have given the stack another thought.

My eyes drifted to the ceiling where light pooled from an etched glass chandelier. On a whim, I held a page to the light, wondering if perhaps there were words hidden in invisible ink.

No such luck.

I sighed and secured the stack with a large rubber band and returned them to the trunk.

What was I doing?

Going crazy?

Yeah, Emily. Yeah.

The more time that passed since the bubble tea incident, the more convinced I was becoming that I had imagined the entire thing. There was no other logical explanation. These were simply words on paper. My notes couldn't affect the future. It was ridiculous that I was even considering the possibility.

Come on, Emily, pull yourself together.

To get my mind off it, I left the office to explore the rest of Gertrude's behemoth house. I started in the parlor. The room wasn't remarkably lighter than it had been when I arrived last night, despite the fact that it was nearly noon. Dim lighting appeared to be a theme throughout the historic mansion. A Moby Dick mural had been painted on the high arched ceiling. At least I thought the illustration paid homage to Melville with its mosaic of cresting waves crashing into a medicine woman morphing into a whale.

The stone fireplace with its carved oak mantel anchored the room. A smoky scent from fires past lingered in the air. I imagined Gertrude curled up in one of the wing-back chairs reading in front of a crackling fire. Marbled blue coasters on the side tables likely held her mugs of tea. How was it that a woman I didn't know had left me this most intimate piece of herself?

As I moved toward the bookshelves the vastness of her collection took my breath away. I became acutely aware of every spine as a warmth spread throughout my body. Gertrude wasn't a casual book collector. She was a true bibliophile.

The complete set of Maud Lovelace's *Betsy, Tacy, and Tib,* one of the series I adored most from childhood, was tied together with a silky pink ribbon. I smiled at the memory of traveling to Minnesota circa the early 1900s through the pages of those books. Grandma Gertrude must have loved them too, from their prominent placement in the center of dark walnut shelves.

There was an entire bookcase dedicated to vintage reads long out of print. These covers were rigidly bound with paperboard and covered with faded cloth, buckram, and soft leather. I inhaled the scent of their yellowing pages, imagining how many fingers like mine had once cracked open these spines. Gertrude's fingers had cracked these spines. Her fingers had turned the pages. She had consumed these books, just like me.

Paulo Coelho's *The Alchemist*, Isabel Allende's *Zorro* and Joanne Harris's *Chocolat* showed me that Gertrude had been a modern reader too, drawn to books with mystical elements set in faraway lands.

Heat radiated from my hands as I ran my fingertip along row after row of familiar titles. It was as if Grandma Gertrude's essence were here, housed not only in her estate but in the millions of words printed on these pages. Is this what she wanted to show me? Was she speaking to me through her books? Books could say so much about a person without actually speaking.

Tears welled. I didn't fight them back.

They fell in hot, wet splotches running down my cheeks.

These books had been well-loved, treated with gentle care. Not a speck of dust lingered on a spine. No pages had been dog-eared. Her books weren't haphazardly piled in random stacks. They were organized by genre and style. Hardcovers, paperbacks, and antique first editions each had their own shelf space.

I brushed away tears and massaged the back of my neck, overcome with a deeper sense of the woman who had lived in the shadows of my memories. I wasn't sure what it meant for me, but I was sure that Gertrude had adored books, revered books, perhaps like me had even worshiped some of these reads.

The thought brought a smile to my face as I wandered into the attached dining room. In addition to being a booklover, Gertrude must have been an entertainer, given the massive mahogany table that looked like it could seat at least twelve people comfortably. Everything about the house was oddly juxtaposed. Traditional Victorian-era furniture like the table was mixed with modern art, books, and Goddess statues. A bust of Joan of Arc in glossy white marble reminded me of a scene from *Alice in Wonderland*. "Off with her head," kept running through my mind as I continued down the hallway to the kitchen.

The kitchen was at the back of the house. Its row of four-paned windows looked over immaculate gardens with benches and fountains tucked in between old growth trees, climbing candy-striped pink roses, ferns, and a pebble pathway that led to a gazebo designed to match the house. Boxwood wreaths strung with gray and cream checked ribbon adorned each window. A low humming sound echoed from the stainless-steel refrigerator.

The long, narrow kitchen gleamed under a canopy of copper pots hanging from the ceiling. I ran my fingers along the white-tiled countertops where someone, maybe Gertrude, had arranged galvanized tins with miniature cherry tomato and sweet pepper plants. Sparkling stemware and red crystal goblets were displayed in a glass cabinet near the sink. A butler's pantry was stocked with enough canned goods to outlast any winter storm. But it was the vintage black and white gas stove that drew my eye. I could almost picture a scene from Dickens with a kettle boiling on the stove and a gaggle of children being shooed out of the inviting kitchen by a cook wielding a wooden spoon.

A salmon vase bursting with fresh cut sunflowers sat in the center of the breakfast nook where an assortment of French, Italian, Mexican, Vietnamese, and Indian cookbooks were displayed on tiered shelves. Lacy curtains allowed filtered light to reach the dining table, enclosed with a circular bench with gray and cream striped cushions and red throw pillows offering pops of color. Across from the cookbooks was an accent gallery wall featuring a barn-red vintage kitchen scale, cake stands, and canning jars.

Had she enjoyed baking? I thumbed through a well-used copy of Betty Crocker's original cookbook. The pages were yellowed and smudged with stains. When I turned to a recipe for chocolate cake with double chocolate frosting, a visceral memory took hold. I could see myself standing at the counter on a step stool helping Gertrude measure ingredients.

"Emily, my sweet, would you like to lick the frosting bowl?" her voice echoed in my head along with a tactile memory of sticky fingers and chocolate lips.

At that moment chimes reverberated through the house,

rattling cake plates and startling me. I couldn't be sure, but the jangle of the bells sounded like "A Spoonful of Sugar" from *Mary Poppins*.

I whistled the tune as I went to see who was there.

A man about my age wearing a pair of khaki slacks, tennis shoes, and a fleece stood on the porch. "I'm Cameron with Humboldt Bay Real Estate. I'm guessing you're Emily?" he said as he stretched out his hand. "Your uncle asked me to stop by. I hope I didn't interrupt your cooking. Baking?"

"Oh, right." I didn't realize I was still clutching the cookbook. "No. Not at all. Just trying to go through some things."

"It must be daunting. I'm sorry for your loss." Cameron sounded sincere.

"Did you know Gertrude?" I moved to the side to let him in.

"Everyone in town knew and loved your grandmother. She was the lifeblood of Cascata. A literary force, so to speak. Small but mighty. Don't know how we'll fill the hole she has left." He put a hand to his heart. "You know, I've always sort of secretly wanted to write a children's book. Gertrude never let me off the hook. Every time I saw her, she would ask if I had started yet. I wish I'd been brave enough to follow her advice while she was alive."

I couldn't come up with a worthy response, so I shifted the conversation. "I'm not really sure how this works. I've never inherited an estate, and I don't know if Danny mentioned this or not, but there are some stipulations in the will."

"Yeah, he told me." He looked up toward the cavernous ceiling with its elegant chandelier. "Is there somewhere we can talk?"

I showed him to the parlor.

"This is a great room." His gaze lingered on the ceiling. "That mural is such a conversation starter. I hope whoever buys this place will keep it, but you know how it goes with real estate." He unzipped his fleece. "Danny says you want to sell? I have to admit that I'm surprised. Not that I don't want your business, but a house like The Ballad doesn't come on the market very often. They tend to stay in families."

Had Danny sent Cameron on purpose? To try and convince me not to sell? I set the cookbook on the side table. "I live in New York. In fact, I just got my first editorial job in publishing."

"Ah, like your grandmother." Cameron offered me a wide smile. He crossed his legs and studied the room. His long brown hair, tied in a man bun, matched the low key Cascata vibe. "Are you going to keep the agency, then?"

I pointed across the hallway. "Lost Coast Literary?"

"It can be done, depending on how we work the contract." He scanned the room, his eyes drifting across the hallway. "You'd likely have to find new headquarters. Although there's always a chance the new owners would be willing to sublet the office space. It's a long shot, but you never know."

"No, I mean, I don't think so. As soon as I can get the estate details wrapped up, I'm heading back to New York." I was feeling like a broken record. "To be honest with you, I didn't even know that she was an editor until last night. How could I keep her agency? I don't even know what sort of work she did."

Cameron was thoughtful for a moment. "I'm not sure of specifics since I'm not a real writer. I'm not published or anything. But I do know some of the writers she worked with, who said that getting an edit from Gertrude was like getting decades of therapy in a re-write. She had a gift for words. She had a gift for changing lives."

His sentiment made the tiny hairs on my forearms stand at attention.

A gift for changing lives.

Did that mean something?

My throat started to close in on itself. I forced myself to swallow.

"Anyway, we should probably get to business." He removed a small yellow legal pad and ballpoint pen from his fleece pocket. "I'll need to run some comps to come up with a fair market value for the property. I'm not sure if Danny told you, or if you're familiar with this information, but the house is on the National Register of Historic Places so there will be a few additional hoops that we'll need to jump through. Nothing major, but I do need to warn you that the local preservation society is likely going to give us some resistance."

"Why?"

"It's a trend here in Cascata. Housing is at a premium with college students. Many of these historic buildings have been torn down and replaced by condos. I don't expect any trouble, but I do want to give you a heads up that you'll probably get a visit from one of the members the minute we put a sign in the yard." He made a note on the pad. "What about the interior? I'm assuming you and your family will go through and take what you want. Will you be interested in an estate sale?"

"Uh, yes. Probably?" My pulse thudded in my neck. I was beginning to feel overwhelmed with the multitude of decisions in front of me. "Actually, I don't know. This is all so new and I'm trying to take it in. I haven't even made it up to the third floor yet."

"There's no rush." He clicked the cap on the ballpoint pen. "Do you have a price point you're hoping to hit?"

"No. I have no idea what the house is worth. I mean, I'm guessing since it's pretty remote out here, that prices reflect that." I couldn't begin to imagine what a property like this would go for in Santa Clara or New York, but Cascata wasn't exactly a draw for industry, its job market, or even tourism for that matter.

"Usually, but not always." He put the pen and pad away. "In that case, if it's okay with you, I'll go ahead and do a quick walk-through. I'll take some pictures, then I'll head back to my office and start putting comps together for you. I understand there are legal issues with the will, but I think it's a good idea to get the process started. That way when you're ready to list we'll be good to go." He stopped for a moment. "I'm assuming you'll want to list as soon as you can, right? A property like this can get expensive—ongoing maintenance, upkeep, repairs, property taxes."

I felt dizzy.

Cameron continued. "I told Danny I would give you a discount on my commission since Gertrude was a friend. She used to loan me books, and her parties, oh her parties. Have you heard about them? They were the stuff of legend." He trailed off for a second.

"Anyway, I can offer five percent if that sounds good to you. And, that way Danny will owe me free pints anytime I stop into the pub." He winked.

Five percent sounded fair. Was it fair? I had no idea, but I was so overwhelmed at this point, I was ready to agree with anything.

"I should have a rough estimate for you by tomorrow evening. Should we plan to get together for a drink? Say five? Do you know The Campout?" He pointed out the window in the direction of downtown.

I shook my head.

"It's a live-fire bar and restaurant on the plaza. You can't miss it. Gaucho-style grills, everything is wood-fired. I'm drooling talking about it. I should go make my assessments before I get carried away."

He stood and began taking pictures of the parlor. I took the Betty Crocker cookbook back to the kitchen, happy to be moving forward on the sale, but stuck on Cameron's words. He had said that Gertrude's edits had changed lives. Was that simply figurative language or could her re-writes, like mine, have had a literal effect on her clients?

CHAPTER SEVEN

$\mathcal{B}$y the time Cameron finished taking photos it was nearing one o'clock. I followed him outside, locked the wood-carved front doors with stained glass panels and iron handles, and headed along Grammar Street toward downtown to meet Danny and the rest of the family. It was hard not to stop and marvel at the painted ladies that lined both sides of the street. Each house was painted in three to four unique colors to enhance their Victorian and Edwardian architectural details, scalloped shingles, sunburst arches, and filigreed trim. From a gingerbread mansion with turrets and cupolas to a sea foam-blue Queen Anne with a dominant denim-blue corner tower and steel overhanging eaves, every residence looked as if it belonged on a postcard.

No wonder the preservation society was trying to ensure that these historical gems weren't bulldozed.

The neighborhood eventually spilled into the plaza where even more people had gathered since my strange coffee encounter, sharing lunch on benches and lounging in the grass on blankets. I took the opposite route around the triangular center park from earlier, first passing the Apothecary, where a wooden sign surrounded by bulk medicinal teas, herbal bath salts and lotions, and botanical soaps caught my eye. It read: No passion in the world is equal to the passion to alter someone else's draft.

I recognized the famed H.G. Wells quote. Was the Universe pushing me toward something? Or was it sending me a message to say that I'd tempted fate by editing the forsaken manuscripts? Since the moment I had received Danny's text that Gertrude had died, I'd felt like I was in some strange limbo, living in a waking dream where I was dancing on a ledge between the real world and other realms. Everything was fuzzy, just out of my grasp, like trying to bottle up air.

I moved on to the next shop. The two-story row houses in the plaza were scrunched together tightly. The Apothecary's gentle red façade quickly transformed into a vibrant pumpkin orange with cascading yellows and reds where an upscale bar was housed. I chuckled at the tagline: Crafts & Drafts—a drinking spot with a crafting problem.

I peered into the cutaway bay windows. Rows and rows of stainless-steel tap handles and expensive glass liquor bottles lined the bar. Industrial crafting tables were dispersed throughout the space along with shelving containing ribbons, bunting, tissue paper, beads, and enough crafting supplies to be the envy of any art teacher.

Cool concept, I thought as I proceeded onward past Tall, Dark & Bagel selling their signature slug slime and bright yellow stuffed toy slugs, plus lunchtime bagels. A line wrapped along the sidewalk with customers eager for a sesame seed bagel smeared with cream cheese and Mission figs. Next was an Italian restaurant and Forage, a boutique succulent shop brimming with dainty cacti, burro's-tail, and houseleeks. At the base of the plaza, signs pointed to hiking trails that led to the marsh and the redwoods. I rounded the last corner and took a long breath before venturing into the pub.

Like last night, the place was packed. I was immediately enveloped in the smell of steeping grains and bright hops. It must be brew day. A server balancing a tray of frothy, overflowing beers stopped to ask if I needed anything.

"I'm meeting Danny, is he here?"

"They're upstairs." He nodded above us.

"Got it." I went to the wooden staircase and made my way to the balcony. Danny was seated at a long table carved in the shape of a surfboard with Keeshawna and my cousins. A wave of nerves washed over me. I stuffed my hands into my pockets.

"Emily!" Danny stood and gave me a half hug. "You remember Keeshawna, Arty, and Shay?"

"Hi, everyone." I wondered if my facial expression reflected how uncomfortable I felt. I wanted to scream, "No! Of course I don't remember them." Instead, I faked a smile. Arty was a few years younger than me and Shay three years younger than him.

Keeshawna waved hello. Her dark natural curls and high cheekbones made me wonder if she had been a model in a previous life. "Please sit." She motioned to the spot across from her.

I slid into the empty spot next to my cousins.

"It's been too long," Keeshawna's voice cracked slightly. She and Danny shared a brief glance. "I think Artemus was five or six and Shay was just starting preschool when your parents moved away."

Shay, my younger cousin who sat to my left, squeezed my forearm. Dozens of tiny earth-toned beaded bracelets wrapped around her thin wrist. They matched her fringed willowy blouse and wide-legged denim jeans. Her relaxed bohemian style mirrored her personality. "We are so excited that you're here. I can show you all around. Have you been to the beach or marsh yet? What about Letter Press or the library? There's also a great library on campus. I mean you're an editor, you have to love libraries, right?"

Arty interrupted before I could respond. "She doesn't need a tour guide, Shay."

The two of them could have been twins despite their age difference. Arty reminded me of a younger, more uptight Trevor Noah. His rigid body posture and permanent scowl made it evident he wasn't thrilled to welcome me to our makeshift family reunion.

"How was your stay in The Ballad last night?" Keeshawna asked. She had a slightly more refined look than Shay. Her romantic paisley print flowing dress complemented her silhouette. A flowering lotus tattoo bloomed on her left arm and a lacy dreamcatcher with tiny ethereal stars ran from her right elbow to wrist.

"Fine. It's a big house." I wasn't sure what else to say.

"Five thousand square feet, right, Dad?" Shay chimed in.

A tug of sadness tightened in my chest as I watched the way she and Keeshawna twisted their bracelets when they spoke.

Would Mom and I share similar traits if she were still alive? Grief had left me with wispy generalized memories. The chemical smell of a hospital room. The way she used to throw her head back when she laughed. Reading in her bed under layers of Pendleton blankets and a down comforter, pillows propped behind our heads and the book light flickering with each turn of the page. Her fingertips brushing my eyebrows as she tucked me in at night. Jasmine. Peaches. Dirt caked on her jeans after hours spent tending the soil beneath the summer sun. She and Dad dancing to Harry Connick Jr. in the kitchen late at night.

"Are you hungry?" Danny asked, forcing me out of my head.

"Uh, sure." I cleared my throat.

Shay offered me a menu. "Everything is awesome, but you should totally get the NorCal pita. It's the best. Because you know when you live on the Lost Coast, it's a requirement that everything comes with guac, a side of guac, or just a whole damn avocado."

"So what I'm hearing is guacamole." I tried to laugh, feeling a touch lighter, thanks to Shay's shift in the tone. I studied the menu, ignoring Arty's continuous glare. The pita sounded delicious. A grilled pita stuffed with guacamole, spicy chicken, red onions, heirloom tomatoes, and lime coleslaw.

"She'll need a Tangerine Squeeze IPA to go with that," Danny added.

I closed the menu and placed it on the table. "Sold." Suddenly I was famished. Maybe it was the smell of bacon and cheese fries being delivered to the table next to us, or the stress of a bizarre morning paired with looming details about how we were going to handle the estate.

"Do you all work here at the pub?" I asked, hoping some of my nerves would fade away with a lunchtime beer.

"It's a family affair, except when one of us tries to break free, like me." Keeshawna pointed to the window. "I don't know how much Danny has told you, but I'm part of a jazz trio. We perform five nights a week at the martini bar across the street. Otherwise, I manage staff here and do payroll. The not fun stuff."

Danny wrapped his arm around the back of her chair. "She's being too modest. This place would crumble to ruin without her."

Shay cleared her throat. She crossed her legs, revealing Birkenstocks and burgundy toenail polish. "Dad, I think you're missing some important details."

"Yes, thanks for the reminder. Arty took over dealing with distributors when he graduated from college a couple years ago. That's given me more time to brew and dabble in the kitchen. It's been such a lifesaver to have him around." Danny shot Shay a playful wink.

She rolled her eyes. "What my dad meant to tell you is that I'm in charge of marketing and social media." She paused for a minute and pointed to a young couple a few tables away who were snapping pics of their food. "See, that's thanks to me. So is our pub trivia night and ugly sweater Christmas crawl. You get the idea. This place is alive because of me and my tweets," she teased.

Our drinks arrived. I wrapped my hands around the chilled glass. The tangerine ale had a lovely apricot color. Bubbles erupted toward the surface of my pint glass, leaving a fizzy tingle on my tongue.

I could feel everyone's eyes on me as I took a sip. Tangy citrus notes came through, immediately followed by a smooth, hoppy finish. "This is amazing," I replied, meaning it.

Danny smiled. Arty refused to make eye contact even after I asked him about his shirt—a simple kayak and paddle. "I take it you kayak?"

"When I have time." His tone was rough and hard.

Keeshawna ignored his rudeness. "Emily, I have to tell you that Gertrude would be over the moon knowing that you're continuing Lost Coast Literary. It makes my heart happy and eases some of the sting of losing her, knowing that you're going to continue her legacy." She rested her hand on her heart to prove her point.

I gulped down my beer. "Wait, what?"

"Danny mentioned that you were considering continuing Gertrude's work." Keeshawna's eyes narrowed as she studied me.

"Nooooo," I looked to Danny for support. He gave me a sheepish shrug.

"I said we had to *help* convince her," Danny corrected his wife. "Doesn't look like we've succeeded yet." He turned to Shay. "You are going to have to show your cousin around town, let her see how great it is."

Why was he suddenly talking as if I weren't in the room?

Arty beat me to a response. He balled up a cloth napkin and tossed it on the table. "She obviously doesn't want it. Why is everyone pretending like this is going to happen? It's not. I can see it on her face, and I told you guys at the reading of Grandma's will. She's going to sell the place to the highest bidder and take off again." He inhaled through his nose. His deep brown eyes lasered on me. "Am I right?"

"Arty." Keeshawna shot him a warning look.

"Hey, I'm calling it like it is. I know you believe that Grandma had a plan, but what if she didn't?" He gave Danny a hard look. "Grandma was quirky. She could have made a mistake. Maybe she hoped that this would be the last olive branch without realizing she was signing everything away to a stranger."

The intensity of his tone cut through me. He wasn't wrong. I had basically said something similar to Danny last night. But an olive branch and deserting them? He was taking too much artistic license with my family's history for my liking.

"Food's here," Shay announced with a brightness that baffled me.

I felt Arty's gaze continuing to burn as the waiter passed around plates.

"Emily, how's your dad?" Keeshawna asked, catching Arty's eye and signaling him to stop.

"He's fine." I picked up a crispy fry coated in spice and sprinkled with garlic. Melted Gouda and bacon bits oozed on the top. Dad's curt text earlier was a reminder that he was not happy that I had made the trip. I would have to try and smooth things over with a phone call later.

"Is he still in Santa Clara?" Keeshawna ran her index finger around the rim of her pint glass.

"Yes. He's busier than ever. I keep telling him that he should think about scaling back or even full retirement, but he won't consider it."

"Sounds like Stephen," Danny said with what I interpreted as a touch of sarcasm.

I bit into my pita, happy for a momentary reprieve. The flatbread was layered with guacamole, tender chicken, and chilled lime coleslaw. I savored another bite, washing it down with the IPA, wondering how he would know what sounded like Dad. They hadn't spoken in years.

Everyone dug into their lunch, allowing quiet to fall over the table.

After devouring a third of my pita, I dabbed my mouth with a napkin. "Listen, I don't want to make this more awkward. I already told Danny that if you want to keep the house in the family, we can figure out how to make that happen. It's an amazing place, but my life is in New York. I just completed an intensive publishing program and landed my dream job."

"I've always wanted to go to New York," Shay said, sipping her tropical pineapple beer. She could barely be old enough to drink. I was impressed with her palate. In my early twenties I hadn't developed an appreciation for craft ales. Maybe that came with the territory of growing up in a family-run pub.

"You're welcome to visit anytime. Fair warning, my apartment is not even four hundred square feet and I have two roommates, so you'll have to sleep in the kitchen sink."

"Less than four hundred square feet?" Shay gasped. "I think my closet is bigger than that."

"Most are," I replied with a nod, trying to lighten the mood.

Danny stirred his bowl of steaming chili. "What if we meet at the house tonight? It might be nice to continue our conversation about what's next there." He addressed Shay and Arty. "Grandma set aside special items for both of you, like we discussed, but we'll need to go through each room together at some point."

"So you're just going to let this happen, Dad?" Arty didn't attempt to conceal his disgust.

"It's not up to me, Art. This is what your grandma wanted." Danny folded his hands on the table. "Come on. Let's enjoy lunch. We have plenty of time to go over details later."

They might have had plenty of time, but I didn't. I found myself in a strange limbo. Part of me longed to be on a plane at thirty thousand feet hurtling my way back to New York. I thought of my meeting with Piper. If I wanted to break out of writing rejection letters, I was going to have to prove myself and I couldn't do that here. But the other part of me refused to lose the thread of Gertrude's story. Of mine. There was no denying that we were tethered together with some sort of invisible string.

A string that linked my future with my past.

Maybe it was wishful thinking, but I wanted to believe I was here to learn something. Did the answers to my past lie in the forsaken manuscripts? In Gertrude's estate? Or somewhere else?

CHAPTER EIGHT

Keeshawna attempted to keep the rest of the conversation light as lunch wore on. By the time we had stuffed our faces with fries and full pints of beer, I was ready for a nap. My head felt like it was being swarmed by dozens of bees.

"Shay, do you want to take Emily to the beach?" Danny suggested. "You've got a few hours before dinner service."

"Sure." Shay stood. Her lanky body stretched in a yoga pose as she waited for me. "It's only a half mile from here. You want the quick tour?"

"Sounds good." A walk might help clear my head. Plus, out of everyone in the family, Shay seemed most likely to divulge missing details about my past and whether I was getting the complete story about the rest of them.

Keeshawna came around the table to hug me. "Don't worry. It's all going to work out. We are so happy you're here," she whispered in my ear. Her gentle touch made my spine stiffen. After decades of only having Dad, who wasn't exactly the most affectionate person on the planet, it was overwhelming to feel so welcomed by most of my newfound family.

Danny followed suit. "Should we meet up at the house later?

Tomorrow night? Say seven? That will give you a day to explore the house and me time to make sure dinner service is going smoothly. Keeshawna performs tomorrow night at ten, but she needs to be there early for sound check."

"Sure." I nodded. "I'm meeting Cameron for happy hour to go over comparable properties, so that should work."

"*Comparable properties,*" Arty scoffed under his breath. "I told you she's going to sell."

"I introduced her to Cameron," Danny retorted.

Shay looped her arm through mine. "Let's go check out the beach." She guided us downstairs and out onto the plaza before her brother launched into a new rant.

"We'll cut through the park." Shay let go of my arm and pointed diagonally across the plaza, which had filled in even more since lunchtime. A photographer snapped pictures of leafy palms and the kaleidoscope of colorful Queen Annes. College students sunbathed on hemp blankets. The faint aroma of cannabis and blooming jasmine lingered in the air. A sax player wearing black pants and a flat-brimmed felt hat busked near the center of the shared community space. I dropped a couple dollars in his case as we passed by. Variegated purple hydrangeas in neatly trimmed rows lined the brick pathway. Shockingly pink flower baskets hung from sturdy lampposts. Three flags fluttered in the coastal wind—the U.S. flag, the California State flag with a bear and a single red star, and a flag of the world.

We turned onto Bayshore heading north, passing narrow alleyways strung with twinkle lights and painted with abounding soulful jazz murals.

Shay stopped to point out one of the murals that depicted a woman crooning into a microphone. "This one was inspired by Mom. Can you see it?"

Sure enough, Keeshawna's image took up half of the yellow building. Her eyes were closed as her hips swayed to the music. The artistry of the life-sized painting made me feel like I was sitting in the front row of a jazz club. "Do you sing, too?"

"Not like Mom." She twirled her curls. "I sing for fun or when we're together, but I don't want any part of the stage."

We reached the end of the brick sidewalk. A two-toned compass in blue and gold took up the entire street. Each direction of the compass pointed to a Lost Coast landmark—the beach, marsh, redwoods, and plaza. "I take it we go that way?" I nodded to my right.

"No wonder you have a smart New York job," she joked as we turned into another tree-lined neighborhood with smaller period houses. "So, tell me everything about you. Single? Dating? Boyfriend? Secret lover?"

"Ha! I wish. Not unless book boyfriends count."

"Totally. Who's yours?"

"Mr. Darcy."

"Oh, come on, Emily." Shay shook her head in disapproval. "That's too cliché. Plus, he's too old. Too stuffy and way too many layers of clothes."

I laughed. "Okay, fair enough. What about you?"

"I'm a John Green girl. Give me modern heartbreak."

"Any non-book boyfriends?" I asked as the sidewalk narrowed. Shay was a good foot taller than me, and even with a casual stroll toward the beach, I had to take long strides to keep up.

"I've been into this guy for a while who has no idea I exist. John Green would be super unimpressed with my uninteresting love story. Basically, I'm pathetic." She threw her hands up.

"Why don't you ask him out?"

"I know. I should, right? I'm a freaking feminist. But is it wrong to want a little old-school romance in my life?"

"Not at all. I'd take a Darcy-style proposal just to go out for sushi."

Shay cracked up. "So we have that in common. Two hopeless romantics. The Bryant cousins."

The Bryant cousins. I liked the sound of that.

"Okay, here's a serious question," Shay said. "Emojis or no emojis?"

"Sure, emojis in text—when used sparingly," I cautioned. "But never in a manuscript. And multiple exclamation points are an unforgivable sin."

That made Shay laugh harder. "You're funny. Quiet but clever. I bet you sneak up on people."

A brood of free-range chickens squawked a hello from their fenced-in coop as we passed by.

"Is it true that you really didn't know Grandma was a book editor?" Shay asked.

"True. I didn't know her at all." I nodded. She had opened the window for me. "What was she like?" I wanted to hear Shay's perspective. My memories were at war with one another, battling for space in my head. Was the Gertrude who had whisked hot chocolate on the stove the same person who cut me out of her life? How could that be?

Shay ripped a stalk of lavender from a wild bush and ran it beneath her nose. "She was super intuitive, like she had this way of knowing what you needed, even when you didn't know you needed it. Does that make sense?"

The heady scent of lavender had a naturally calming effect. I allowed myself to breathe it in. "How so?"

The temperature shifted as we descended the hillside and the ocean came into view. Another flood of memories washed over me as I took in the coastline. I remembered the smell. The dampness of the temperate forest. The horizon that stretched for miles and miles until it eventually evaporated, consumed by clouds in the distance.

The bay was calm and still. Kayakers and paddle boarders cut through the glassy waters leaving tiny wakes in their trail. A pod of pelicans performed an acrobatic display as they dipped and dived toward the shallow waves in search of fish. Rocky prominences jutted out in the middle of the bay, serving as landing spots for flocks of seagulls. It was as if the jagged rocks had been dropped from the heavens. In the distance a bank of clouds rolled closer.

Shay glanced at me and then to the sea. "It's pretty awesome, isn't it?"

"I'd forgotten how different the north coast is from the boardwalk and packed beaches by Santa Clara. I grew up going to the amusement park at Santa Cruz. This is so." I struggled to find the right word. "Rugged. Organic?"

"Totally." Shay strolled down the hill. "Except it's usually raining and judging by those clouds looming out there, it will again soon, so don't let the sun fool you."

I laughed.

"Anyway, about Grandma, what do you want to know?"

I pressed my index finger and thumb firmly together. It was time to rip off the Bandaid. Here goes nothing. "Anything. Everything. I don't understand why she left the house and literary agency to me. I can see why Arty is pissed, even though it's not my fault. I didn't write the will. She did. And for the record, it's been me and my dad for years alone without any contact from the family. Then suddenly I get a text out of the blue from your dad telling me that I've inherited her property and I need to get out here as fast as possible. My dad told me not to come—not to trust your dad. I don't get what went so wrong with them that they didn't talk for almost twenty years."

Shay rubbed the lavender between her fingers. "Me neither. I wish I could tell you what happened. I honestly have no idea. I was so young at the time. It wasn't something any of them talked about in front of me. The topic was basically off limits because it made Dad and Grandma too sad."

I took her words in. It made them sad. That was something.

We made it to the shore. Shay kicked off her Birkenstocks and dug her toenails, painted the color of glossy wine, into the sand. I kept my tennis shoes on but bent down to pick up a handful of the fine dusty particles worn down from years of thrashing waves crashing into the jagged coastline. I drank in the briny scent of the sea and the way the sun reflected on the water.

Shay rolled up the edges of her bell bottom jeans, revealing a small tattoo on her ankle.

"What is that?" I asked, squinting to get a better look at the female figurine.

"My Goddess, Sige."

"Sige?"

"Yep. She's the goddess of quiet. I have a tendency to spend a lot of time in my head, so she serves as a reminder to help balance me out. I'm learning to surrender to that chatter and to listen. I'm not good at it yet, but hey, I'm a work in progress, right?"

"Aren't we all?" I chuckled.

"I hope so." Shay changed the subject. "Your dad never talked about what happened either?"

"Never." I shook my head.

"I wonder what could have gone wrong. My parents are pretty chill, and like I said, Grandma was one of the wisest and calmest women I've ever known. She just had this way of making you feel okay. Whenever I had a problem, I would go to her. She'd make me a cup of chai tea or her amazingly awesome hot chocolate and toast a slice of her cinnamon bread with butter. She would sit me down at the kitchen island and just let me talk. I can't really say exactly what it was, but after a conversation with her I just always knew things were going to be okay."

"She sounds great." I hoped my tone didn't sound too bitter. I would have liked to have had Gertrude in my life. Not that I wasn't close with my maternal grandparents. They were sweet and kind, and had given me anything I wanted growing up, but the enigma of the Bryant family had always left me feeling incomplete.

Shay must have picked up on my irritation. "She talked about you. She knew what you were up to. Once she gave me a stack of books that you had re-written when you were young. I still have them."

"You do?"

"Mmm hmm. This might sound weird, but they made me feel connected to you. I never had other cousins, and I always wanted a sister. I especially loved your ending for *Little Women*. I mean, why did Beth have to die? And, of course, Jo *should* have married Laurie." She made a squiggly heart in the sand with her big toe.

I felt surprised but warmed by her admiration. "That was thanks to my mom. I remember crying all night after she read me *The Giving Tree*, so she told me to re-write the ending. I'm not sure she knew what she was getting into, but it sort of became an obsession for me."

"You know, I'm a writer. Well, not officially. But that's my goal. I want to tell stories and share stories. I've been working on some short stories, and some personal essays and even a novel, but damn, I had no idea how hard it was going to be." She reached into her tote bag and removed a purple journal with a peace sign on the cover. "See, this is where I keep my notes."

"What's the novel about?"

Shay flipped through the pages which looked to be filled with notes and doodles. "That's the problem, I'm not sure. I get started and then I get about a quarter of the way into the story and I have no idea where it goes next."

"That's a universal struggle," I assured her.

Her face lightened. "Really? Grandma used to tell me that you and I were going to make the perfect team one day—editor and writer. She said that I would write stories and your editing would help bring them to life."

"What?" I pressed my index fingers into my temples. Had I misheard Shay? "She said that?"

"I swear." Shay made an X over her heart. "Grandma was sure that you and I were destined to be like sisters."

We sat in a comfortable silence for a bit, watching the waves slide up the sand and recede again. A natural fiber kite bobbed in the offshore wind. Its puppeteer released more string, allowing the kite to begin its graceful ascent toward a cluster of pristine white clouds overhead until its tether line disappeared against the sky.

Shay waved to a group of young women setting up a beach volleyball net. I recognized Kenzie and her friends from the coffee shop. "How was it growing up in a small town like this? You must know everyone."

"Pretty much." She tossed her head from side to side. "There are pros and cons, especially since I stayed here for college."

"Do you know them?" I pointed to Kenzie, who stood to the side directing traffic while her friends labored over rolling out the net and staking it in the sand.

"Yep. They're a couple years younger than me, but the college like everything else in Cascata is small, so you end up hanging with everyone."

I hesitated for a moment. The uncomfortable buzzing had returned to my body. It felt like hundreds of bees were humming beneath my skin. "This might sound strange, but I witnessed a weird encounter with them at the coffee shop."

Shay waited for me to say more, but Kenzie called her over. "Hang on a sec. I'll be right back." She tucked the journal back in her tote bag and stood up, kicking sand with her toes.

I watched her approach the group, thinking again of Tamir. But my attention quickly shifted farther down the beach where a fluffy golden dog chased the waves foaming on the shore.

A woman wearing a flirty floral running skirt and lightweight jacket jogged toward the dog, who immediately followed after her.

"Dashwood! Dashwood Toad, get back here!" A man sprinted through the sand.

I blinked twice. It was Cameron the real estate agent.

The woman slowed her pace to let him catch up, bending over to pet the dog licking her exposed leg.

"Dashwood Toad—knock it off!" Cameron yelled louder.

My heart thudded in my chest. This can't be happening. This can't be happening.

I glanced around, trying to center myself in reality. Shay was chatting with Kenzie and her friends, who were still struggling to secure the net against the wind blowing in off the Pacific. A couple strolled in the surf searching for beach treasures. Two surfers paddled out to catch the next wave.

Breathe, Emily. Breathe.

I dared to look back toward Cameron. He had caught up to his dog and the jogger. He looped one hand through the dog's tie-dyed collar and clutched his taut stomach. Exhaling with force, he took a good minute to catch his breath. "Sorry about that."

"No worries." The woman brushed her hands on her Lycra jogging skirt. "Is his name Dashwood Toad?"

"Yes. This is the extraordinary Dashwood Toad, named after two of my favorite literary characters."

Oh, my God. Not again. I dug my fingernails into my forearms, leaving a mark. *Wake up, Emily! Wake up!*

I concentrated on the smells around me—a faint hint of coconut sunscreen, the wet sand, a woody tone of a bonfire far away. If I were dreaming, my senses weren't failing me. This certainly didn't feel like a dream. I watched in disbelief.

The woman jogged in place. "Dashwood, as in the Dashwood from Jane Austen?"

What was wrong with me? I stuffed a finger in my ear and closed my eyes, trying to block out the sound of their voices.

I dislodged my finger and stared with a slack jaw as Dashwood yanked on the leash. Instead of letting him chase after a beagle, the woman massaged his wiry head. I couldn't tear my gaze away as the same words I read on the page spilled out in front of me.

"I'm Sienna, by the way. This is going to seem forward but since you have me craving cookies talking about *Frog and Toad* would you want to meet at The Campout and split one of their chocolate chip cookie skillets with a huge scoop of vanilla bean ice cream?"

Cameron grinned. "Sure. That sounds great. How's tomorrow?"

"Good. It's a date." Sienna jogged away. Cameron, with Dashwood in tow, went the opposite direction.

My stomach dropped. An impending sense of doom came over me. My heart raced in my chest. I tried to take long and slow breaths, but I couldn't seem to fill my lungs with enough air. My breathing felt shallow and forced.

This couldn't be a coincidence. Not twice.

I scanned around – was there a camera crew filming me? Was I on some sort of reality show? *And what sort of bizarre reality show would that be, Emily?* I grabbed my legs and rocked back and forth on the sand, trying to soothe myself. What was I going to do? Who could I tell? Who would believe me?

I needed to get out of here. I didn't know what strange phenomenon had occurred in Gertrude's office, but I knew that I didn't want any part of it.

CHAPTER NINE

"*E*mily, are you okay?" Shay stood over me, her frame blocking the light and casting a long shadow on the fine sand.

"Huh?"

"You don't look so good." She sat next to me. "You're really pale. Did something happen?"

I threw my hand on my forehead and mopped sweat from my brow. What was wrong with me?

"Emily, you good?" Shay repeated.

The nape of my neck felt ice cold. I gulped down air and forced myself to give her a nod.

"Do you need something? Water? An ambulance?" Shay dug her phone out of her bag, readying herself to make a call.

I had to do something. I had to tell her.

"Shay, you're going to think I'm crazy with what I'm about to tell you." I stopped. *No, this is a terrible idea. I barely know her, and I'm going to confess that my editing pen has some kind of a curse that inscribes a new future.*

"Tell me what?" she prodded. "It's okay."

"It's crazy. Like seriously crazy, but I have to talk to someone."

"Okay." Her voice was thick with concern. "You can talk to

me. I won't think you're crazy. I know you probably don't believe me, but I really have idolized you since I was eleven years old and I read your re-write of *Little Women,* and like I said, it was the best thing I'd ever read. You're the reason I majored in English Lit."

"The thing is, I'm pretty sure I might be losing my mind." My fingers wouldn't stop shaking and my feet felt numb as the words escaped my lips.

"How?"

Everything came gushing out. The forsaken manuscript pile. Tamir's story. What I'd just witnessed.

When I finished, I expected Shay to march me straight to the hospital to be examined for a rare neurological condition that had to be responsible for blurring reality and fiction, but instead she bombarded me with dozens of questions. "How does it work? Has this happened before? Do you think it's some kind of magic?"

"I have no idea, other than I must be losing my mind."

"No way! It's the magic of Cascata." She clapped her hands together. "Emily, this is amazing! You have a gift. I would die to be able to re-write everyone's future."

"No, you don't get it. It doesn't feel like a gift. This is terrifying." I wrung my hands together, trying to get them to stop quivering.

"No, really. Think about it. Tamir should *not* be with Kenzie. She's a totally self-absorbed granola beauty. You know why she called me over there?" Shay's gaze drifted to the college students who had finally managed to erect the net. They had stripped down to their bikinis and were lobbing a volleyball back and forth, but mainly trying to catch the attention of a group of surfers.

I shook my head.

"Because she's 'woke'—her word by the way—and wanted to invite me onto her podcast where she's raising awareness on race issues on the Lost Coast. It would be great to have a 'mixed-race' (her words again, definitely not mine) person like me on to share my experiences." Shay pretended to gag. "She's the worst. You did Tamir a favor with that re-write."

"Maybe." I wasn't convinced.

"No, I'm serious—this is huge! It's like you're editing everyone's best life for them."

"Shay, I'm definitely not qualified to edit anyone's best life. I can barely edit my own life. That's way too much pressure. It's like playing God. I don't want that kind of responsibility." I reached my hand into the sand in an attempt to ground myself, forcing the tiny granules between my fingers. Continuing to edit the forsaken manuscripts was a bad idea. Sure, it was clear that Kenzie and Tamir were wrong for each other, but that didn't give me the authority to dictate the course of their futures.

The weight of my decision to come to Cascata was as heavy as the thick sea air. Is this what Gertrude wanted? For me to dictate a random stranger's fate?

No. No way.

I dug my hands deeper in the sand.

I couldn't do this. I shouldn't do this.

Who has the right to make decisions that alter someone else's life? Certainly not me.

This was too much.

I stared at the waves lapping on the shore as Shay's voice broke through.

"Yeah, I get that," she said, studying my face. "That's a lot of pressure, but why else would this be happening? There has to be a reason, right? It's like Grandma knew this was your destiny and called you here. She wouldn't have left you The Ballad and her agency if she didn't trust you to do the right thing."

"You realize that in this case, we're talking about the 'right thing' being me scripting out a future for complete strangers."

She twisted one of the bracelets on her wrists. "True. True, but hear me out on this. Maybe you're supposed to get to know these characters in real life. Grandma knew everyone in town. She used to say that her job was more like therapy. That she could pull the pieces that weren't authentic or working out of the manuscripts she edited because she could see where writers were holding back and know what story was actually meant to be told."

"You think this happened to her, too? That she edited her clients' future—literally?" A tiny glimmer of hope welled inside. For the first time all day I considered that maybe I wasn't completely out of touch with reality.

Shay shrugged. "I don't know. She never said anything to me if it did, but that doesn't mean it's not possible. Think about the beach story. Imagine if you hadn't edited it. The runner and dog guy might never have met. They could have been destined for each other and their stars never aligned. You fixed that. You might have created love. And even more importantly, you saved Tamir from the *wrong* love. Maybe your job is to help people live their best lives. That's insanely cool. I want an editing pen that fixes all of my mistakes."

"I don't know." The quivery feeling in my stomach had eased since telling Shay, but nothing made sense. Even that I was sitting on the banks of Humboldt Bay, let alone that my editing pen appeared to have some mystical touch.

"I know! I have an idea!" She clapped twice. "Let's test it. You have to try to do it again. See if it happens with me. You know, like give the Universe a nudge. You've got to give it a chance." Shay tried to tug me to my feet. "Let's go. I'll help."

I dug my heels in the sand. "No way. I can't touch the stack again. This is so creepy. It doesn't feel right. No one should be able to change the direction of someone else's life."

"But you already have." She met my eyes and held my gaze. "It's too late to turn back now."

"Not really. I can make a choice right here, right now to stop."

"Can you, though?" Her gaze turned more probing. "Isn't there a part of you that wants to understand this? To see where it leads?"

I hesitated.

"Come on, Emily." Shay yanked my arm hard. She was

surprisingly strong. "It will be a test. If I'm with you when you edit the next manuscript and this happens again, you'll have tangible proof."

She did have a fair point. Proof. Confirmation that this wasn't in my head. Maybe she was right. I was already seeing things that shouldn't be happening. Things couldn't get much worse, could they?

"I can't edit with you sitting and watching me," I protested, brushing sand from my hands. The grainy particles stuck between my fingers and left a dusty residue.

"Don't worry about it. I'll keep myself occupied." Shay practically ran up the hillside past the neighborhoods with white picket fences and wind-battered evergreen trees until The Ballad was in sight. She didn't waste any time unlocking the magnificent stained glass paneled door or pushing me into the front office. "You go do your thing. Call me when you're done." She held up her purple journal. "I'll work on my book. You won't even know I'm here."

After she left, I closed my eyes and leaned back in Gertrude's chair, letting out a long, slow breath and trying to center myself in space and time. This was probably in my head. The result of an overactive imagination and years of devouring too many novels. Maybe I should have listened to my therapist and spent more time with real friends instead of bookish friends.

Did I even know what I was doing? My six-week intensive publishing course hadn't prepared me for this level of editing.

I opened my eyes and opened the trunk, feeling a familiar sense of anticipation. The next manuscript reminded me of the Pulitzer Prize-winning *A Visit from the Goon Squad* by Jennifer Egan. At Columbia I had been assigned the book for a reader's report and was completely captivated by Egan's use of shifting narratives and an actual PowerPoint presentation as a storytelling device. The forsaken manuscript, *The Opt Out Clause*, featured smart and savvy Martine Francois, who had spent over a decade building an enviable digital marketing client list for an ad agency stuck in the Mad Men era. Her bosses, both old white men, took her for granted and paid her less than her junior male colleagues.

～

Martine fumed. She wanted to rip the proposal into shreds, but instead sucked in her cheeks and listened to her boss try to mansplain geotargeting.

The man couldn't figure out how to turn off his flashlight app or set up an automatic out-of-office email. This should be rich.

"Now, Martine, what I'm going to need is a PowerPoint on my desk by Monday about this new geotarget. We need to get on this ASAP for our clients."

She considered explaining that PowerPoint presentations were digital. Unless he wanted her to print it out and deliver it to his desk, which she knew he did.

"As luck would have it, I have a PowerPoint already prepared for you." Martine clicked a file and turned her laptop so the screen was facing him. The first slide bubbled out and turned blue. Two words popped in the center—I quit!

～

Hmmm. I tapped the tip of my pencil on the page. Too easy. Too cliché. I scanned the next few paragraphs confirming my suspicions. In the manuscript, Martine quits and magically her clients abandon the firm and follow her. What did Martine want? What did she need?

I re-worked the scene with Martine agreeing to have a completed PowerPoint by Monday and then receiving a call from a big-name marketing agency in Silicon Valley interested in hiring her, as long as she committed to poaching her client list, which would definitely be lawsuit worthy. That should add some much-needed tension to the manuscript and give Martine a moral dilemma to deliberate.

"Shay, I'm done," I hollered when I had finished the edit and packed the forsaken manuscripts in the trunk.

There was no answer. The house creaked and sighed a not quite silent reply. The drafty corridors were oddly welcoming as I checked the powder room with its tile floor, pedestal sink, and clawfoot tub. I searched every room on the main floor, checked the covered porch, and even peered into the immaculate gardens where the wind shook the heavy blooms of nectar blue salvia and white flower clusters on dogwood trees. I checked the bedrooms on the second and third floors, hesitating in the doorframe, half expecting a monster from *Where the Wild Things Are* to jump out at me.

Another memory glittered along the edges of my mind. Stuffed animals. Notes from Max, the original wild thing, tucked into a cupboard near the stairs?

Was it real?

I shook it off and continued on in search of Shay.

There was no sign of her.

"Shay!" I called again, dragging my footsteps along the hand-woven hallway rugs. Had she left? Did she disappear? Was she even here to begin with? Am I going crazy?

Probably.

Relief sank in a few moments later when I heard a faint and muffled, "Up here!"

"Up where?" I yelled to the embellished concave ceiling. Its plaster cast panels reminded me of royal wedding cake.

"Attic. Use the round staircase at the end of the hallway."

I followed her directions to a set of stairs concealed by an arched door. The hobbit-like entrance twisted in a spiral to an attic hideaway with a sharp peaked roofline and an unobstructed view of the sea. Shay was stretched out on a wooden bench, her long, thin legs taking up the entire space and draped in a gray cashmere throw blanket. "Isn't this the best view ever?"

I came closer to take a better look out the curved windows. I remembered this space. It was as if we were floating above the deep churning waters on the wings of a seagull. Waves rumbled into shore propelled by obsidian clouds. The soft foam lapping the sandy shore that we'd seen earlier had been replaced with angry cresting water barreling into the coastline.

"I told you a storm is brewing." Shay shifted her feet to make room for me on the window seat. "How did it go? Tell me every detail."

I sat on the edge of the comfy window seat cushions and relayed my edits. "Do you know anyone named Martine?"

She was thoughtful for a minute. "Hmmm. No, I don't think so and I don't think there's an ad agency in town either. Maybe in Eureka, but I can't think of a swanky digital agency anywhere on the Lost Coast. You've seen this place. It's granola hippies, surfers, and artists. There's still a film processing shop and freaking video rental place on the south side of town that rents DVDs and VHS. VHS—what the hell is that?"

I laughed.

We sat in silence for a moment, gazing at the approaching storm. "What do we do now?"

"We wait." Shay pushed a long curl away from her face. "Isn't that how it's happened so far? You make the edits. You re-work the scene. Then, voila!" She waved her hands. "You see it unfold in front of you." She sat up, stretched, then patted me on the back. "This is going to be fun."

I wished I shared her enthusiasm.

She glanced at her watch. "I should get to the pub. I promised Dad I would take pics of tonight's dinner special to share on social media. If I have time, I'll swing by my apartment and get the old books that you re-wrote as a kid. If not, I'll get them to you tomorrow." She stood and slid on her bronze suede Birkenstocks.

I followed her downstairs, as she pointed out secret panels tucked in the tongue-and-groove walls beneath the spiral staircase.

"When I was a kid, I used to stash candy bars in here," she said, pressing her finger into one of the dark redwood panels which swung open to reveal a hidden compartment. "Grandma must have caught me in the act because then I started finding notes and little treats and surprises tucked away. For a long time, I thought I had a special fairy friend who was communicating with me."

I clasped my hand over my mouth. Max. The stuffed animals. My memory was true. I froze, remembering my fingers making contact with the paneled wall. Remembering the fluttering feeling in my stomach when I would peek inside to find a secret note waiting for me.

A flush of adrenaline pulsed through my body.

It was true for me too.

Shay continued on, chattering about how it wasn't until she was in high school that she realized her fairy friend was actually our grandmother.

I continued behind her. The hallway creaked and popped under the weight of our footsteps. Old plumbing moaned and hissed, rubbing against the studs. "Didn't you get scared?"

"Scared?" Shay's eyes bulged. "No. Why?"

"Can't you hear the groans and the creaks in this place?"

"Oh, sure, but you get used to it." She waved a hand in front of her. "Grandma made this space feel so warm and inviting that I never thought about being scared."

Yet again the grandmother who had abandoned me didn't match up with Shay's memories.

We made it to the foyer. Shay held up her little finger. "I pinkie swear that I won't tell anyone our secret, but I'm so glad you trusted me, and you have to promise to text or call the minute something happens, okay?" She left me with a hug and strolled away.

I hadn't pinkie sworn in more than fifteen years. Maybe telling Shay was a mistake, but I didn't care. I needed an ally, a confidant, someone who didn't think I was entirely out of my mind because at the moment all signs pointed to the contrary.

CHAPTER TEN

$\mathcal{I}$ spent the remainder of the day after Shay left orienting myself with the property, mainly the gardens. The late afternoon sky saturated with color as I traversed the extensive pressed pebble pathways and iron archways dripping with wisteria and ivy. Anna's hummingbirds with tiny pink gorgets flitted from fountain to bubbling fountain. Bunches of yellow calendula flowers and rows of raspberry sherbet and fiery tangerine dahlias bloomed in neatly arranged patches. An entire portion of the garden was reserved for seaside botanicals and herbs. Another paid homage to the Lost Coast with fairy forest mushrooms, benches carved from driftwood, and collections of rocks designed to resemble the tidal gradient.

There were hammocks and hidden benches perfect for lounging with a book under pinkish unicorn clouds. Copper flower spinners caught the wind, and honeybees buzzed in wooden hives mounted to the sides of splendid oaks.

A red and black speckled brick retaining wall divided the back half of the grounds, where there was a large stone terrace with wicker couches and chairs interspersed with fairy bird baths, Goddess statues, decorative mirrors, and glass balls.

Time slowed to a crawl in the hallowed grounds that had

been cultivated with Gertrude's signature. I lingered late into the night until the sun made its retreat and moonlight washed over the sea.

The next morning, I woke with renewed focus to try to reconcile my memories, Dad's narrow lens, and the feelings that The Ballad was stirring inside me. My first stop was Letter Press. Danny had said it was Gertrude's favorite shop, so that seemed as good a spot as any to continue to try and excavate the truth of my past.

In the plaza I passed the record store where old vinyl disks hung from fishing wire in the front window. The spa next door was offering specials on bee and pine pollen facials and hot stone massages. Mountain bikers trekked past me, emerging from the nearby trails in a happy mess of caked mud and sand.

But my eyes were set on Letter Press, which sat like a bookish beacon lighting the way inside. Book bunting and pastel string lights hung from the ceiling. Display cases with bookish stickers and individual sheets of artistic wrapping paper flanked the entryway. Cubbies with colored and charcoal pencils, fountain pens, rainbow Sharpies in all shapes and sizes, and stamps filled the far wall.

"It's adorable, isn't it?" A woman behind the counter beamed as I scanned racks of hand-drawn cards, leather bound journals, and inspirational notebooks.

"It's gorgeous. This is the stuff of dreams. I'm speechless." I didn't know where to look. There was too much to take in.

The woman emerged from the counter and came up to me. "I'm Sienna. I own the shop."

Oh, God, it's her. The woman from the beach. It's the woman from *Dashwood Toad*. Blood rushed through my ears like waves crashing into the shore. My knees wobbled. "Hi, I'm Emily," I managed to squeak.

"Great to meet you." Sienna's wide smile made her entire face light up. She wore a crafting apron covered with enamel book pins. "Are you new in town?"

"Yes, sort of. I'm here for my grandma's estate. Gertrude Bryant, did you know her? I heard this was her favorite shop."

Sienna placed her hand over one of the pins, a black and gold book that read: WHEN IN DOUBT GO TO THE LIBRARY. "Unfortunately, not as well as I would have liked. I bought the shop shortly before she died. She came in a few times and we were just getting to know each other. What a loss. She was larger than life around here."

"Was she?"

Sienna nodded. "Yeah, everyone adored Gertrude. All of my customers. She was the lifeblood of Cascata. I'm so sorry for your loss. Is there anything I can do?"

"That's very kind, but I'm fine."

"You know what they say, the way to keep people alive is through their memories. It's uncanny that you came in this morning because I've been thinking about a way to try to keep Gertrude's memory alive here."

I forced a smile. Her gesture was sweet and given the sincere look on her face, I believed it was well intended, but it was the words she had uttered that made the ground beneath my feet feel shaky. The way to keep people alive is through their memories. How could I keep someone alive who I'd never been given the chance to remember?

"I should have guessed it when you first walked in. You look like Gertrude. Well, a much younger version of Gertrude, obviously. Gertrude and Ginny Weasley from Harry Potter." She pointed to an assortment of Harry Potter gifts like butterbeer tea, dragon egg bath bombs, and Dobby socks.

"Check it out. This is an original letter press. Can you believe it?" Sienna moved to the far window and ran her hand along the antique machine on display in the front window. "One of my goals is to make this a writing museum of sorts, and it seems like there has to be a way to tie in Gertrude with that." She adjusted the straps on her navy crafting apron. "I have a friend who's going to help me get another card catalog from the library and I

have a connection in Eureka with a guy who wants to sell me his grandfather's old printing press. I'm thinking of offering some workshops on the techniques used before we all became glued to our phones. I think it might resonate with the community here, and it's in the same line of Gertrude's writing workshops and literary parties, so I was thinking maybe the first event could be dedicated to her memory. What do you think?"

"It's a wonderful idea. I'm sure my family would be touched." That was true. What I didn't say aloud was that I would have little to offer in terms of Gertrude's memories. I picked up a Mark Twain library candle in a silver tin. It was scented with tobacco flower and vanilla. A sticker with his clever quote about procrastination read: Never put off till tomorrow what you can do the day after tomorrow.

Is that what I was doing? Procrastinating? I knew what had to happen. At some point soon, if I really wanted to understand our family's difficult past, I was going to have to confront Dad.

The door jingled and Sienna went to greet another customer. I wandered through the shop, picking up origami stars made from the pages of old books, fancy paper clips, and writer's charm bracelets, wondering which items Gertrude would have loved the most. Any of them? All of them?

I waved goodbye to Sienna, promising I would be back soon, and spent the rest of the afternoon going from shop to shop. Locals and college students congregated around outdoor fire pits at restaurants. I ended up buying a canvas beach tote, screen printed with pastel botanicals found in the redwood forest, and rose petal hand lotion.

Later, when I returned to The Ballad before my meeting with Cameron at The Campout, I decided it was time to rip off the Band-Aid and call Dad.

The line rang and rang until it sent me to voicemail. I left him a pleading message to please call me as soon as he could. Then I hung up and took a few minutes to splash some water on my face. Trying to tame my unruly waves was a challenge, but I managed to smooth them down and change into something warmer for the evening. Shay had been right about the shift in the weather. Granite clouds blocked the sunlight that had been streaming in through the stained-glass windows. I opted for a pair of jeans and my favorite book junkie sweatshirt in a soft heather gray. To think I had considered packing a blazer and tailored skirt when I left New York. They would have been useless here. Although I did regret not bringing an umbrella.

On my way out, I checked the coat closet and discovered that Gertrude had an umbrella for every day of the week. There were black and red oversized golf umbrellas, stylish pin-striped and polka dot umbrellas, and even a Raven umbrella with a quote from Edgar Allen Poe. Yet another moment of kinship between me and the grandmother I barely knew. Gertrude's collection of literary knickknacks was another reminder of how similar we were despite not having a relationship. What did that mean? Was it merely genetics or something more?

A tightness stretched across my chest. How had she left me?

I sighed and went with the Raven umbrella, tucking it under my arm and heading out into the cooling evening air. There was no rain as of yet, but the darkening clouds threatened to unleash a deluge of water. I had a feeling I would be glad for the umbrella later.

The Campout was only a few blocks away on the south end of the plaza. I could smell it before I could see it. A swooning sensation threatened to consume me as I smelled woodsmoke and the dreamy aroma of grilled meats and charred breads, and I placed my hand over my stomach to control it. The restaurant's rustic chic aesthetic, red camp lanterns, an entire wall composed of log slices and woodsy furniture, made me feel like I'd been transported to an upscale urban steakhouse. A large tree wrapped in flaxen twinkle lights dazzled as a centerpiece for the bar.

Intoxicating smells erupted from the live-fire grills, spitting out brilliant orange flames. I spotted Cameron at a two-person booth near a forest wonderland mural. He was deep in conversation with none other than Sienna.

Two empty wine glasses and the remnants of a cookie skillet sat in the center of the table. Cameron leaned his head on his elbows, gazing into Sienna's eyes. They appeared to be hitting it off. I almost didn't want to interrupt the moment, but Danny and the rest of the family were going to be at the house in a couple of hours.

"Hi, sorry to cut in," I said, with an apologetic grin.

Cameron startled and sat up. "Emily, hey! Is it five already?" He looked around for a clock. "This is Sienna—uh, uh." He fumbled over the introduction.

"A friend." Sienna beamed at him and then looked to me. "We met earlier." She had ditched her craft apron for a slinky low-cut red dress and dangling silver earrings. Definitely date attire. "I was just on my way out," she said, gathering her black leather purse. "Cameron mentioned that he's going to list your property. I've always loved the look of that place."

"Thanks," I responded, feeling awkward about accepting the compliment.

She slid out of the booth. Cameron's eyes followed her every move. "This has been nice," she said to him. "Let's do it again soon."

"Yes, I'd love to." He half-stood watching her go, then waved the waiter over to clear their dishes. "I had dessert first. What can I get you? Wine, a cocktail? Dinner?" Cameron had transformed since I'd seen him last, too. His long hair looked as if he had slicked it down with gel. He wore a short-sleeve shirt and a pair of khakis.

I took the seat that Sienna had vacated. It was still warm, and her floral perfume lingered in the air. The Campout's menu resembled a campground sign. "The Forager sounds amazing, and I could go for steak frites." I drooled over the cocktail's description of bourbon served chilled with foraged wild berries and a drizzle of honey.

"Good choice." Cameron placed our order.

"Sienna seems really nice," I offered, hoping he might expand on their meetup. Was Shay right? Had my edits created a love match? Was I supposed to play matchmaker?

"She is. We just met on the beach yesterday and ended up here." A flush the color of his wine spread across his cheeks.

"In the book industry, especially the romance genre, we call that a 'meet-cute'."

Cameron's face burned hotter. "Oh, no. No. No. It wasn't a date. Strictly professional. You never know where you might bump into potential future clients—the beach, the grocery store, you know, anywhere. No, that wasn't a date. I don't know why you would think that. Definitely not a date."

His protest didn't line up with the boyish grin I'd seen a few minutes earlier when he and Sienna were deep in conversation. Could my edits actually be a force for good? Did Sienna and Cameron's connection have anything to do with me? Or was this merely another coincidence?

CHAPTER ELEVEN

Cameron slicked his hair down with his fingertips, staring after Sienna as she crossed the plaza and disappeared out of sight.

"Sorry. Okay. Where were we?" He sounded distracted.

After he took a moment to compose himself by gathering a collection of real estate fliers from his bag, we reviewed the list of comparable properties he had compiled. "Now remember, these are preliminary numbers. Houses like your grandmother's don't come on the market often, so I want to expand my query to surrounding towns. I want to give you a general sense of price. This is a starting point because nothing that compares with the luxury, the attention to historical detail, or the square footage and lot size of The Ballad has come on the market here for at least ten years."

I leafed through the glossy fliers he had printed. They showed unique beachfront villas and exquisite Spanish style architecture.

"My range right now, which again is subject to change once we have a broader base of comps from the entire Lost Coast, is between three and a half and four million dollars." He paused and leaned closer, studying me for a reaction.

I gulped. "I'm sorry, what?" Had I heard him wrong?

His chin tilted down. He shook his head repeatedly. "Is that not what you were expecting? Like I said, I know there are similar properties in terms of architecture, history, condition, and size that have sold more recently in Ferndale and Eureka. I need to pull those in and talk to a few colleagues. This is a once in a lifetime property so we may be able to get much more. I wouldn't be surprised if we could push to five; we just have to see what the market will bear."

Words escaped me. Three or four million? I exhaled with long, slow intention. Holy crap. That was a lot of money. A lot of money.

"What are you thinking? I can't read your face." He leaned on his elbow and squinted like the dim light was hurting his eyes.

My voice cracked as I tried to form a sentence. "Millions? I had no idea."

"So you're happy with that price range?" Cameron wrinkled his brow and bent closer as if trying to get a better angle on my face.

"I'm stunned." No wonder Arty had been an asshole at lunch. I would have been, too.

"That's only for the property and grounds. There's also the matter of the business. I have a friend who can evaluate that and once we have a sense of the value of Lost Coast Literary, we can determine whether we want to list everything in one bundle, split them up, or include language to let potential buyers know that we're flexible."

Numbers swirled in my head. Coming from exorbitant housing markets in Santa Clara and New York, Cameron's estimate shouldn't have shocked me, but I had assumed that given the remoteness of the Lost Coast and the lack of industry and viable jobs, the price range would have been much lower.

"You're not attached to the literary agency, correct?" Cameron held his wine glass for the waiter to refill.

Wynston Marsalis's soulful trumpet lulled the bustling restaurant like a mother soothing a newborn. I sipped my cocktail,

letting the news sink in. "The agency? Uh, no, I'm not attached."
Or was I? I still hadn't solved the mystery of the forsaken manuscripts. The thought of seeing Gertrude's book collection and
literary agency sold off to a stranger made my throat constrict. I
gulped down another sip of the cocktail, trying to force it open. "I
don't know, actually. I'm not sure."

"No problem. I'll leave it up to you. You can think on it. As I
said, we can be flexible in the language to ensure that we keep our
options open." He patted the file folder. "Go ahead and keep
these. I'll have even more for you within a few days. There is one
thing to be aware of that I want you to know upfront."

"Okay."

He collected the fliers and stacked them in front of him. "I
mentioned this before, but I do need to warn you that properties
like this can take time to sell. But I'm confident that we'll find the
right buyer. I'll be doing broad marketing in the Bay Area and
Southern California. Likely throughout the Pacific Northwest—
Portland, Seattle. Since it is a special property, connecting with the
right buyer could take a while. In the meantime, there are going to
be some upkeep costs. I'll want to get a general contractor out to
look at the house, so we don't have any surprises down the road
when it comes to repairs. If it takes a while to sell, we'll want to
make sure we have a plan to keep the property in good shape
while it's listed."

"How much time are you thinking?" My mind flashed to
Piper. I'd been so eager to start building my list. I'd pictured it
hundreds of times, walking into the conference room wearing my
favorite skirt and outfitting my desk with my bookish treasures—
my Mr. Darcy framed quotes, my antique book pen holder, and
my Irish bookshop wall art, and dazzling my colleagues with a
brilliant pitch as to why the book I wanted to acquire was going to
become an instant bestseller. But now the picture was getting
fuzzier. Was there a life here in Cascata for me? My errant memories of this place were so different than the reality. The shades of
black and white that I'd learned about our family and the Lost

Coast from Dad were morphing into a kaleidoscope of brilliant grays.

"It's impossible to come up with a firm range. If this were a starter house or even a single-family home under four or five hundred thousand, I could basically guarantee we'd have offers within a month or less, but obviously when you're talking about multi-millions, the potential buying audience gets tighter the higher we go. I can't even guess because I don't want you to be disappointed if I say I can sell it in six months and it takes me a year."

A year?

"That's understandable," I said to Cameron, plunging a fancy bamboo stir stick into my drink. Our shared plate of steak bites and truffle fries arrived. Cameron dished up slices of seared steak, fries, and harissa ketchup for me. "I don't have to be here, though, do I? When I return to New York we can do this remotely, right?"

He dipped a fry into the thick sauce. "For sure. That's not a problem at all. We can do everything remotely. I'll keep you updated via email, text, FaceTime, whatever you prefer."

That was a relief.

"We may want to consider consulting a stager about how best to show the house, especially if you end up going the route of an estate sale. Empty houses tend to sit longer. Buyers don't like that vibe, and I would fear with a house the size of The Ballad that the creepy factor could be a deal breaker. We want warm and cheery. Or I guess more like high end and luxurious."

I cut into the tender steak. It melted like butter in my mouth. But my throat still felt tight and narrow. "Do you think it's better to hold off on the estate sale? Wait until we have an offer?"

Was I trying to buy myself more time?

He considered my question for a minute, swirling his wine and watching its legs cling to the side of the glass. I got the sense he was buying time to come up with a response. "Uh, yeah. Good question. Let me think on that. I'll reach out to a friend who is a home stager in Eureka. Hopefully, she can swing by in the next few days and give us her opinion."

The cocktail had warmed my body. Rain lashed the windows, spattering into the glass like tiny missiles. I was glad for the heat from the open-flame grills and the delectable food.

This was progress. This was movement. The estate had been valued for more than I ever could have imagined. But my role in its future still felt unclear.

Cameron provided me with a brief oral history of the region's architecture. "I always wished I lived in the pages of *A Study in Scarlet*," he said with a wistful quality to his voice. "That's one of the reasons I was drawn to this area. There's nowhere else on earth where you'll find stately Queen Annes hugging the cliff-sides. This place was made to be a novel. You should give this place a chance. I promise the longer you're here, the more it gets under your skin."

I didn't disagree with him, and I also hadn't pegged Cameron as so bookish. "You know your classics."

"Blame my mom. She was a children's librarian. In fact, Gertrude was a real mentor to her when she was starting out. She still volunteers three days a week at the library. Books were the lifeblood in our house. She had me reading the greats from a young age—Dickens, the Brontë sisters. I guess that's why I've always been drawn to write children's stories, but you know, life gets in the way." He stopped himself. "I'm sorry. I should be asking about you, not commandeering the conversation to talk about me. Sienna and I had the same conversation. She's a book lover, too, so I guess it's sort of the theme of tonight—books connect us."

"I could talk about books forever," I assured him. "Reading is and always has been my greatest love." What I didn't say to Cameron is that I wasn't sure I had ever really been in love. At almost thirty I'd had a couple of short-term boyfriends, but no one who lived up to the unrealistic expectations I'd created in my head thanks to the fictional characters I'd fallen for. No one who shared my passion for words. No one who made me feel like it was worth the risk of opening my heart.

I pushed the thought away. "You know when I was growing up what my punishment was?"

He shook his head.

"On the few occasions when I got in trouble my dad would ban me from nighttime reading. Seriously. He would take away my books. He knew it was the worst possible punishment imaginable. And obviously it was."

Cameron chuckled. "Oh, God. Don't take away our books."

"Exactly." I laughed.

We chatted about classics, poetry, our favorite modern writers and sci-fi titles that altered our perspective on the genre and reshaped our lifeviews. *The Left Hand of Darkness* by Ursula Le Guin for me. Ray Bradbury's *Fahrenheit 451* for him.

"Did you say you're meeting your family at the house?" Cameron asked when the waiter brought the check.

I glanced at my watch. "Yes, I should probably get moving. Thanks for the drink and dinner." I picked up the paperwork, my purse, and umbrella.

"I'll be in touch tomorrow." He stood as a show of respect. "I'm looking forward to working with a fellow book lover."

I left the restaurant feeling more conflicted about what to do. As Shay had promised, the rain fell in wet sheets from every direction as I stepped outside. A stinging wind made each drop feel like a bullet from the sky. I used Gertrude's umbrella as a shield without success. It blew in upon itself, bending the wire frame and looking like an archaic weapon or some kind of torture device.

I gave up. Instead of trying to stay remotely dry, I cinched my hood as tight as it would go, stuffed my purse and the file folder with the comps under my sweatshirt, and sprinted three blocks. Standing water pooled on the brick sidewalks, soaking through to my socks. A squishing sound oozed from my tennis shoes. The cold rain on my face felt like I was getting sprayed by a pressure washer.

Lumbering clouds blocked out any sliver of late evening light. They hung so low on the horizon it was if I could almost reach out and capture them. Howling winds bent the rain-laden branches of velvet ash trees and Monterey pines, sending debris and leaves scattering.

There was no reprieve until I skidded up the front steps of the house where the rain had found a way onto the covered porch, soaking the cushions on the rocking chairs and creating a tiny stream that trickled between the weathered floorboards. I kicked off my drenched shoes and ditched the mangled umbrella.

"Hello?" I called when the door handle twisted easily. A welcoming sound of crackling logs and the scent of smoke greeted me.

"Hey, Emily." Danny popped his head out of the parlor. "I hope you don't mind. I let myself in. I figured we might need to warm up this creaky old lady. She tends to get drafty when the wind kicks up like this. Keeshawna is making tea."

"Great." Yet again I was struck by how comfortable, how familiar Danny and his family were in Gertrude's house. They belonged here. Did I? I wanted to give them a chance, but I felt like an intruder.

My wet socks left imprints on the hardwood floor. I tugged my purse and paperwork free from my waterlogged sweatshirt. "I'll go change real quick." A thick pair of wool cabin socks, soft sweats, and my thickest fleece later, I returned to the parlor to find everyone gathered around the fireplace. Arty leafed through a volume of Keats poetry. He was the only person who hadn't removed his coat.

"Tea?" Keeshawna handed me a steaming mug. "It's herbal lemon with a splash of cream and Gertrude's secret ingredient."

"What?" I shot her a grateful smile as I took the tea.

"Maple syrup." Shay grinned. She lounged on a comfy chair, holding a ceramic mug. "Sounds bananas but it's delish."

The tea was too hot to taste. "I'll take your word for it."

"How did it go with Cameron?" Keeshawna stood in front of the fireplace. She had changed since lunch, I assumed for her performance, since she'd donned three-inch heels and a tight black turtleneck dress. Her hair was tied back in a twisted braid, accentuating her graceful neck and giant gold hoop earrings.

"Good." I clutched the mug tighter, thankful for the heat generated from it and the fire. Goosebumps had broken out on my arms. I stifled a shiver. How had I gotten so cold in just a few blocks?

"The rain gets into your skin, but you get used to it," Shay commented. "You can move a chair in front of the fire."

"Or come stand by me." Keeshawna moved to make room for me next to her. "I can't sit before I go on stage. Have to move the nerves through my body."

"Haven't you been performing for years? You still get nervous?" I stepped cautiously so as not to spill my tea.

"Always. I don't believe performers who say they don't. It's not like it was when I started, but there are usually helpful butterflies that remind me I'm about to put myself on display. Singing in front of people is the ultimate act of vulnerability."

I appreciated that she wasn't jaded or trying to pose as something other than her artistic self.

Thin smoke wafted into the room. Not enough to force anyone into a coughing fit. Just enough to center me in the reality that I was in a completely different world than I had inhabited a few days ago. I tried to imagine a roaring fire burning in my New York apartment. Or sipping tea spiked with maple syrup. Or how quickly my sense of family was expanding.

"Mom's seriously solid. She's dope. Don't let her fool you." Shay beamed at her mom, pride sneaking out the edges of her dark eyes. Keeshawna returned her gaze, like this was the way they always interacted.

It was almost unbearable, the easy tenderness between them.

Arty, who had been silent until now, caught Danny's eye. He

slammed the book of poetry shut and returned it to the bookcase, ruining the moment. "Are we going to sit around or are we going to talk?"

Danny crossed one leg over the other. He let his head rest on the back of the chair. "Can you give your cousin a minute to catch her breath?"

"Why? I don't know why everyone keeps pretending we're one big happy family. I want to know what we're going to do about Grandma's will." His piercing stare sent a new round of shivers through every cell in my body. "You're all thinking it. I'm the only one saying it. It's bullshit. I don't understand why Grandma would do this to us. It's total crap that she," he gestured at me, "gets everything, and that the pub is on the line."

I started to reply, but he cut me off.

"Do you know how much The Ballad is worth? Millions. It's not fair that you're inheriting everything. It's not what Grandma wanted. She wanted to keep this place in the family. It belongs to us. We can't just sit around and let her sell everything to total strangers."

Did they all feel this way? Danny, Keeshawna, and Shay had been so open and kind, but were they faking their enthusiasm for having me in town because they were worried about losing the pub?

If I were editing my own story, I would have written dozens of questions in the margins. What was their financial status, for starters? Yes, they owned what appeared to be a successful restaurant and pub, but how did that compare with a multi-million-dollar estate? And why wouldn't Gertrude have left something to the only family she'd known? The more I thought about it, the more none of this added up.

CHAPTER TWELVE

*D*anny shifted uncomfortably. "Arty, don't."

"Ask her. Ask her how much of Grandma's money she's going to pocket. This house is worth millions, and she doesn't care. She admitted that at lunch. I'm not going to let it happen. Grandma worked so hard to make The Ballad what it is. *She* doesn't care that this house has our history. She's seeing dollar signs. She cares about the millions. Not that these walls contain our heritage. Every room in this house is a reflection of her. This wallpaper." He slid his hand along the teal and cream accent wall where spindly water birds waded in marshy rushes and poppies and reedy flowers twisted amongst slender trees.

My pulse sped up. I crossed my arms and tried to tamp down the heat rushing through my body. How dare he accuse me of only being here for the money.

Arty massaged the wallpaper, gliding his hand along its smooth surface. "Grandma picked every detail of this house. Every swatch of paint, piece of artwork was intentional. You guys are okay with seeing her legacy destroyed? Selling this place off to some Southern California investor who will rip down this wallpaper and shred every remaining reminder of Grandma? Because

I'm not." His cheeks expanded, tinged with red, like a bottle of over-carbonated beer about to explode.

"And I don't care if I sound like an asshole or entitled. It's not just about the money. All of my best memories are in this house. Grandma is alive in this house." His pitch changed. "The Thanksgiving when the power went out. Remember when the turkey had only been in the oven for an hour and we ended up eating peanut butter sandwiches and pie right here in front of the fire? Birthdays in the garden. Grandma's homemade chocolate cake with sprinkles and raspberry ice cream. Her literary weekends when we got to dress up like our favorite characters and the entire town showed up for the salmon bake outside. How is no one else saying this out loud?" He looked to me. His face was so intense with a wash of anger and sadness that it made me move back. "Listen, it's not personal, but you left. You and your dad ditched us, and you don't deserve a dime of Grandma's money."

"Hey, enough." Danny got to his feet. "Arty, you don't know the whole story."

"Wait a minute." I threw my hand in the air. I didn't need Danny to protect me, and I didn't have to take this. "I didn't leave. I was a kid. I didn't have a choice. That's not on me." Anger formed a tight knot in my throat. "And I didn't ask for any of this. I'm supposed to be in New York right now. Do you know how hard I worked to follow that dream? Do you know what I gave up?" I paused just long enough to get more air. "Do you think I want to be here? I'd rather be tucked into my cramped apartment sticking ice cubes down my bra and fanning myself like I'm Mrs. Bennet trying to stay cool. You think this is a dream for me? Quite the opposite. I'm just getting to know you all. I have no idea where I stand." I lasered my focus at Arty. "You're pissed at me, and my dad won't return my calls. I'm as clueless as you about why Grandma left the house to me. But if I had to take a guess, it probably has something to do with guilt for abandoning *me*. It's awesome that you have such great, intensely personal memories of her. That must be nice. She's a stranger to me. Do you know how that feels? Let me tell you, it's pretty crappy."

"I'm not pissed at you," Shay jumped in. She placed her tea on the side table and stood up too.

"No one is," Keeshawna said in a soothing tone. She eyed Arty. "It's an impossible situation for Emily. Blaming her is only going to make things worse."

"Like it can get worse." Arty clenched one hand into a fist. "I'm out. I can't do this. Not here." He thudded to the front door and intentionally slammed it shut, causing the windows to rattle.

Awkward silence fell over the parlor.

"Look, why don't I just sell the house to you?" I asked.

"I'm not sure it's that easy," Keeshawna replied with a sad smile. "You have to understand that Arty and Gertrude were extremely close," she tried to offer as an explanation for his outburst. "We all grieve differently."

"He's not wrong, though. It sucks to bear the brunt of his anger, but I agree with him. Why did she leave everything to me? And why are the rest of you being so calm about it?"

No one answered. Logs cracked in the fireplace, lapped by the flames that devoured them. I finally tasted my tea. It was heavy on the lemon with a sweetness from the syrup.

"This was a bad idea." Danny looked to Keeshawna for confirmation.

She set her tea on the mantel. "Yes, this is our fault, Emily. We shouldn't have pushed Arty. I thought if we were all in the house together, it might put everyone at ease, but I was wrong. I'm sorry."

"But my point is that he's right. We do need to talk about this, even if it's hard. I'm not sticking around forever. We have to figure out what to do with all of her things." I swept my hand across the room. "As soon as I can get my dad out here, I have to get back to New York. Cameron is working on pulling comps from a broader region. He wants to bring in a home stager to talk about whether it makes sense to leave everything as is until we have an offer or move forward with an estate sale now and stage the house for showings."

"Oh, my Goddess, it's starting to feel real." Shay chomped her fingernail. "It's going to be so bizarre to have another family living here."

Danny reached for the fire poker. I moved to the side as he pushed the logs around, causing tiny embers to float up the chimney like a sea of fireflies. "Let's table this for tonight. I have a feeling we'll just go around in circles."

"But we need to talk about plans," I insisted. I got the sense that neither he nor Keeshawna enjoyed conflict. If left to their timeline, we might go on pretending for months on end. "This isn't going to magically fix itself. There's five thousand square feet of stuff we have to discuss."

"We will, soon. Let's give it a day or two." Keeshawna picked up empty teacups. "Would you like to come to the club? I can put your name on the guest list."

I glanced to the windows where the rain continued to fall, spurred by the screeching winds. "Can I take a rain check? I'm wiped out. I think I'm just going to call it an early night."

"Sure. Anytime." She gave me a gentle smile before taking the dishes to the kitchen.

"You can let this burn down." Danny returned an ornate iron gate to the front of the fireplace. "Keep the flue open tonight, and it will be fine."

"Thanks."

Keeshawna wrapped on a scarlet raincoat. She belted the waist and then stepped closer to kiss my cheek. The touching gesture made me clench my body tight. I fought back tears as she said, "Please don't worry about Arty. He'll come around, and we'll figure this out. We *really* are so happy to have you here."

Danny seconded her sentiment. "We are. Mom would have done anything to see us together like this. That's why I'm choosing to believe that Mom knew what she was doing, and you'll figure it out, too."

Shay started with them toward the door but stopped herself. "Oh, I almost forgot! I found your old books. I put them in Grandma's office. You're going to crack up when you see them." She gave me a big hug. I could smell her peachy shampoo as she squeezed me tight.

I couldn't remember the last time I'd been shown this much physical affection by anyone. It was oddly comforting and uncomfortable at the same time. I tried not to hold my body too rigid.

"Let's get together for lunch or something tomorrow. Catch up on stuff, you know? Cool?" Shay asked. Her eyes motioned to Gertrude's office.

I agreed and locked the door behind them. I went to grab the box of books that Shay had brought for me and took them back into the parlor. The fire burned low, logs smoldering above a bed of crimson embers. I found the pounding sound of the rain against the side of the house soothing. I tucked myself under a velvet throw blanket and took the books out of the box.

The first book was a hardbound copy of *Charlotte's Web*. I flipped through the pages, taking in the wonderful illustrations and E.B. White's remarkable story of an unlikely friendship between a spider, Charlotte, and a pig, Wilbur. My feminist roots must have been planted in early childhood because as I looked over my purple penciled notes for a better ending, I realized that even at eight or nine I had been confused and frustrated with the unhappy ending for the strongest female character in the book. Charlotte saves Wilbur only to write her own death sentence? No way. Not in my re-write. In my version, Charlotte's web weaving did indeed rescue Wilbur from being served up on a platter for Christmas dinner, but she also went on to save herself by hitching a ride on the tail of Templeton the rat to the farmhouse after laying her eggs, and living out a long and happy life with her children in the barn's rafters.

I felt pleased with my childhood editing lens. My version of the story offered Charlotte a new narrative. One she deserved.

After all, she was and should be the heroine of her own story. It made me feel more connected to Mom. Without her suggesting that I could re-write a different ending, would I be an editor today?

I held on to the thought as I leafed through the next book, a cartoony paperback copy of Roald Dahl's *The Witches*. I remembered how disappointed I'd been after reading the book the first time. All women could potentially be witches—disguising our disgusting and cruel witchy tendencies behind masks. I didn't understand misogyny at the time, but clearly my younger self had not been impressed with Dahl's slant on female leads. My penciled-in ending had the grandmother saving her grandson from an ill-fated life as a mouse by casting her own spell. Instead of the Grand High Witch Coven seeking out a mission of destruction, my re-write had them brewing potions for good. I must have borrowed themes from a few other childhood favorites like *Cinderella* and *The Candy Witch* because rather than having the witches strike out on a mission to eliminate children, the witches in my adaptation sprinkled kindness and chocolate bars to villagers, casting spells on mice to transform them into carriage drivers who delivered books to happy readers throughout the countryside.

I ruminated on my naiveté and my quest to enhance the endings that hadn't resonated with me to better match my world view. Reading through my re-writes made me acutely aware of my current responsibilities as an editor. Nothing had really changed since my first attempts at fixing a book. That was my job. To take a work in progress and change it, hopefully for the better. Could I do that for myself? I was more than a work in progress. I was a mess. I was confused. I was lost. And yet I could feel a tiny part of me starting to fracture, like the jagged coastline around me. This house, these books, Gertrude's warmth, none of it added up. None of it made sense. How could the Gertrude I was getting to know be so capable of love and not have loved me?

CHAPTER THIRTEEN

The storm blew strong for the next morning. I woke to howling winds and debris battering the bedroom windows. It sounded like a hurricane roaring onto shore. I dragged myself out from beneath layers of blankets and took a long shower. Long because it took what felt like twenty minutes for the water to reach a temperature anything near acceptable enough to step inside the tile surround. After the shower I dried my hair and pulled on a sweatshirt and jeans. The stack of clothes I had packed was starting to thin. Soon I was going to have to figure out where the laundry room was hiding.

I padded downstairs into the kitchen. Gertrude must have shared my love for good coffee. I found a French press and an expensive espresso machine with a built-in grinder, along with an entire cupboard filled with bags of whole beans from Guatemalan roasts to cinnamon-flavored coffee. I opted for a dark roast and took my coffee to the glassed-in sitting room to watch the storm while I tried to decide what to do next.

What was the best way forward with listing the estate? I couldn't delay forever, yet the conversation with Arty and everyone kept replaying in my mind. I wasn't in this for a money grab, as Arty seemed to think. Gertrude had put me in the middle of this family drama. If Arty wanted to be upset with anyone, it should be her.

Blaming our dead grandmother probably wasn't going to get us anywhere, though. I needed to talk to someone. I needed input from someone older and wiser than me. There was only one person who filled that role in my life—Dad.

I could almost hear his disapproving tone, but I called him anyway, hoping this time maybe he'd pick up.

To my surprise, he answered on the third ring. "What's going on, Em?"

The sound of backhoes in the background made it hard to hear him. It was barely after eight and he was already on a job site.

"Hi, Dad, how are you?"

"I'm okay. How are you, Em?"

"I've been better. Do you have a second to talk?"

He mumbled something. The rumble of machinery stopped. "What's going on? Is it Danny? Is he pressuring you to stay?"

"No, I mean, I don't know."

"Emily, I'm worried about you."

Maybe this was a bad idea. I swallowed hard.

"I know, Dad. It's just that I'm in the middle now, and I need your help." I wondered if he could hear the desperation in my voice.

He sighed. "What have they done now?"

"It's not what they've done. It's the whole thing. Gertrude left The Ballad to me, but I can't sell or do anything with it until I finish editing these manuscripts she left me."

"Manuscripts?" His tone was harsh. "What manuscripts?"

"A stack of manuscripts she left me in the will. I don't know what to do. I'm supposed to edit all of them, but I need to get back to New York and it's super complicated with the family. Arty is pissed at me. He thinks I'm taking advantage of the situation. Do you know how much this place is worth?"

"Does it matter?"

"Yes, it does to me. I need answers. I need your help. What

should I do, Dad? I spoke with a real estate agent yesterday who can put it on the market as soon as I finish editing, but he thinks it could take a while to sell." I cradled my coffee cup. "And I'm not sure now. After being here for the last few days I'm starting to wonder if maybe I should stay."

Dad interrupted again. "No, Emily, please don't put your dreams on hold. It's not worth it."

"Why didn't you tell me that Gertrude was a book editor, Dad?"

He was quiet. For a minute I thought he might have hung up.

"I thought it would complicate things." His voice softened. "This isn't your battle, Em. It's mine."

I wanted to protest. It was my battle, whether I wanted to engage in family warfare or not.

"Did you know that she had died, Dad? Danny told you, didn't he? Why didn't you tell me?"

"You were busy with the new job. I didn't want to bother you."

I clutched the edge of the kitchen table. My heart rate raged like the storm outside.

He paused to talk to someone. "Listen, Emily, I'm sorry that you're in this position. It wasn't fair that Gertrude did this to you, but I'm not shocked by it. Anything she left you is going to come with strings. You're going to have to ask yourself whether you want to be tethered to the Lost Coast. Whether you want to spend your adult life tied to people who gave up on us."

Gave up on us. What did he mean by that?

"I love you, you know that. If Mom wanted to write a crazy will, that's on her. Not us. It's not your responsibility." He paused for a second. "Listen, I have to get back to work. As soon as I can wrap up a couple things on this job, I'm coming up there to get you out, okay?"

"Okay." After we hung up I stared at the phone, feeling worse than I had before I'd called him. My stomach churned.

I finished my coffee and returned to the kitchen to see if the pantry or fridge contained anything I could scrounge up for breakfast. I decided on instant spiced apple oatmeal and a Greek yogurt. The black skies and heavy sheets of rain looming outside and blocking my view of the gardens matched my mood. There were no easy answers.

He was coming. I felt equally relieved and terrified. How would Danny and Keeshawna act after all this time? Could they all be civil or was I setting the scene for an epic battle?

One thing that would definitely alienate Arty, Shay, Keeshawna, and Danny was selling The Ballad. The truth was I barely knew them. Did I owe them anything? Technically speaking, no. Morally speaking, I wasn't so sure.

Let them in, Emily, the persistent voice in my head whispered. *Let them in.*

I ran my fingers through my hair, twisting a strand around my pinkie. I needed answers before I could make any sort of decision. Why had she left everything to me? What was her connection to the forsaken manuscripts? To me?

There was also the issue of money. The Ballad was worth a lot of money. Money that would set me up for my future. I wouldn't have to worry about retirement. I could get my own apartment in New York. I guess Arty had raised a fair point that I was motivated by money. I couldn't deny that there was a piece of me that didn't want to walk away from that.

Which memories did I trust?

Could these walls speak? Were the answers to my past hidden in another secret passage somewhere in the endless hallways of The Ballad?

I set my dishes in the sink and went to explore more. My hesitation about going through the house had vanished. I had Dad to thank for that. Our conversation was proof that he wasn't going to budge on telling me his side of the story. I could either be pissed or I could take matters in my own hands.

Or both, I thought as I opened cupboards and drawers with more force than I intended. I rummaged through rows of spices, a cupboard devoted entirely to sprinkles, and a library's worth of cookbooks. Unlike the pristine collection of books in the parlor, many of the cookbooks had miniature sticky notes flagging favorite recipes. I scanned a cake book with glossy pictures of hummingbird cake layered with decadent cream cheese frosting, and peach bourbon cobbler. Gertrude had noted different baking temps and minor adjustments to lists of ingredients on pastel sticky notes.

I felt my jaw go slack as I flipped to a recipe for red velvet cake where Gertrude had noted: "Emily's 8th birthday. A birthday in red for our little red."

Images of bunches of red balloons filling the kitchen, a three-tiered cake on a pretty white stand, and Little Red Riding Hood decorations surged forward. I had worn a velvet candy apple-red cloak. There had been a basket with snacks and sparkling cider. A scavenger hunt that led me and my friends on a search for treasures in the garden, and a piñata filled with candy and fake plastic rings shaped to resemble the big bad wolf.

I could hear the sound of the smack of the baseball bat pounding the piñata and the shrieks of happy laughter as its papier-mâché base ripped open, spilling brightly wrapped candy onto the grass.

I had been happy, delightfully so.

I closed my eyes for a moment, placing my hand on the picture of the red velvet cake and the inky smudges of Gertrude's handwriting, letting that truth sink in.

I had been happy here. I blew out a long breath and closed the cookbook.

My body hummed with restless energy. I needed to move. I returned the cookbook to its spot on the shelf. Next I found the laundry room on the opposite side of the pantry. Like the other rooms on the first floor, it was painted in tawny sand tones with natural wood wainscoting. A picturesque four-paned window faced the garden. Lavender and eucalyptus sachets made the room smell like it had invited the herbs inside. The space had been modernized with a freestanding washer and dryer and outfitted with neatly labeled bins for towels and sheets for each of the guest rooms. It reminded me of something straight out of Downton Abbey. Clean blankets, towels, and pillowcases were stacked in plastic bins reading SECOND FLOOR OCEANSIDE GUEST ROOM and THIRD FLOOR BATHROOM.

Who took care of The Ballad? Gertrude couldn't have managed this space alone. And yet since I'd been here I hadn't seen a housekeeper or gardener.

The front door chimes rang out the upbeat *Mary Poppins* tune. I went to the front, and found Cameron standing on the porch shaking rain from his black golf umbrella.

"Good morning. I hope this isn't too early." He was dressed in jeans, a rain jacket, and a pair of ankle-high boots. His long damp hair fell loose on his shoulders. "It's a soaker today."

"Nope, I'm up. Come on in."

He stopped in the foyer to take off his boots. Then he followed me into the parlor. Smoke from last night's fire lingered in the cozy room.

"I have some news," Cameron said, taking his phone from the inside pocket of his raincoat. "I heard back from a colleague in Ferndale. There's a property very similar to yours that just came on the market. I thought you might want to take a trip down that way to check it out. It's probably our best comparable." He offered me his phone. "Go ahead and scroll through the pictures. They should give you a good sense of the condition of the estate, but nothing makes up for touring a house in person. I told my colleague that we can be there in thirty minutes, if you're interested. She doesn't have a showing until later this afternoon."

I looked through the pictures. The Victorian had a similar style to The Ballad, and perhaps even more property with three outbuildings and a private pathway to the beach. "It's impressive," I said to Cameron, giving him back his phone. "But I don't think I need to go see it."

"Are you sure?" He sounded disappointed.

"I mean, I trust you. Is anything likely to change if I tour the house?"

He used his fingers to hold his wet coat away from his phone when he tucked back into his pocket. "Not a problem. I can head down there and take a look. It's always good for me to have a real sense of condition when it comes to finding comps. Pictures can be deceiving. Lighting and angles can make a big difference. Once, I convinced a client I had found the perfect property for them based solely on the photos that the agent had posted online. We arrived at their dream house to find that it sat two feet from train tracks in the front and next to a porn shop in the back."

I laughed.

"I don't need you to come, but I thought I would at least extend the offer." He ran his fingers through his damp hair.

"Thanks. I think I have plenty to do here." I wanted to get back to the house and my searching.

Cameron must have sensed how overwhelmed I was because he glanced around the parlor and nodded. "How did the talk with your family go?"

"Not great. My cousin thinks I'm a soulless gold digger, and I can't get anyone to commit to starting the process of going through Gertrude's things. I think we're stuck in some kind of standoff. Part of me has fallen in love with this place, too. I get it. It's magical, but I also have a life that's waiting for me in New York. I don't know. I don't want to make any authoritative decisions, but it might have to come to that. What about the lawyer who put together her will? Do you think there's any chance we can find a way around having to edit the manuscripts?"

What I didn't say to him was that the thought of making any more changes made me queasy.

"Uh, I don't know. That's not my area of expertise, but it's worth a shot." He frowned and sucked in his cheeks. "I've heard nightmares about family fallouts over estates like this, though. It could get messy. The good thing is that it sounds like Gertrude made her wishes crystal clear. You shouldn't have to worry about getting drawn into long legal battles with the extended family, if you can get the edits done."

I wasn't sure he was right about that. Arty had sounded like he was ready to fight.

The doorbell chimed again.

"You're popular," Cameron said.

I went to answer it. A woman in a sleek tan raincoat greeted me with a sheepish smile. Her long chestnut curls fell in lush thick waves. She wore a stylish pair of ankle-high boots under skinny slacks. Light maroon shadow dusted her dark brown eyes.

"I'm so sorry to bother you, but I'm looking for Cameron." She was naturally tall, but made even more so by her three-inch boots. Her meticulous stylish outfit, manicured nails, and expensive leather purse made her seem out of place on the gloomy Northern California coast. "He accidentally took my car keys this morning," she said, stretching her neck to see inside.

"Your car keys?" I was confused.

"Oh, how rude of me." She extended her hand. I noticed a sparkling diamond resting on her ring finger. "I'm Martine. I'm Cam's wife."

"Cameron's wife?" I repeated like a parrot.

"Yes, you must be Emily." She smiled, revealing unnaturally white teeth. "Cam's thrilled to be listing Gertrude's house for you."

I tried to take it all in. Cameron was married? To a woman named Martine?

Martine.

The Martine from *The Opt Out Clause*. Here we go again. I braced myself.

CHAPTER FOURTEEN

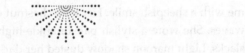

*P*anic rose in my chest. My heart thudded so loud it reverberated through my ears like a ping-pong ball bouncing back and forth.

"Is he here?" she asked, trying to get a better look into the parlor.

Now I was the one being rude. "Uh, sure, come on in." I stepped to the side, trying to remain calm.

"This is such a beautiful property," she commented, gazing at the arched ceiling. "If we were going to stay here much longer, I would be the first person putting an offer in. Not that we could afford it, but a house like this makes you want to deal with the devil."

"You're not staying in Cascata?" Why would Cameron have agreed to list the estate if they were leaving?

Cameron jumped up from the couch and hurried to the entryway. "Martine, what are you doing here?" He kept his eyes averted from mine and went to greet her with a hug.

"Sorry to interrupt your meeting. I know how important this is." Her voice was as smooth and silky as vanilla ice cream.

Too silky. Too smooth. Was it my imagination or was there tension between them?

I stared at them feeling dumbfounded that Cameron was married. I had assumed that he and Sienna were meant for each other.

Cameron was married.

Holy shit. Cameron was married.

"You took my keys, babe," Martine continued. "I have to get down to San Francisco by three for that meeting."

"Yeah, right." He dug through his coat pockets until he found Martine's keys. He rubbed the back of his neck, eyeing the foyer like he was trying to figure out a way to make a quick exit. "You met Emily?"

Martine unzipped her purse and stashed away her keys. "I just did. I was telling her that I would love to put an offer in on this place."

"We could." Cameron sounded hopeful.

"Cam, we've been over this. I can't keep commuting. It's killing me." She turned to me and rolled her eyes. "This guy. He's such a dreamer. I can't ever get his head out of the clouds."

Cameron stared at his feet.

"Cascata is a sweet little town, but I work for an ad agency in the Bay Area Monday through Thursday and then come home for long weekends. The commute is the worst."

Not that I needed more confirmation but, yep—she *was* Martine from *The Opt Out Clause*. For the first time since I'd made changes in any of the forsaken manuscripts, I was less disturbed by reality and fiction mashing together than with the fact that Cameron was *married*. What about Sienna? They had had such obvious chemistry last night.

What had I done?

Their meet-cute wasn't a meet-cute at all. I had written it wrong. They should have gone their separate ways. Instead, my edits had sent Cam on a date with another woman.

"You work in the Bay Area?" I asked Martine, hoping my gaping stare wasn't as obvious as it felt.

"Yeah, and like I said, the commute is killing me," Martine

admitted. "It wasn't so bad at first. It's a gorgeous drive along Highway 101. Have you ever done it?"

I shook my head.

"Not many people have," she continued. "There's rarely traffic, but it's a six-hour haul. I fly sometimes, but that's expensive. That's why I've been trying to twist this guy's arm for the last year to make the move with me." She squeezed Cameron's wrist.

Cameron tried to smile but his eyes held a faraway, wistful quality.

"I keep telling him that just the sun alone is worth it. We are going to be so much happier out of this sunless forsaken town."

Forsaken. Had she just said forsaken? Did it mean something? Was I missing some kind of secret code?

"That's true," I agreed, nodding to her. "I lived in Santa Clara for years."

"You did?" Martine perked up. "Why did you leave?"

I told her about my previous job writing mind-numbing tech copy and how an online ad for Columbia's Publishing Program had completely altered my career.

"I would love to take you out for a cocktail when I get back this weekend and pick your brain about Santa Clara. I've had my eye on a few neighborhoods. Now I just need to get Cam to come look at townhouses with me." She nudged his waist. "It's time to ditch the cold miserable drab drizzle. I have so much more energy when I'm in the valley. There's really something to this whole vitamin D thing, you know? It's no wonder that everyone here on the Lost Coast is so depressed."

Were they? Could that be part of the reason my parents had left? Danny and his family didn't seem depressed. Maybe Arty. But I had a feeling that was due to me.

"I keep telling Cam he could write. There are great grad schools in the area." She caught his eye and stopped herself. She strode with purpose toward the fireplace and ran her finger along the edge of the mantel. "I keep dreaming of the sun and orange trees and a swimming pool and my own clients."

Cameron shifted uncomfortably, fiddling with the zipper on his coat. "But now you get the best of both worlds." His voice was tinged with caution.

I wanted to disappear into the wallpaper.

"I wish it were that easy," she said with a hint of a sigh. Then she pulled me back into the conversation. "You see, I've been working for two terrible bosses for way too long. I have to do something else. My commute is only part of it. I can't keep working for these assholes. I'm talking movie quality bad bosses. Think ass-grabbing Mad Men era. They're the worst, and yesterday I literally almost quit. I was this close." She scrunched her thumb and index finger together. "I had put together a Power-Point letting them know that I was out for good."

"A PowerPoint?" I heard myself saying, knowing exactly what Martine was going to tell me before she spoke another word. Was my face betraying me? A damp sweat formed on my brow. I blinked rapidly, trying to focus on what she was saying.

"Don't ask. They think PowerPoints are the second coming. It's like SpaceX technology to these guys. I'm not exaggerating when I say that they are stuck in the past. Two martini lunches, admins (who they still call their 'secretaries') in short skirts. They come back from their private club reeking of cigars. It's nauseating. I've put up with it for way too long, haven't I, babe?"

"Yes, you definitely have." Cam nodded in agreement but didn't move away from the wall. Since Martine's arrival he had shrunk into himself. Even his broad shoulders appeared smaller as she continued. I noticed a familiar self-soothing gesture as he reached for his hair like he was going to tie it up in a bun, but let it fall again.

"What's so weird is that I've been plotting this for weeks. Yesterday the perfect opportunity arose." She picked up a small Buddha statue from the mantel and examined it. "I was inches away from clicking the file on my laptop when a text came through. I've been attending as many ad conferences as they'll let me under the premise of networking. The only networking I've been doing is for myself. I almost felt like some greater power was controlling my movements because if I had launched the Power-Point and quit on the spot, the job offer that's now on the table wouldn't be here. It's like divine intervention."

"Except you don't know anything about this new company," Cameron countered. "Like I've been telling you, maybe this is your chance to do your own thing. You have so much experience now. You could start your own agency here, and we could go visit whenever you want."

Martine blew him off. "That sounds good, but you know the reality isn't that simple. Venturing out on my own means paying for insurance and retirement. I don't want that risk. This is the opportunity we've been waiting for—we need this. This offer ensures that we can buy property in Santa Clara which has great schools for any future kids. You won't have to work if you don't want to." She gave him a half smile. "You can finally devote all your time to working on your book."

Cameron's cheeks flamed. I couldn't tell if it was because Martine had outed his secret or if he was worried about making a good impression with me. "I want to work. I like what I do." His voice was so low it was barely audible.

"I know you say that, but think of the time you could actually devote to writing children's books. But of course, if you want to continue with real estate in Santa Clara, I'm sure that will be very lucrative." She glanced at her gold-rimmed smartwatch with a rose band. "Sorry, I've got to hit the road." She kissed Cameron on the cheek and gave me a wave. "Let's do cocktails soon."

Cameron didn't speak for a few moments after Martine took off. A weighty silence filled the parlor with a heaviness as dark as the clouds outside.

"Sorry about that," he finally said, massaging his forehead with two fingers.

"No worries. I didn't know that you were married." I let the words linger, fairly confident that Cameron would pick up on my meaning.

"Yep. Going on ten years now. Martine and I met in college here. She was studying copywriting, and I was a creative writing major. We thought we might open a writing studio. She was going to freelance for ad agencies, and I could host writer retreats and workshops on the beach, but life, well, bills got in the way. She hates her job and the commute, which I get and I feel terrible that she feels like she has to keep doing it, but." He didn't finish his thought.

"But what?"

"Uh." He sounded surprised that I had asked more. "I guess it's that I can't imagine leaving this place. I love the moodiness of the weather. The storms, the rain, fishing off the shore, walking everywhere. My family is here. My mom hasn't been doing well, and I can't imagine leaving her."

"Have you said this to Martine?" I nudged. I was probably overstepping my bounds, but then again, I had re-written their story. Maybe if she had quit yesterday, she would have given up the commute and found happiness here in Cascata with Cameron. Of course, that didn't explain Cameron's date with Sienna.

"We've been talking about it until we're both out of words. She thinks that I'll get over it. She wants me to come spend a few weeks in Santa Clara, and then she's sure she'll convert me. What she doesn't understand or maybe isn't willing to see is that this is my home. It's hard when the person you love doesn't share your dreams anymore. I could never be happy in a big city, and I can take some vitamin D if I'm starved for the sun. Honestly, I'm not, though. People here aren't depressed. You've seen that already, right?"

I wasn't sure how to respond. I hadn't been in town long enough to take the emotional pulse of the community, but no one I had met had seemed depressed until now. "It doesn't seem like it," I said to Cameron and changed the subject. "Tell me more about your dreams—you want to write a children's book?"

His face burned again. "Someday. Yeah. Everyone says they want to write a book, don't they? Everyone I meet has a novel in them, it's only a very select few who actually do the work to see their ideas on the page. That's what my stack of 'how to write' books tell me anyway, although I don't know why I'm saying this to you. You're the book therapist. Isn't that what everyone called Gertrude?"

Did they? I wished I could answer that question.

"I prefer editor," I said to him. "You're correct about the vast majority of the reading public dreaming up book ideas and never following through."

"Do you know that Martine hasn't read a book in five years?" He shook his head in disbelief. "She says she doesn't have time with the commute, but she's hyper-focused on her career."

"It sounds like she's passionate about her work," I offered.

He blew out a long breath. "Listen, you're a new client. I shouldn't be dumping my personal issues on you. What I need to do is go get in the car and drive down to see this comp. You're sure you don't want to come?"

"No, thanks. I think I'll keep wandering around here." I glanced up to the ceiling mural. I had barely begun to scratch the surface of The Ballad, but I intended to change that later.

Cameron hesitated for a moment. "Hey, before I go, I just want to say thanks for being cool with Martine. I'm sure that was weird for you after seeing me with Sienna last night. It's not what you think, though. We talked about books and my dog."

"You don't have to explain anything to me." In fact, I hoped he wouldn't say more, especially since I knew I was ultimately responsible for their connection.

"Cool. Yeah, thanks. Anyway, I'll be in touch once I've toured the Ferndale property."

I showed him to the front door, locked it, and let my back fall against it until I slid all the way down to the cold hardwood floor, half expecting that the vintage wooden slats might break open and devour me. My mouth went dry. I tried to swallow, but my throat cinched tight. I wasn't imagining this.

Each of the forsaken manuscripts was playing out in real life, and all three storylines were headed for disaster. Tamir had been eviscerated by his crush, Sienna had been set up with a married man, and Cameron and Martine were on a miserable path of potential self-destruction.

Obviously, I was doing something wrong. The question was—what? And could I fix it?

CHAPTER FIFTEEN

*I*nstead of exploring more of the house, I returned to Gertrude's office and retrieved the stack of forsaken manuscripts. My body moved like sludge. I felt like one of the gooey slugs slithering in her garden. I had to fix this. I'd clearly done a hack job on my first round of edits. This couldn't be what Gertrude had intended. What was it about this stack? What was I missing?

The answer had to lie with the forsaken manuscripts. Maybe they needed a complete re-write. Maybe they needed to be shredded or burned in the fireplace. But what would that do to the characters? If I burned the stack, would they die in a horrible fire? How much power did my editing pencil actually have?

I had always believed that any book could be salvaged. It was a personal challenge to take on books in need of deep repair and unearth the nuggets of beauty and wisdom within. Maybe this was a sign that it wasn't possible.

My heart thudded in my chest as another thought invaded. Was this a sign that I had made a mistake? A reflection of my life choices? I'd been so confident, so convinced that publishing was where I was meant to be, but maybe I was wrong. Maybe this entire experience was meant to teach me that.

I sank into the chair and ran my finger along the picture of all of us on the desk. Was there a reason I was meant to be here? What did Gertrude know? My lips trembled as I stared at the photo. My hand instinctively went to my locket. I held it tight and said a silent prayer to Mom or whoever was listening to offer me some kind of guidance. Any kind of guidance.

I leafed through the stack, running my thumb against the edge of the pages. To my surprise when I landed on a short manuscript, I was stunned to see a sticky note taped to the front. The rectangular note was oyster pink with a butterfly on the top right edge. Gertrude's handwriting in beautiful calligraphy filled the page. It read:

IF THE LIGHTEST FLUTTER OF A BUTTERFLY'S WINGS CAN SEND RIPPLES OF WIND ACROSS OCEANS, SO TOO MUST BE THE TOUCH OF AN EDITOR'S PEN.

Was she speaking to me from the other side of the grave?

I carefully pried the note from the manuscript and set it on the desk.

Tears stung my eyes as I read her words again and again. The lightest touch. Was that my lesson?

Thank you, Gertrude, I need that.

I exhaled slowly and studied the manuscript. Unlike the others it was only a few pages in length. The forsaken manuscript was titled *Tip Jar Karma*. I read the short story in a matter of minutes. It was a cautionary tale about second chances. Lindi, the heroine, has recently been released from a women's prison after serving time. Her path of self-destruction was painful to read with abusive relationships, massive gambling debts, and a young son whom she was forced to abandon. In *Tip Jar Karma*, Lindi works toward redeeming her life by taking a job at a restaurant. The reader believes she's on her way to recovery, working a stable job and finding a way to reconnect with her son. Except there's a twist. Lindi witnesses a customer accidentally leave a huge tip. The story doesn't have a conclusion. It's up to the reader to decide if Lindi pockets the cash or returns it to its rightful owner.

When I finished the story, I leaned back against the chair and studied the ceiling. Wooden slats ran parallel toward the curved windows. Each slat had been stained with a Sahara gold varnish. How did Gertrude keep this place clean? Dusting the vaulted ceilings alone would have required an extension ladder and hours of time. Someone must have been tasked with the job because it looked as if the ceiling had been buffed smooth enough to skate on.

My eyes returned to the manuscript. It reminded me of a short story I had read in high school, *The Lady or the Tiger*, an allegorical tale about choice or lack thereof when faced with impossible situations. The story had stuck with me long after I had turned in my essay to Mrs Greene, my high school English teacher. Even as a teenager, I remember the idea resonating, and being fascinated with the story's intimate examination of personal morals. It was the first book I remember reading that left choice completely to the reader to decide.

In *The Lady or the Tiger* a princess has fallen for a commoner who is beneath her in status and situation. Her father, the king, makes her choose her beloved's fate. Behind one door lies a tiger who will consume him in a bloody massacre. Behind the second door waits a young maiden whom he must marry. Either option drags him away from her or forces her into a life without him. I distinctly recalled a vision of Mrs. Greene standing in front of the class holding a piece of worn-down chalk in hand as she paced in front of the blackboard, asking us a litany of leading questions like—What should the princess choose? Why did the author leave it up to the reader to decide? What would you choose for someone you love? What would you choose for yourself?

Tip Jar Karma didn't need a re-write. I understood what the author was trying to achieve in leaving the ending open for interpretation. It allowed the reader to put themselves into the pages. Would you reach into the tip jar and take the cash? Or would you alert the stranger of their error?

Mrs. Greene likely wouldn't approve of what I did next, but

since I'd made such a mess of my first attempts at editing these strange manuscripts, I picked up my editing pencil and made Lindi decide for herself. If this is why I were here like Shay had suggested, if this were Gertrude's legacy and something I had to finish, then I was taking charge of my edits. It was time to let the characters on the page decide their own fate.

❧

My eyes darted from the tip jar, a piece of paper taped on it with the words "TIPS ARE JUST HUGS WITHOUT AWKWARD BODY CONTACT" written in black Sharpie.

Had she meant to drop what looked like a few hundred dollar bills into the jar? I took a minute to check her out. Fancy sweater, skinny jeans, black and white polka dot rain boots, and a pair of aviator sunglasses. Odd choice for a drizzly day, but who was I to judge? She could be a famous celebrity trying to hide out from the paparazzi on the Lost Coast for all I knew. That would explain the sunglasses. I felt wide awake suddenly, as if I were on a caffeine high, as I eyed the tip jar again. That money would pay for Brayden's medical bills and leave enough left over for me to buy him the train set he'd been begging me for every time we walked past the toy store on the plaza. If she were rich, she'd probably dropped the bills on purpose.

❧

The manuscript ended a paragraph later with Lindi considering her choices. There was one simple way to end this bizarre experiment. I gave her a nudge, a light nudge. With one eye on Grandma's butterfly note, I penned Lindi making a choice. What it was, was up to her, but this manuscript wasn't going to end on a cliffhanger. Maybe if Lindi could make a decision, then I could hold out a glimmer of hope that her story might bring me some much-needed clarity, too.

I returned *Tip Jar Karma* along with the other forsaken manuscripts to the trunk and decided to venture out in the rain for a cup of coffee and some fresh air. If I sat inside, I knew I would over-think everything. Dad. The manuscripts. What I was going to do about The Ballad.

I grabbed my coat and stepped onto the covered porch. Debris from the storm lined the front pathway. Limbs from the redwood trees littered the grass and sidewalks like some sort of barbaric old-world brawl where contestants ripped each other to shreds. Even though Gertrude's house was a few blocks from the beach, I could hear the waves crashing violently against the shore, the same way my stomach had felt since I boarded the plane to come out here.

Two young guys in wetsuits balancing surfboards raced past me as if they might somehow miss the giant swells. I resisted the urge to follow after them. The inner adventure geek in me loved the thrill of extreme sports, not that there was a single cell in my body actually willing to put myself at risk. I preferred watching other people from a safe distance. That's what I loved about reading. Cracking open the pages of a new book meant transporting myself into new worlds and new ventures without ever having to leave the comfort of the couch. My therapist had once asked if books had become a crutch for dealing with my grief.

"What if you took an adventure yourself, Emily?" she had asked.

"I don't need to," I replied without having to consider her suggestion. "That's what books are for."

Had I been wrong about that? I'd spent the bulk of my twenties being pretty much miserable in a job I hated, taking respite in long weekends spent at my favorite bookstore and in the library. Was it respite, though? Or had it been an escape? Since coming to Cascata I'd been surrounded by books but I hadn't disappeared into them.

Rain rushed down the storm drains like a mini whirlpool. I had to use both hands to keep my raincoat hood secured on the top of my head, even with the straps cinched as tight as they would go. The heady scent of brewed coffee was a welcome relief from the miserable weather when I stepped inside Oceanic. Tamir stood behind the counter, taking orders and pouring mugs of hot coffee.

I felt skittish as I glanced around like a scared rabbit, waiting for another fictional character to appear at any moment. There was no sign of Lindi or celebrities in sunglasses lurking at one of the tables adjacent to the steamy windows, dripping with humidity.

"Hey," I greeted Tamir. "What's your special today?" I nodded to the chalkboard where the daily special was missing.

"Huh?" He turned around and looked at the board. "Crap. I forgot to put it up. It must have slipped my mind." He flipped through an old-school order pad until he landed on the page he was looking for. "We have a sweet and savory sandwich. Brioche with honey ham, Swiss, and my mom's famous apple chutney." He fiddled with the strings on his apron. I wondered if he'd slept last night. His hair was disheveled, and his eyes were bloodshot.

"That sounds good. I'll take that and a cup of the morning roast." I made sure no one was around us before leaning closer and whispering, "Have you seen the podcast crew again?"

"What?" His brows slanted. The way his nostrils flared made me wonder if it were from confusion or because he'd caught a whiff of something burning in the kitchen.

I inhaled deeply, realizing I had probably given myself away. "Uh, nothing... Sorry... I just happened to overhear your conversation about a podcast."

He took a minute to study my face, his dark eyes piercing into the back of my brain as if he were trying to mine it for information. "Oh, that's right, you were here when that went down. I forgot."

I tried to think of the right thing to say. "I mean, that was quite a scene. I was just hoping that there weren't any more incidents."

Tamir wandered over to the coffee pot and then returned

empty-handed. "No. It's fine." He tapped the screen of the iPad secured to the counter and punched in my order. While I waited for him, I scanned the counter. Next to it was a small pastry case with pre-wrapped slices of banana slug bread and lemon pound cake. There were collections of quirky coffee mugs and a station at the end of the counter with cream and sugar. The one thing missing was a tip jar.

Good. That was a relief. At least I didn't have to worry about seeing a scene from *Tip Jar Karma* play out for the moment. I felt my jaw unclench and my shoulders soften.

Tamir filled a cup with coffee and eyed me with a hint of suspicion as he handed it to me.

I paid for my order and scurried away, opting for the same empty window seat. Oceanic was quieter than it had been yesterday. An older couple read the newspaper at a table nearby. The husband orated tidal reports while his wife paid no attention. She was focused on the local news section. "Honey, did you hear that the library is hosting a benefit dinner in Gertrude's honor next month?"

He kept reading aloud.

She snapped in his face. "The tide doesn't matter. You're not listening. There's a benefit for Gertrude at the library, which is odd. I wonder why the family wouldn't have it at her estate?" She thrust the paper in his face.

The man appeased his wife with a nod, but he folded his tidal report with a reverence typically used for military flag ceremonies and tucked the paper into his coat pocket. It was surreal to think that probably the vast majority of customers in the coffee shop (if not all of them) had known my grandmother. It was yet another reminder that she had been loved by this town but hadn't loved me enough to keep in touch.

A woman with long dark hair worn in a braid and kind eyes delivered my breakfast sandwich. I guessed she must be Tamir's mother, given the strong family resemblance. I thanked her and scrolled through my phone. There was an email from Piper, checking in on me and asking me if I had an update in terms of when I might return. How quickly things had changed. I should have been excited about getting back to New York, but instead the thought of leaving Cascata brought a touch of sadness and nostalgia. How was that possible? I'd been here less than a week. And yet, with every passing day this place was getting under my skin.

My thoughts drifted to the forsaken manuscripts. I found myself surveying the room every few minutes, on high alert for anyone with an entourage or aviator sunglasses.

No one from *Tip Jar Karma* materialized. I enjoyed my breakfast watching the wind bend the leafy palm trees in the plaza. Residents weren't fazed by the rain. People yanked up their hoods and trooped on, seemingly not bothered by the deluge of water and gusty winds.

I emailed Piper, letting her know that I wasn't sure when I would be back. As I hit send, a text from Cameron buzzed.

AMAZING TRIP TO FERNDALE. HAVE SOME GREAT IDEAS FOR THE ESTATE.

THAT WAS FAST. GREAT IDEAS?

YEAH. IT'S ONLY 30 MINUTES AWAY. ARE YOU FREE FOR LUNCH TO TALK ABOUT IT?

SURE.

MEET YOU AT CRAFTS & DRAFTS IN AN HOUR?

I agreed, although my stomach wasn't going to forgive me. I had polished off every last bite of the breakfast sandwich and slugged down two cups of coffee. I couldn't possibly eat again all day. What was I going to do? My dream job loomed large in New York, but I was just starting to piece together the clues of my heritage. Of a family who seemed like they really loved me.

a n hour later, I walked directly across the plaza to meet Cameron at Crafts & Drafts. The rain had let up a bit, swallowed by clouds so thick that I almost had to use my hands to carve a pathway through the soupy fog that had rolled onshore. Mud seeped in large pools where the cobblestones met the grass. I was careful to stay on the sidewalk. The grassy area in the park looked like a post-Coachella mosh pit.

Crafts & Drafts reminded me of an artist's gallery when I stepped inside. Massive drafting tables took up one half of the room. Ribbons and yarns in every color of the rainbow hung on spools on the far wall. Floating shelves held craft paper, charcoal pencils, calligraphy pens, glitter, felt, and organic materials like straw, shells, and assorted smooth rocks and pebbles. The inner pre-school artist in me screamed in delight as I took in plastic bins filled with LEGO bricks and high-end crafting tools—laser cutters, 3D printers, and a screen-printing station.

Opposite from the crafting area was a long walnut bar with at least two dozen tap handles. Rustic seating wrapped around the bar. Cameron waved from a barstool. Behind him on the tawny-colored walls was a gallery of identical paintings. As I approached the bar, I realized the artwork must have been from a pint and paint night advertised at the counter. Each of the individual masterpieces featured a beach sunset with the jagged Lost Coastline. It was interesting to see how the artists had used the same color palette and yet every painting had its own unique slant.

"How was your morning?" Cameron asked. He had tied his hair up. A few loose strands fell from his bun. His knee bounced on the bottom rung of the barstool.

"Good, I mean, I just saw you a couple hours ago."

"True. True." He reached into a worn leather satchel and handed me a flier splotched with rain. "Check this out. I've got a really good feeling about this idea. In fact, I can't sit still. I'm pumped about what I came up with on the drive home." His entire body nodded in rhythm to his words as he spoke. "Okay here's the thing. The property in Ferndale is impressive, but still not on par with Gertrude's estate. They're selling it as an investment opportunity, which I think is something we could do for you. Or, if you want to think out of the box and get really creative, we could even have a discussion about me managing something like this for you."

"Something like what?" I asked as I scanned the flier.

He ran his teeth over his lips in a show of nervous hope. "High end Airbnb. The revenue they're generating just during the summer season covers all costs and expenses for the year— staffing, cleaning, maintenance, and property taxes."

"I don't understand." I set the flier on the bar.

"The Ballad could become this, but better." He tapped the flier. "What if you take the concept of Lost Coast Literary and turn her estate into a book lover's paradise? You love books. I love books. This town loves books."

"Huh?" I frowned.

"Just hear me out on this. Many of the rooms already have book themes and décor. Expand that. You could go all in with the great California writers like Steinbeck and John Muir. Or give a nod to the classics. You could have an ode to Agatha Christie room where you serve traditional English tea in the afternoon. I'm thinking writer's retreats, workshops, literary parties—everything books." His energy was electric. His knee shook so hard that I thought he might topple off the barstool. His eyes were wide with enthusiasm. "I know an amazing baker we could hire to cook beautiful breakfasts in that gorgeous kitchen. People would eat up this concept, pun intended." He let out a little chuckle. "But no, seriously, you could stand to make a lot of money. I'm talking long-term income here. Not just money from a sale, but an ongoing investment that could set you up for life. You wouldn't have to worry about taxes, or things getting awkward with your family. It could be the perfect solution."

"What?" I wrinkled my brow. Could I keep The Ballad and turn it into something like this? I chomped on my lip, imagining the possibilities. The idea filled me with a palpable excitement, but that was a huge undertaking and would mean giving up on my dream of New York for good.

"Our conversation about Gertrude's will got me thinking. This could be a way to avoid family conflict. You wouldn't be selling. It's a way to keep the property in the Bryant family." His eyes became even wider as he tried to pitch me on the idea. "Seeing the property in Ferndale really opened my eyes. It's booked every night solid through the end of October. There is some serious cash to be made in the short-term rental market. I know you're heading back to New York as soon as you've fulfilled your editing require-ment here, and that's why I'm saying I could manage the property remotely for you. And on the plus side, that way anytime you come to visit your family, you'll have a built-in place to stay. I need to run some firm numbers, but I think you can gross a really nice profit." He paused and picked up the flier. "That's stable income for decades. There's already a shortage of hotels here, especially during the summer and when families come to visit for parents' weekends, homecoming, and graduation. The Ballad is one of a kind and guests will pay top dollar to be able to stay in the historic mansion. If you do some book themed add-ons, we, uh, *you* could stand to make a lot of money."

A waitress interrupted us to take our order. Her face was pretty with high cheekbones and plump lips, but her eyes held a weariness as if the world had beaten her down like the storm outside. Her dusty blonde hair was cut short at a blunt angle like it had been sheared off with a straight edge razor. "What can I get you?"

Cameron ordered lunch. I opted for a cup of lemon herbal tea.

"You're not going to eat?" he asked when she left to put our order in.

"I just had a big breakfast." I paused for a minute, trying to think of how best to tell him that owning an Airbnb on the opposite coast wasn't any part of my future vision. "Look, I appreciate your enthusiasm and wanting to think through every possibility, but I don't know if I can take on a project like this now. I'm supposed to be back in New York next week."

"That's why I would run it for you." His pale brown eyes were almost pleading. I could sense what felt like a manic desperation pulsing off of him.

"Right, but there's so much more that would go into a project like that. Firstly, the renovations. Do you know how much it would cost to outfit each room with a book theme? Not to mention the level of staff who would be required for upkeep—cleaners, a cook, grounds people. Do you know if she had hired help?"

He shook his head.

"I mean I love the idea, I really do, but I'm not sure. That's a huge project to take on right now." It was true. The thought of turning The Ballad into a bookish retreat was more than compelling, but could I handle that on my own? What about the conversation I had witnessed earlier between him and Martine? For all I knew, he was planning to take off for the Bay Area. Did he really want to help me with this, or did he see me as his ticket to stay in Cascata?

His face fell. He reminded me of a young child who'd been told that he couldn't keep a puppy. He tried to recover by clearing his throat and shifting on his barstool. I saw through him. "I understand. It's a lot to think about. Maybe you should take the rest of the day and then tomorrow we can get moving ahead with the listing if that's the direction you want to go."

Before I could respond, the door blew open, and a woman rushed in. She shook an umbrella unsuccessfully, sloshing water onto her cable knit sweater and skinny jeans. "This place is so wet," she fumed as she tossed the umbrella in a galvanized tin by the front door and left a trail of footprints from her black and white polka dot boots as she tromped to the bar.

Oh, no.

It's happening again.

I curled my toes around the barstool. The woman's outfit was a dead giveaway. She shielded her eyes from the grayscale tone behind a pair of aviator sunglasses.

"Be with you in a minute," the waitress said, as she came to deliver my tea and Cameron's lunch.

I tried to steady the shaky feelings assaulting my body by grasping the mug. Its warm, smooth surface did nothing to quell the familiar swirl of nerves in my stomach. I already knew what was going to happen, but I watched anyway. A feeling of distance invaded my body, like I was observing a film from far away and couldn't quite make out the sound.

"I'll take an Irish coffee," the woman in the aviator sunglasses said to the waitress, cutting a direct path to the bar and making sure everyone around her took notice. "Double shot. Make it strong. I hate this place."

The room began to sway. Or was it me?

I could hear Cameron crunching on his chips, but I couldn't tear my eyes away from the scene I had re-written. The woman in the sunglasses dug through her expensive black leather purse and pulled out a wad of cash. Her cell phone buzzed at the same time, distracting her from the task at hand. Without paying attention, she handed the waitress payment for her drink and then she stuffed a bunch of crisp bills into the tip jar before she moved to the far side of the room to take the phone call.

The waitress, who I now realized must be Lindi, stared at the tip jar, which I noticed for the first time had a piece of paper with the words "TIPS ARE JUST HUGS WITHOUT AWKWARD BODY CONTACT" on it exactly as it had appeared in the forsaken manuscript.

Lindi removed the money from the jar and carefully peeled the brand-new bills apart.

"Excuse me," Lindi called to the woman.

The woman pointed to her phone and shot daggers at Lindi.

"I think you left too much money," Lindi continued. "These aren't ones." She pointed inside the jar.

The woman on the phone glared even harder. Then she held up her index finger. "Excuse me. I'm on a call."

Lindi held her hands up in surrender. "I'm trying to tell you that you tipped me too much."

"It's fine. Keep it." The woman let out an exasperated sigh and shook her head repeatedly at Lindi before continuing with her call.

I watched with interest. This was as far as I had edited the scene. What happened next was entirely up to Lindi.

The sound of Cameron's voice made me almost fall off my barstool. "How's your tea? You sure you don't want something? They make the best chips in town here. You should try them."

"I'm okay." I didn't make eye contact, keeping my focus on Lindi, who had backed away from the tip jar like it was a bomb about to go off.

"Seriously, they are so good," Cameron said with a mouthful of chips. "You have to have them with the aioli dipping sauce. It's spicy and has a hint of sweetness. So good."

"Uh-huh." I was barely listening to him. I wanted to see what Lindi was going to do with the money. He must have taken my lackluster response as a request for chips because the next thing I knew he was waving the waitress over. "Hey, can I put in another order?"

"No, really, I'm fine," I insisted, but Lindi had grabbed her order pad and approached us.

"What do you need?" She had a pen in one hand and an order pad in the other, but her eyes kept darting back to the far end of the bar where the tip jar sat with crisp hundred dollar bills. Was she considering her options or worried that the woman on the phone was going to realize the mistake and come back for her cash?

"Can we get a second order of chips and aioli?" Cameron asked, clearly oblivious to what just happened.

"Sure." She made a note and then caught me staring at the tip jar. "Did you see that?"

"The tip?" I nodded.

"Yeah." Lindi's eyes had lost their dullness. "She stuffed a bunch of hundreds in there. That had to be a mistake. They were stuck together. I think she must have thought they were ones."

"That's my kind of mistake," Cameron chimed in. He seemed to take notice of the woman on the cell phone for the first time. "She looks like rich Hollywood to me. I'd pocket that cash if I were you."

"You think?" Lindi looked to me.

I shrugged. "You told her about it, right?"

She bit her bottom lip. "Yeah, but she didn't listen."

"Does it matter?" Cameron munched on another chip.

Lindi hesitated. "I don't know. It feels wrong. I don't know why, but it gives me a bad feeling. When I give her her drink, I'm going to ask her again."

Miss Sunglasses began screaming into her phone. "No! Do *not* do that. I'm telling you not to do anything until I get back. Are you listening? Can you hear me?" She stopped and held her cell in the air, trying to get better reception. "Hello? Hello? Can you hear me?"

She must not have received an answer because she stormed to

the front of the pub, grabbed her umbrella, and slammed the door behind her.

"Well, that takes care of it, doesn't it?" Cameron said to Lindi. "Looks like today is your lucky day."

I heard Lindi murmur, "It doesn't feel lucky," as she went to get our chips.

A day or two ago I might have agreed with her, but now I wasn't as sure. There was something about the Lost Coast that made me feel like my luck was starting to shift.

CHAPTER SEVENTEEN

ameron hadn't exaggerated about Crafts & Drafts chips. I tucked into the basket as Lindi went to take another order. They were crispy without being greasy, with a touch of sea salt and vinegar. When dipped in the spicy aioli they were undeniably delicious. I found myself polishing off the entire basket despite still being full from breakfast. I watched Lindi the entire time I stuffed my face. The space had filled in with a group of retirees who were attending a ceramics class. Lindi navigated the crowd, carrying trays of frothy pints and platters of burgers and chips to each table. She shuffled as she delivered food, keeping her head down and making minimal small talk.

The tip jar continued to fill with loose change and dollar bills, pushing the stack of hundreds to the bottom, like some kind of buried treasure waiting to be unearthed. Or was it that the treasure was cursed? Lindi avoided the jar as if she anticipated the opening of a pharaoh's sealed tomb releasing deadly plagues and seas of spiders onto her path.

"Told you the chips were addictive," Cameron noted when Lindi came to clear our plates. He didn't appear to notice the distress etched on her face. Her body moved like a rabbit fleeing from a predator. Her face revealed her struggle. I watched as her eyes would briefly drift quickly to the tip jar. Then she'd give her head a quick shake and pour a pint or take an order. I felt like I was invading a personal conversation, intimately watching her vacillate between stuffing her hand in the jar and shoving the cash into her jeans before making a break for it, or letting it sit there and fester like an open wound.

"So what do you say, take some time, think about my idea, and in the meantime, I'll finish putting the listing together and send out my photographer. Sound good?" Cameron pulled out a well-worn wallet stuffed with receipts and business cards to pay the bill.

"Will do."

"Just keep in mind what we talked about in terms of expenses, too. If things go south and your extended family drag this out in court, you'll be on the hook for everything in the meantime." He paid the bill, then turned to me after he had settled the tab. "Sorry, I'm not trying to freak you out. I swear I have your best interest at heart." He tucked his credit card back in his wallet. "And hey, I wanted to apologize again for earlier with Martine. I'm sorry if that was weird, but like I said, the other night with Sienna wasn't what you think. Martine and I have been talking about separating for a while now."

"It's really none of my business." I shook my head and held up my hands to stop him from saying more. Although given that I could have had a hand in his narrative, I wasn't sure that was entirely accurate.

"Anyway, I appreciate it." Cameron stood. "Can I give you a ride?"

"No. I'll walk." The truth was that I wasn't sure what to do next. I sat at the bar nursing my tea, which had gone cold. Lindi came over twice to check on me and ask if I needed a fresh pot of water or a new tea bag. The third time she asked, I thought she was going to politely suggest that it was time for me to vacate my seat, but instead she leaned her chin on her callused hands and glanced around to make sure no one was listening.

"You're new here, aren't you?" Her hands were cracked and dry. Tattoos in dark shades of black and blue spread along her forearms, almost like bruises. "I haven't seen you around."

"I'm here for some family business." I shifted in my seat, not wanting to elaborate at the moment.

"Okay, that's why I didn't recognize you. I'm Lindi, by the way." She held out her hand.

"Yeah, I know." The words came out before I could stop them. I returned the handshake as she gave me an odd stare.

"Your name tag." I pointed to the name tag pinned to her shirt.

"Oh." She drummed her fingers on the bar. Her black nail polish was chipped and her nails had been chewed down, leaving open cuts on the tips of her fingers. "I guess I could use some advice. I know it's supposed to work the other way. I'm supposed to be offering wisdom from this side of the bar, but you saw what happened earlier, and I'm not sure what to do."

"You mean about the tip?" I nudged, hoping she would say more.

"Yeah." Her eyes returned to the jar. "I have a kid and I've been gone and not able to take care of him. I could really use the money to help him, but it doesn't feel right to take it, you know?"

I wasn't sure how to advise her. In my re-write she had attempted to return the money, but I hadn't anticipated that Miss Hollywood wouldn't accept it.

"It's like a test. A weird test," Lindi continued, pounding her fist lightly on the bar. "A test I'm going to fail." The Edison style bulbs lining the bar reflected in her sky-blue eyes, giving them soft angelic halos. I got a closer look at her face. She wasn't as young as I had first thought. Soft lines creased her forehead. A small scar cut from the base of her lip to her chin. Her cheeks had a dull tint to them, as if her skin had been deprived of natural sunlight. Her short bob accented her cheekbones, but it wasn't a particularly stylish cut. It looked more like she'd taken a pair of kitchen shears and cut it herself. Her blonde ends were split and frayed.

"How so?" I asked.

"It's a long story." She sighed. "I've made a lot of mistakes. Big ones. I've paid for them, though. I'm not afraid to admit that, even to you—a stranger. In fact, my therapist said it's important to own my past. I'm trying to do right by my kid. That money feels like it could be a gift or it could ruin me. I'm not supposed to touch the money, but we're short staffed today."

I'd never had anyone be so forthcoming with me. Was it because of the manuscript? Did Lindi intuitively know that I had nudged her to a new future?

I should have left it up to chance, as Mrs. Greene would have scolded. After all, wasn't that the author's intention? To let each reader determine what came next. I should have trusted my instinct that *Tip Jar Karma* had been written in the same vein as *The Lady or the Tiger*. It hadn't been my place to tweak it. A wave of guilt washed over me as her cheeks sank deeper into her face.

"How would it ruin you?" I asked.

She gnawed on her bottom lip so hard I thought she might cut straight through it. "I've had some problems with money, you know, and it's probably better that I don't have a wad of cash hanging around, you know?"

Maybe if I played devil's advocate, I could help her figure out the best choice. "But didn't you say that the money would pay for necessary things for your son?" Had I made a mistake? I knew that from the manuscript. What had the manuscript said about overdue bills? The real world and my edits were starting to blur together.

She appeared unfazed. "It would help a lot. I have a kid and I've been gone. I could really use the money to help him, but you know." She trailed off. The way she continued to stare at the tip jar as if it might grow legs and walk away was unsettling. She moved from chewing on her lips to biting her thumbnail. "I just need to take it and get out of here, you know, because it would be pretty easy to double it."

"Double it?"

"Yeah, the casino's just a few miles down Redwood Highway." She pointed behind us. "If I could double it, that would pay for half of next month's rent."

"Or you could lose it all," I countered.

She nodded in agreement, but her eyes remained glued on the tip jar.

One of the women attending the ceramics class approached the bar. "I should get back to work," Lindi said. "Thanks for listening. I needed to talk that through."

"No problem."

Part of me wanted to stay and watch what she decided to do, but I'd been sitting on the hard barstool for too long. My left foot had gone numb. I shook off the tingling sensation as I put on my raincoat and walked outside. The rain had let up, giving way to gray skies with tiny spots where the sun struggled to break through. Garbage cans had been blown over. Tree limbs sagged under the weight of the rain and wind. Pale purple hydrangea petals littered the cobblestone pathway. Streams of water gushed toward overflowing storm drains, creating miniature rivers adjacent to the sidewalk.

"Emily! Emily!" A voice called behind me. I turned to see Shay sprinting toward me. She looked like she belonged on the cover of a travel ad for Cascata with her black leggings, candy apple-red rain boots, and matching red rain jacket with oversized black buttons and a black and white striped hood.

"Hey, I was heading to the house to find you," she said as she caught up to me. Water sprayed with each of her long strides.

"You found me." I held my hands out in surrender.

Shay's cheerful disposition wasn't dampened by the rain. "Yay. I'm so glad. I totally need an update about..." she lowered her voice and glanced around us. "The manuscripts."

"You want to come back to the house with me?" I didn't want

to talk about it in the middle of the plaza. I had the sense that news traveled fast in Cascata, especially since it appeared that the entire town had adored our grandmother.

"Sure." She slowed her pace to match mine. Her legs were so long I had to take two steps for every one of hers. "How was last night? You didn't lose power, did you?"

"No. Why? Is that normal?"

She nodded. "Sometimes. Depends on the storm."

I made a mental note to check my bedroom for flashlights or candles. The thought of being plunged into complete darkness in the rambling mansion sent a shudder down my spine.

"Before I forget, what are you doing tomorrow?" Shay asked. We passed the hotel and turned right toward the beach.

"No idea."

"You want to come with me to a taping of the podcast?"

"*The* podcast?"

"Yeah. It's not a big deal." Shay waved me off. "But I thought you might be interested in coming to see what goes down between Tamir and Kenzie. I still don't get why he likes her. She's such an ass." She made a gagging motion. "Just wait until you see how sickly sweet she is to the audience."

"She has an audience?"

"Yep, can you believe that? Some people. I guess that's what money buys you. Her parents own a bunch of restaurants in SoCal, and her mom is a reality TV star. The rumor is that they gave the college a donation in exchange for the show. It's a pretty big show. They record it in the auditorium on campus. It's broadcast live twice a week. She gets some decent names to come on as guests. Mainly any speakers who are already coming to campus, but still. It sucks that she's bitchy because Cascata could use a decent podcast."

I frowned. "I thought that's why you turned her down."

"I did, but I changed my mind." She winked. "You've inspired me. I decided it's better to be part of the narrative and try to shape it versus just reacting to it. That's why you have to come for moral support."

"Okay." I was surprised that Shay had had such a dramatic shift of heart. Then again, everything about Cascata had surprised me since my arrival. Shay's shifting attitude shouldn't be any different.

We arrived at the house, and Shay immediately made herself at home, kicking off her boots, hanging her coat on the rack, and plopping onto the couch in the parlor. Her body had a familiar connection with the estate. It was obvious that she'd spent many hours lounging in the same position.

Envy welled inside me. How many times had she spent rainy afternoons reading in the cheery parlor with Gertrude? I could almost picture Gertrude bringing them a tray of hot chocolate with mini marshmallows and chocolate chip cookies. I could hear their laughter and how they had conspired to convince Keeshawna and Danny to let Shay and Arty sleep over and stay up late watching movies in Gertrude's king-sized bed. Could I have had that, too, if it weren't for Dad? But then, why had Gertrude let him take me away? Why hadn't she tried harder? Why hadn't Danny and Keeshawna made more of an effort to connect with me?

"So, tell me. What happened? Have you found a mysterious woman named Martine?" Shay dangled her feet off the edge of the couch like her toes were skimming the surface of the surf which roared in the distance.

"I found Martine, and it's not good." I locked my eyes on her, waiting for her reaction.

"What! You found her? Already? Damn. That was fast." Shay sat up straight. "What? Why are you looking at me like that? It isn't good? I don't get it. Isn't this what we wanted to happen?"

I shook my head. "Well, for starters she's *married* to Cameron."

"What?" She threw her hand over her mouth. "Married? How can that be? I know my dad and Cameron have done business together but I had no idea he had a wife. Crap. What does that mean for the manuscript? I could have sworn you had edited the perfect meet-cute. A dog on the beach. That's like romcom gold."

"Nope. Our meet-cute on the beach was actually a complete mess. Cameron and Martine are married. She works in Silicon Valley for part of the week and commutes here on the weekends."

"Oh, shit." Shay's mouth hung open. She tapped her fingers to her chin. "Married, really? Shit. I didn't see that coming."

"Neither did I. It was super awkward. She showed up here this morning because she couldn't find her keys, and Cameron turned as white as a ghost. He knew that *I knew* he and Sienna had been on a date last night. It's so messed up." I paced in front of the bookcases.

"Crap."

"Nothing that I've edited has helped, Shay. Nothing! Everything I've changed has gotten worse."

"You don't know that." Shay stood up as if she were going to try and hug me, but instead she moved to the fireplace. "Give yourself a little more credit. I'm telling you that Tamir is way better off without Kenzie. She's the worst. He deserves so much better. I've already said this, but I swear to the Goddess that you did him a massive favor."

"I don't know about that. You should have seen him this morning. He looked like he'd been run over by a truck."

She started to protest, but I motioned for her to hang on. "But there's more. It's not just Tamir and Cameron." I told her about *Tip Jar Karma* and my interaction with Lindi. "I think she has a gambling problem. I thought she was weighing her choices when she kept staring at the jar, but now I think she was calculating how she could double the cash. This woman is on a path to rebuild her life and with my re-write, I may have destroyed her only chance at happiness."

"No, come on. You're being dramatic and way too hard on yourself." Shay's tone was pleading.

"I can promise you that I'm the least dramatic person I know. Think about it, Shay. Every edit that I've made has backfired. This is a disaster. I haven't written a single happy ending. If I were reading any of these books, I would want to toss them in the fireplace and torch them."

"Emily, you don't get it. You're a professional editor. You know as well as anyone that tension is what makes good fiction. This is the murky middle. This is the place in a manuscript where everything is supposed to go wrong. What if you've gotten it right? Maybe this is exactly what was meant to happen. I'm more convinced than ever that this was Grandma's plan for you. This has to be why she left you the house. She knew you would have to come out here. She knew you would find the manuscripts. She knew you were the only person who could fix them."

"You're giving her and me a lot of credit, Shay."

"No, I'm serious. You can fix this. You know books. You've trained for this. You studied for this. Books are your life, am I right?"

I shrugged.

She rolled her eyes. "Of course I'm right. Do what you would do with any other manuscript. The tension has been established. It's time to move the plot forward. Get back in Grandma's office and do the next round of edits." She pointed across the hallway.

I clutched the bookshelf. "I'm not sure. Do you really think it's a good idea? What if I just make things worse?"

"You don't understand, Emily. You have to. Don't ask me how I know. I'm not sure, to tell you the truth. Maybe it's reading all of the books that you fixed when I was young, or the way that Grandma talked about you, but I'm pretty sure that this is your purpose."

"Shay, that's easy for you to say. You're not the one responsible for ruining people's lives. This isn't fiction anymore. It's happening, and I don't know how to make it stop." Panic bubbled up to the surface. What if I were wrong about my edits only happening in the forsaken stack? What if I couldn't make it stop? What if I were stuck seeing fiction play out in front of me for the rest of my life? Or what if I ended up getting assigned a serial killer's memoir? I didn't want to see bloody edits play out in real life. If I couldn't control this, how was I going to function in any job?

"Exactly." She smiled with confidence. "That's why you have to keep going." She reached out and grabbed my arm. "Come on. I'll help." With that she dragged me across the foyer and into Gertrude's office.

CHAPTER EIGHTEEN

"*S*hay, I really don't want to do this." I froze in the doorway, feeling anxiety begin to churn in my stomach. She was already opening the trunk. "You're in too deep now. We have to fix them." She undid the rubber band and began leafing through the stack. "Which one is Tamir's story? Oh, wait, I've got it. *The Egyptian and the Alabaster*, right? Such a bad title, by the way." She waved me inside. "Come on, sit down. Trust me on this. You know these people now. We're going to find a way to fix it together. I've got your back."

Did she? I was wading into unfamiliar territory. I wanted to trust Shay's unwavering confidence. Was she onto something about knowing the people whose stories I had altered? They were more than words on a page now. They were living, breathing people. I glanced at the butterfly sticky note, repeating Grandma's phrase like a mantra. The lightest touch.

"Sit, Emily. I'll help." Shay patted Gertrude's desk chair.

I sat down, massaging my temples. I appreciated her pep talk. I really did. Ever since stepping foot into The Ballad for the first time, I had felt a spark of joy that I hadn't even realized I had been missing. But being caught between two worlds had left me feeling tugged in two directions. Which narrative about my past was true? There was Dad's story. Gertrude's story. And the truth, which was probably somewhere in between. Isn't that something that books had taught me? That the past had more than one inter-pretation.

Shay pulled the chair on the opposite side of the desk around so she could sit next to me. Our knees touched as she laid the manuscript out in front of us. "Okay, so what's the theme of the story? Finding love?"

I hesitated. "I'm not sure I would say that."

"But that's his goal—his ultimate quest, right? Every hero needs a journey and Tamir's is to find love and not settle for the wrong person, don't you think? You said yourself he was crushing on Kenzie only to have his heart broken. Now you need to re-write so that he finds the right love." She drew Tamir's name in the margin and then drew a heart around it.

"I don't know. I think the central theme might be about finding his voice. Not love."

Shay frowned. "How so?"

"It's too obvious. Romances are light and fluffy. Even in the early sections where he's pining for her, there's a depth. There's something more." I flipped through the pages of Tamir's story. "He confronts the woman he's been dreaming of because he can't remain silent. His quest is to find his voice. It has to be."

Shay bumped her fist on my knee. "See! This is what I'm saying. This is why we have to go through each of the manu-scripts again. You totally get it. You see the big picture." She reached for a pencil and offered it to me. "Write that. Write him using his voice."

What if I were wrong? What if another round of edits made things worse?

"Don't overthink, Emily. That's something my creative writing professors told us over and over again. Trust your gut." Shay held the pencil for me.

She could be right. There's only one way to find out, I heard a voice echo in my head.

Without waiting for more internal dialogue, I took the pencil from Shay and crossed out paragraph after paragraph of text.

The manuscript's original author had written a scene after Tamir and Kenzie's initial interaction over bubble tea with the two of them joining forces on her podcast. It was a cloyingly sweet passage of young love where Tamir gazed in her eyes as she expounded on her struggles with white privilege. The manuscript was a mess. In a burst of inspiration, I took a different route, having Tamir crash the podcast and create a scene, embarrass Kenzie in front of her friends and professors, but then I left it to Tamir to take it from there.

Isn't that what Gertrude's note suggested? My job was to make suggestions without being prescriptive.

I lost track of time as I made changes to the pages. Is this how Gertrude had worked?

When I was done, I handed Shay the pages to review.

"Harsh." She let out a long whistle. "I wouldn't want to be on your bad side, but I love it. If Tamir's growth arc is finding his voice, then I would say he's found it."

"You think?" I was already starting to have doubts.

"For sure." She must have sensed that I wasn't feeling confident because she snatched the rest of the manuscript, bundled it together, and shoved it back into the trunk. "That one is done. This has to be it. We're on the right track. I can feel it. Do the next one." She shoved *Dashwood Toad* into my free hand.

"I don't know about this one." I stared at the manuscript. "I mean, it's not exactly a love story either, is it?"

Shay shrugged.

"Maybe I'm reading into it because I know Cameron now, but I think his journey is about finding his truth or maybe defining what home means to him." I thought for a minute. "At first, I assumed that the beach scene with the dog was supposed to be a meet-cute, but now I'm not sure. In getting to know Cameron, I think he's really at odds. He obviously loves Cascata, but Martine wants to leave. He's being pulled in two directions. They say that opposites attract, but is that true when they want two very different futures? He said they don't have the same dream anymore. Maybe that's what he needs to explore. Martine, too. How do they follow their dreams, even if it means they take different paths?"

Shay whistled. "True. True."

"I swear if he could afford to buy this place, I think he'd do it in a heartbeat. He loves this life, but the question is, does he love his wife?" I didn't elaborate on my conversation with Cameron where he offered to manage the property for me.

"Does he?" Shay twisted a silver bracelet on her narrow wrist. "Do you think he does?"

"I don't know." I thought back to his first interaction with Sienna. They had much more in common, namely a deep love and appreciation for literature. Did he and Martine share the same passions? "They seemed so different. So mismatched," I said to Shay. "Apparently he wants to write children's books, and she hasn't read a book in five years. Can you even imagine? I think I would have serious withdrawal and need like around the clock therapy if I hadn't read a book in five years." I made a funny face and pretended to shake my fingers like I had just downed too many shots of strong espresso.

"Wait, what?" Shay threw up her hands. Her bracelets clinked together and slid down her arm. She contorted her face in disgust. "What kind of monster doesn't read? No, you gotta fix that. He's definitely not supposed to stay with a woman who doesn't read." She shook her finger like a schoolteacher scolding a student.

"I don't think she's a villain in his narrative. I just don't know if they're a good match."

I flipped through the pages of the manuscript.

"How does the story continue?" Shay peered over my shoulder.

I read the next few pages aloud. In the original manuscript Cameron and Sienna's paths hadn't crossed on the beach. For days they continued to come close to meeting, brushing past one another at the grocery store, in the plaza, at a paint night, and even at an open house. They finally have a moment in the library where they reach for the same copy of *Mansfield Park*.

"It seems like they're meant to be together," Shay commented when I came to the end of the chapter.

"Yeah, maybe." I doodled in the margins, unsure where the story should go next. "Is Sienna the catalyst for change or a roadblock in his ultimate quest?"

"I feel like we need to call in my creative writing professor. Or I should grab some paper and start taking notes for my own story themes." Shay dumped out a tin of paper clips and began sorting them by color. "What's Cameron meant to do? Stay here, right? If you send him to the Bay Area, isn't he going to be miserable?"

"Sometimes characters have to be miserable to find their truth."

"So you're going to send him away?"

I crossed out the passages and considered my options. "No, but I am going to give him a little push." I proceeded to write a new section where Cameron embraces his love for literature and then he could take it from there.

"If you're going for subtle change, this is good," Shay said after reading the new section.

"I think that's what I'm supposed to do."

"Good. Then let's keep going." She didn't give me a chance to reconsider. Instead, she grabbed the next manuscript, *The Opt Out Clause*. "So are Cameron and Martine on the same path?"

"No. I'm pretty sure their paths are divergent. She needs to follow her dream. She's desperate for change, for something new. Cameron's the opposite. He's content at home." I was finding it easier to take my pencil to the pages. For Martine, I had no trouble nudging her toward her dreams. She couldn't give up her dreams for Cameron. She had to find herself first.

Does every book need a happy ending? No, but every book needs resolution. And I could argue that I was creating resolution if not happiness. There might be angst, depression, or regret with giving up her marriage for her career. That was life. That was reality.

That kind of writing attracts readers who see themselves, their struggles and conflicts through the eyes of fictional characters. This was the kind of editing that filled my soul. None of the forsaken manuscripts were fairytales. They didn't come with a prince sweeping in to save the day on horseback. They came grounded in the moment, the reality that each of our choices builds on the next, for better or worse. They came with the knowledge that sometimes finding happiness, our true north, our way home, means giving up something or someone we love. For the first time I realized that was the theme that connected each of the books.

The manuscripts paralleled my own journey into discovering a different version of the grandmother Dad had painted in my head. My choices had been building, too. With every new detail I uncovered about Gertrude and Cascata, my past was coming into clearer focus. It was more than clearer focus. It was shedding away the layers of contorted truths. The stories I had invented. The stories I didn't believe. This place was calling me home. Like the dappled light sneaking into the office from the stained glass windows, I was beginning to realize that this experience was about so much more than crossing out words on a page. It was reshaping my story. It was ripping off the blinders I'd worn like dark tinted sunglasses for the past two decades. The manuscripts were showing me that it was time to reconcile my memories and Dad's bitterness if I were going to find my way forward.

"Okay, last one." Shay handed me *Tip Jar Karma*. "What are we going to do about the gambler?"

Lindi's storyline was the most unsettling for me. I couldn't stop seeing her sunken face as she talked about her son. Her quest was about redemption. It was about the same things—finding her way back to herself and to her son—that the other manuscripts shared in common, yet I felt a different weight trying to figure out how best to shape her story. Was I supposed to lend my insight?

Did I have any? Or was the moral of her story meant to be an enigma?

"Shay, I'm stumped on this one." I held the manuscript away from my body, hoping that some physical distance might provide space for a revelation.

"You already changed it,though," Shay noted with a wisdom I hadn't expected. "I think you have to finish what you started." Her body shifted. She became quiet and introspective. "I feel Grandma so deeply in this room right now." Her eyelids closed gently as she inhaled through her nose and allowed her head to tilt toward the ceiling, rocking in rhythm with music that I couldn't hear. "This is right. This is what we're supposed to do," she barely whispered, with a small nod.

I set the manuscript in front of me and studied it. There was nothing that came next. The short story didn't have a conclusion, only what I had scripted, that Lindi made a choice. And maybe now her story was about living with the rewards or consequences of that choice. Again, I left it up to her free will, writing one simple sentence: "Lindi made her own choice."

"That's it. I'm done," I announced, dropping the pencil on the top of the pile. Shay was still in a state of meditation. She gave her upper body a shake and blinked rapidly as if trying to bring herself back to earth. "Whoa, that was intense, did you feel it?"

I nodded. "I did. I think I really did." I couldn't believe it as the words escaped my lips.

Shay placed her hand over her heart. "Oh, she is here. Grandma is here, and she is so happy with what we're doing."

The fact that my cousin was channeling our dead grandmother didn't faze me. It would have a few days ago, but after everything that had happened it seemed appropriate. I put the final manuscript in the chest and closed the latch. My hands shook slightly. I wasn't sure if it was from relief, dread, or a combination of both.

"All right. Now what?" Shay stood and stretched. "Oh, my Goddess, I almost forgot I have to get up to the pub. You're still coming to the podcast tomorrow, right? I need you there for moral support."

"Of course." I wanted to be there for Shay, but I had just nudged Tamir toward this. I had to see it through.

I followed her to the foyer, closing the door to Lost Coast Literary behind us. Whether or not Gertrude approved, I felt an undeniable sense of relief. It might be temporary, but at least I had done something. I knew enough about literature to understand themes. Each of the manuscripts shared one similarity—they needed to find their central theme. I had edited them with that in mind. Whether or not I had done so successfully was up to fate.

CHAPTER NINETEEN

The next morning, I found myself in the plaza waiting for Shay. She showed up shortly before eleven.

"Be honest. How do I look?" She twirled in a half circle, showing off her wide-legged pants and a cropped black and orange tie-dye sweatshirt that revealed a gold bellybutton ring. "I'm calling it beachy boho. It feels right for today."

"You look great." It was true. She did. Not because of the outfit, which certainly flattered her tall, slender frame, but because she practically glowed.

"Let's do this." She looped her arm through mine as we headed away from the plaza.

If you weren't looking for Cascata College, you would miss it. The campus was secluded amongst dense redwoods on a steep hillside. Shay took me through town, past neighborhoods and parks until the street curved and made a sharp turn.

I panted to keep up with her as we trekked up the hill at a breakneck pace.

When we finally reached the top, I stopped to catch my breath. The campus stood like a hidden old-world fortress with one-hundred-and-eighty-degree views of the sea. Pathways and mission style buildings with red tile roofs peeked out from an endless canopy of greenery. A row of palm trees lined the main entrance, a reminder that despite our remoteness we were still in the Golden State.

"This way," Shay said, leading me past a quad where students gathered to study next to a domed glass herbarium that housed leafy ferns, palms, along with mosses, algae, and lichens.

I huffed as sweat dripped from my forehead. "I guess you stay in shape walking between classes."

"Huh?" Shay didn't look or sound winded as she reached the entrance to the auditorium first and held the door open for me.

My cheeks were hot from exertion. The auditorium was equally warm from dozens of bodies squished together in the foyer. Posters advertised an upcoming performance of *Pippin*, a string concert, and a lecture series on reducing your carbon footprint. Cascata College had a national reputation for its focus on ecology and sustainable living. I knew this from Dad. It was one of the very few things he had ever shared about our early years in Cascata. Long before climate change had become a household phrase, he had taught adjunct classes at the college on the importance of utilizing native plants in home landscaping and advocating the removal of water-wasting lawns.

I asked him once when I was on a job site with him why he didn't put lush green lawns into his clients' plans like some of his competitors. The one way I'd been able to break through his tendency toward silence was to get him talking about work.

His eyes would brighten as he would launch into a passionate explanation of his mission to save the planet one lawn at a time. "Because lawns are invasive, Em. They're not native and in addition to sucking up huge amounts of our water resources, they don't support local habitats. If a client asks me for a lawn, I tell them I'm not the right landscape architect for them. My job is to bring in native trees, plants, shrubs, and flowers that will attract birds, butterflies, and bees. Plants that don't tax our already depleted water supply. Did you know that if everyone in the U.S. took out half of their lawn and replaced it with native plants, that would be the equivalent of all of our national parks combined? That's how we change the world, Em. That's how we write our future."

I imagined him standing on the stage at the podium and imparting his passion about the planet and our dwindling resources to environmental science students. I'd never been able to count on Dad for much conversation, but the exception to that rule was to get him talking about his vision for how subtle changes like tearing out a section of grass and replacing it with buckwheat, wild cucumber, and milkweed could have a dramatic impact on generations to come.

"Quite a turnout," I noted as we worked our way past nearly life-sized headshots of Kenzie and a line queuing up for drinks and snacks to find our seats.

Shay pointed to a couple of empty seats a few rows from the back. "Take those. I'll come meet you after my segment. Wish me luck." She clenched her teeth in a nervous smile and danced toward the front.

I squeezed past college students and a handful of professors and took a seat. The crowd was predominantly made up of twenty-somethings wearing beanies and stocking caps. I caught a whiff of stale pot and clove cigarettes. The first two rows were reserved for guests. I watched Shay mingle with the other speakers. There was no sign of Tamir, but unless I was mistaken it looked like the woman who had left the generous tip was seated in the front row. I recognized her expensive highlights and model-like posture. Had she flown into Cascata to be a guest on Kenzie's student podcast?

The lights flashed twice and a voice came on the overhead speakers announcing that the show would start soon and everyone should take their seats.

Kenzie pranced onto the stage a few minutes later. She wore a pale blue V-neck T-shirt with the saying: *White Silence IS White Violence* across the chest. Her blonde curls were styled in what could only be described as a failed attempt at an Afro. She pumped her fist in the air as she took a seat at center stage and the lights dimmed.

The set-up reminded me of a cheap talk show production. There was a long folding table with three snowball microphones and a vase of flowers. Three plush chairs that looked as if they'd been purchased at a second-hand store sat behind the table. Kenzie's spot was outfitted with a laptop and sound board. Stage lighting beat down on her as an AV guy balancing a camera gave her the signal to get started.

"Welcome, welcome to like the totally beautiful Cascata College. We're here in the Redwood Auditorium with a killer crowd! You guys are like the cutest. I'm so super stoked to see so many familiar faces in the audience. Say hello, everyone." She paused and waited for the audience to respond. "I want to like thank Lost Coast Blooms for providing today's flowers and to the Cascata College audio visual department for the livestream. You can like catch this podcast again on any of your favorite services. I'd love it if you'd subscribe to my channel and smash those likes."

She sounded older as she spoke, intentionally trying to morph her voice to mirror the style of an NPR interviewer. It was an odd choice and a strange juxtaposition between her throaty, serious tone and her overuse of the word *like*.

"We have like such a monumental topic to cover today, and I have an amazing lineup of guests here to share their perspective, but before we get to that I want to give you an introduction to why I picked the controversial topic of race on the Lost Coast. As a white woman, I need to stay woke. It's my responsibility to give voice to those who don't have a voice."

A few people clapped. Otherwise, an uncomfortable pall fell over the musty auditorium.

Kenzie's attitude might have been well-intended, but she came across as a white savior, as if she could single-handedly solve centuries old issues on an hour podcast.

"Maybe it's your job to share the mic!" someone shouted.

I glanced in the direction of the sound to see Tamir standing on his chair in the second row.

Shay pumped her fist in the air and let out a whoop.

Kenzie laughed uncomfortably and adjusted a dial on the soundboard. "That's like exactly what I'm doing today. Using my platform to raise awareness about the heart-wrenching issues impacting people of color right here in Cascata." She fanned her face as if she were trying to fight back tears.

"How many people of color live in Cascata?" Tamir yelled back.

She forced a smile, but her eyes were wild with rage. "If you could take your seat, please, sir. We're live now, and I know our listeners are eager to hear from my *scheduled* guests."

"Great." Tamir jumped off his seat and raced up to the stage. Before Kenzie could respond, he put on a pair of studio headphones and spoke directly into the snowball mic. "I'll tell you how many people of color live in Cascata, a whopping two percent of the population. And you know why the numbers are that high? Because of collegiate athletics. Without the student athletes on campus, it would be an abysmal less than one percent of the population. Why? Have you ever asked yourself that question? Why?" Tamir's entire demeanor had shifted. He made strong eye contact with the audience. No one moved. Everyone watched in awe.

Kenzie frantically tried to kill Tamir's mic. She was so flustered she turned off hers instead.

"Right, no response. Shocker." Tamir addressed the audience. "Raise your hand if you identify as anything except white."

Shay's hand shot up along with a few others. People shifted in their seats as they looked around to see who had raised their hands.

"Yeah, that's what I thought," Tamir said into the mic. "Go ahead, come on up. All of you." He waved everyone who had raised their hands forward. Then he turned to Kenzie. "If you want to have a conversation about race relations in Cascata, then I suggest you go find a seat in the audience, and we'll take it from here."

The crowd let out a collective gasp.

Kenzie sat frozen. "Um, this is like my podcast." Her voice echoed, but her mic was still shut off.

"And it's so kind of you to share the mic." Tamir pointed to the front row. "Now take a seat."

I had choreographed the entire scene. I felt like a puppet master controlling Tamir's every move, but then something shifted. As he took command of the podcast and directed the tone, he changed. He stepped into himself, going off script and speaking from the heart, sharing what it was like to go weeks without ever seeing anyone who looked like him. The verbal abuse he'd had to suffer from customers at Oceanic, on campus, and even from professors who lowered their expectations of him or graded him down for no reason. His dark eyes traveled across the room from person to person. "I didn't realize I was different until we moved here." A slight wobble broke through his voice. He took in a long, controlled breath and continued. "Do you know what it's like to have people ask you every day where you're from and when you answer here—America—they smirk and say, 'No, but where are you *originally* from? Where is your family from?' Or you know what's even worse? To be the one token friend of color. The friend who makes you feel better about your own privilege because you can say you have a Muslim friend."

Kenzie didn't take a seat, but she did leave the stage. Instead of heading to the front row as directed, she stood to the side recording the entire thing on her phone, pausing every few minutes to add her own commentary. I could hear her making exasperated groans and yelling into her phone to be heard over Tamir.

She's livestreaming this, I thought as I listened, like everyone else, with newfound empathy for the constant assault of challenges that came with being brown in a white community like

Cascata. Shay followed after Tamir, sharing how it felt to be called cruel names due to her mixed race, like half and half, and mulatto, and struggling with straddling both pieces of who she was.

"My father is white, and my mother is black. What does that make me?" She pointed to her chest and posed the question to the audience, not waiting for a response. "Racial sensitivity is about looking inward. What lens do we see the world through? The answer is going to be different for each of us."

She too seemed to find her stride. She crossed her long legs and leaned closer to the mic. "Here's what I want you to know. If you have questions about race, it's your job—not mine—to educate yourself. Ask questions. Read a book. Watch a YouTube video. The stories are out there. You have to find them. You have to do the work."

"Yeah," Tamir added, catching Shay's eye. "Get uncomfortable with your relationship with race and privilege. Each of us has to examine our responsibility."

Shay gave him a fist pump. "Preach."

The discussion continued long past the allotted time Kenzie had scheduled for the podcast. Tamir opened the floor for questions, and this time hands shot up everywhere.

I felt grateful to witness his transformation. None of it was due to what I'd written. He owned the space. He owned his voice.

What had changed? How had he found the courage to speak up?

Kenzie never returned to the stage. She pouted from the side of the stage until Tamir dropped the mic—literally. He finished by standing to take a bow and knocking over the snowball mic. She stomped off, followed by the woman in the aviator sunglasses. Shay chatted with Tamir for a while as people began filing out of the auditorium.

"Holy hell, did you see that?" Shay bounced with adrenaline when she finally came to find me. "That was off the charts. He totally slayed her. Did you see her face? Oh, my Goddess, I love it.

I think I love him." She glanced up to the stage where Tamir was talking to a couple of professors. "He's hot, right?"

I couldn't tell if she was serious.

"Do you feel better about your edits now? Tamir didn't hold back, you have to give him that." She snapped twice. "That was the best thing I've seen here in forever."

"True." My phone buzzed. I recognized the New York area code.

"Sorry, one sec. I need to take this call." I stepped outside and answered the phone.

Piper's voice came over the line. "Hey, Emily, just checking in to see how you're doing. No pressure, but also wanted to loop in on how those reader's reports were coming."

Crap. I hadn't even touched the stack of work I'd brought with me from New York. I stared at the view in front of me. From this vantage point I could follow the curve of the river as it spilled into the ocean. The women's soccer team was practicing on a grassy field below. I could make out the shops and the Queen Annes near the plaza. Towering redwoods nestled in the sleepy downtown, offering a protective barricade from the outside world. I was starting to fall in love with the quirky little town.

"Emily, are you there?"

"Huh? Oh, sorry, yeah," I sputtered. "Sorry, I've been so busy with family stuff I haven't had a chance to get to the reader's reports."

Piper cleared her throat. "No worries. When can we expect you back?"

"Probably another week or so."

"Okay. Just keep me in the loop."

"Will do, and I'll try to get to the reader's reports, too," I said, before hanging up.

I had bought myself another week. Now more than ever, after watching Tamir step into his truth, I knew that I needed to do the same. Cascata's magic was changing me. I was starting to believe that Gertrude's plan was going exactly as she intended.

CHAPTER TWENTY

Shay tried to convince me to come out for a celebratory drink with her, Tamir, and some of the other impromptu guests from the podcast. I declined. I needed some time to myself to try and sort out what to do next.

On my way down the hill, a voice hollered out to me. "Hey, Emily."

I turned to see Arty barreling toward me. The severe look on his face matched his attire—black soccer pants, a black warm-up jacket, and a black stocking cap pulled tight over his head, allowing a sliver of his curls to escape. "Hey, I want to talk to you."

I slowed my pace to let him catch up. "Were you at the podcast?"

"No. I had practice." He pointed to the gym bag hanging from his shoulder.

"Do you play for the college?"

"Does it matter?"

"Just trying to make conversation," I retorted.

He kicked a rock, sending it tumbling down the hillside. "If you have to know, I help coach. I played in college. Most guys don't stick around Cascata, so coach asked if I could come by a few days a week and help develop some of the younger players."

There was a touch of resentment in his tone. I wasn't sure if it was his usual surly mood whenever I was near or if there was part of him that wanted out of Cascata too. That could explain some of his attitude.

"What's going on with Grandma's place?" He took a step forward, not waiting for me.

"Uh, that's a big question. What do you mean, specifically?"

He shifted his soccer bag onto the opposite shoulder. I had to take longer strides to keep up with him. Like Shay, he had a long torso and even longer legs, but I suspected he was intentionally power walking to make me have to practically run to keep up. There was one easy solution. I could stop, and yet as the thought passed, I felt my legs move as if controlled by some external force.

"Everything, but first I want to know what you're planning to do with all her stuff. Some of that is meant for me, you know."

"Yeah, I'm aware. It's spelled out in the will. It's not like I have some master plan to keep it from you."

He scoffed. "That's not what I heard. I heard that you're planning an estate sale."

"From whom?" My voice came out shriller than I had intended, but this was getting out of hand.

"Does it matter? Why would you do that? You might not care about her things, but some of us do."

We were almost to the bottom of the hill. I pointed to Grammar Street. "Look, you can come over right now. Take anything you want. Regardless of what you seem to think, I don't have a hidden agenda or some sort of secret plan. I didn't ask for this. I don't want to be in this position any more than you want me to be. But that's where we're at. We can keep fighting, or you can come get what's important to you right now."

"Fine," he huffed. "I will."

"Good."

We walked the rest of the way in silence. As soon as we were inside, Arty tossed his gym bag by the front door and made a beeline for the parlor. "I'm grabbing some books first."

"Go for it." I almost made a snarky comment about being surprised that he was a reader but decided against it.

"Do you want me to make a list of what I'm taking?"

"No. Like I said, take whatever you want."

There was the briefest flash of remorse on his face before he shot me a nod and headed toward the bookshelves. What was the deal with him? Was it just the money or was there some other reason for his anger at me?

I considered confronting him about it, but I had a feeling that might backfire. Instead, I gave Arty his space and went upstairs to read. The minute my head hit the pillow in the guest room I fell asleep—hard. When I awoke again it was pitch black outside. How long had I slept? I reached for my phone, noticing that I had missed three calls from Dad.

Shit.

It was after nine, which meant that he was already in bed. Dad tended to start his days early, as in before-the-sun-even-rose early, which meant that growing up I tucked myself in and would hide under my Eloise blanket reading with a flashlight until well past midnight.

I got up and stretched.

A message notification popped on the screen. "Emily, it's Dad. Call me."

Classic. He was a man of few words on a good day.

I had often wondered what my parents' relationship had been like. They had obviously loved each other deeply, but what had their day-to-day routine been? I couldn't remember. Two memories of them together played on constant rotation. The first was of them dancing in the kitchen to Harry Connick Jr. The other was Dad delivering Mom's coffee with one lump of sugar and a healthy splash of cream to her in bed every morning before he left for work. It was the simple gestures that made me sure their love must have been real. That and the crater her death had carved in his heart.

Thinking about her last days brought a well of emotion to my body. I tried to fight back the panic. The fluttery feeling in my chest. The vision of her in a barren hospital room. The funeral. The never-ending silence.

Dad had tried to hide his pain from me in the days after her funeral, but I heard him sobbing in the bathroom when he was pretending to shave. I saw the piles of discarded tissues, soaked with his tears, hidden in the kitchen garbage can. I remembered silence. A silence that was different from his usual lack of words. This was a silence that permeated everything. A silence that signaled it was too painful to speak. As a kid, the deafening quiet used to scare me. Books became my retreat. I found solace in the pages of my favorite reads, returning night after night to the warm cozy Murry family kitchen in *A Wrinkle in Time* or trekking back in time to cold Minnesota with *Betsy-Tacy and Tib*. I learned that I wasn't alone when I had a book; characters became my family, my circle of friends.

I realized sometime in my twenties that his silence was likely because he couldn't afford himself the luxury of letting his internal thoughts escape his tongue. They might swallow him whole and drown him. As a teenager the pervasive quiet had felt personal. No amount of self-reliance mattered. He never seemed to notice when I took it upon myself to learn how to make scrambled eggs for breakfast, shop for school clothes, or plug in a pair of headphones to listen to an audiobook at the dinner table while he read the evening paper.

You don't have to do this now, I told myself, blinking back tears.

I tugged on a pair of cabin socks and shoved the unhappy memories aside.

Since I'd slept through the evening and missed dinner, I went downstairs to see if Arty was still around and if there was anything I could scrounge up in the kitchen. Hunger rumbled in my stomach. Creaky noises in the house rumbled right along with it. I flipped on the golden glowing lights as I descended the grand staircase.

Arty must have left.

The kitchen was dark, but an immediate warmth spread over the countertops when I turned on the lights. I found soup and crackers in the pantry. They would tide me over until tomorrow, and given the constant damp chill outside, soup and the coziness of Gertrude's breakfast nook sounded like the perfect retreat.

I heated it in the microwave and dug through the cupboards and drawers. Gertrude had been organized. Each drawer was lined with pretty beach-themed contact paper. There was one drawer entirely devoted to spoons—soup spoons, teaspoons, expensive silver spoons, and everyday dinner spoons. Plates were stacked by size and color. Dish towels were neatly folded in tight squares. There wasn't so much as a junk drawer, although I did find a drawer filled with pens, scissors, matches, and flashlights. None of it was loose or scattered. The pens had their own plastic tub to keep them separated from the matches and scissors.

It made me wonder if Gertrude had had slight OCD.

I ate the soup and crackers acutely aware of how alone I was in the rambling mansion. Who would want to live like this?

Not Dad.

But me?

I could easily live with the hum of the fridge, the creaking floorboards, and books around every corner as my only companions.

But a space like this deserved to be shared. Cameron's proposal was certainly compelling. Could I do it? Could I give up on New York and transform this place into a literary getaway? I could almost hear the sound of happy laughter around the giant dining room table for communal breakfasts and picture guests strolling through the gardens, taking in the afternoon sun and the sea breeze.

Of course, I was operating as if there weren't a huge elephant in the room. Dad. I needed answers and soon.

After cleaning up my dishes I padded back upstairs and browsed through the assortment of books in the guest room. Was there a room in the entire house that didn't contain bookcases stuffed to the edges with an abundance of titles? I landed on a favorite read from my late teen years, *I Capture the Castle*, a coming-of-age story written in the form of diary entries from a seventeen-year-old girl, Cassandra. The book had captured my heart the first time I'd read it, and I was immediately transported to the English countryside and a crumbling castle when I tucked myself in bed and cracked open the pages.

I'd forgotten how beautiful the narration was in the book and was struck by how many themes resonated with me. Not that I'd grown up in a house of physical disrepair, but my childhood had felt equally unsteady and isolated. In the novel, Cassandra's struggle to build connection with her father (a writer who saw a fleeting flash of fame with his first novel and had been in a state of crippling inaction ever since) paralleled my challenges with Dad. As did the fact that we had both lost mothers young and been left with fathers who wouldn't or couldn't move past their own grief.

I stayed up for hours, devouring the familiar read. When the purple blushing light of dawn crept through the windows, I had finished the book and fallen into a semi-dream-like daze. There was no point in trying to sleep now, so I got up, showered, made a pot of French press, and went for a walk on the beach.

The storm had blown onward, leaving Cascata under calm thistle and periwinkle skies. I inhaled the misty ocean air. I had forgotten that living this close to the ocean meant that my body was constantly being rejuvenated by healing ions, the remnants of the particles that created Mother Earth, washing ashore and over me. Mom used to tell me that whenever she felt sad, she simply sank her feet into the sand, letting the minerals seep into her skin. I could see her silhouette staring into the waves in a trance, then turning to me to say, "Emily, isn't the sea such a lovely reminder of how small we are in perspective to the greatness of the ocean?

That fills me with such joy. There's something mighty and powerful in being small."

Was that true? The memory of her voice triggered an image of her. Only not the usual image that I had to fight away of her pasty skin sagging away from her brittle bones and the ache behind her eyes.

Her face as I remembered it from Cascata came into mind. The soft curl of her hair at the nape of her neck. Her twinkly brown eyes that held a hint of mischief. The way she used to throw her head back and laugh at Dad's silly jokes. It had been too long since I had smelled her peach perfume or heard her voice reading *Little Women* aloud.

Being in Cascata these past days had a way of making her feel whole again. I'd spent decades trying to block images of her ravaged by cancer, her gaunt cheeks and blueish skin stretched tight over her bony skeleton. The struggle to speak. Her turning down sips of water. Grasping my hand while she gasped her last breath.

Without even realizing it, I replayed visions of her chasing me through the foamy surf, her face lit from the sun and glowing with happiness. Racing at a full sprint with the waves lapping at our heels until we collapsed in the sand in a fit of giggles. Hours spent with buckets in hand crisscrossing the beach in search of treasures—mussel shells, jade, and shiny glass floats. Windy picnics on a Pendleton blanket, our sandwiches gritty with sand and never more delicious. Her tote bag filled to the brim with library books. Some for her. Some for me. Some we'd read together.

Grandma was there.

I paused in mid-stride. That's right. Grandma was there. She had joined us for impromptu lunches, bringing a wicker basket packed with caramel snickerdoodles and chocolate snack cake.

They would talk books for hours while I read my way through the entire Nancy Drew series.

How had I forgotten?

I forced dusty memories forward.

There had been tears. Grandma's hand with its long fingers and her collection of turquoise and aquamarine rings on Mom's knee. Mom leaning into her shoulder as Grandma dabbed her tears with the edge of a paper napkin. What did it mean?

Did Mom not want to leave?

Had she known then that she was dying?

Why did we go?

I paused as I caught a glimpse of a bob of seals frolicking in the waves cresting off the shore. *I wish I felt that free*, I thought. This new barrage of memories threatened to drag me under.

It didn't make sense. If Mom had already known that she was sick, why not stay and surround ourselves with support? It was only a single memory, a slice in time, and yet, the image was so strong in my mind that it was like stepping into the scene. I could hear their muddled whispers, trying to spare me. Mom's gaze out of the corner of her eye, checking to make sure I was still reading. Grandma's hand massaging the small of my back.

This felt important. I strained to recall their words. *Terminal. Experimental treatment. Emily.*

Why hadn't I paid attention at the time? If only I hadn't been a kid concerned with Nancy's next sleuthing antics.

The story I'd made up had been that Mom and Grandma must have had a falling-out. Or worse. That they'd hated each other. I'd written pages and pages in my head over the years with Grandma starring as Cruella de Vil, the antagonist from *The Hundred and One Dalmatians*, that coincidentally had been written by none other than Dodie Smith. How she crafted a childhood fairy tale so drastically different from *I Capture the Castle* would always remain a mystery to me, and proof that she was one of the most under-appreciated women writers of the twentieth century.

But that was a story that a broken-hearted little girl had told herself to survive not only one loss, but two. I wasn't that little girl any longer. I was a grown adult. A grown adult who felt the women who had loved me in every square inch of this space.

My own internal narrative had been wrong. I had written myself into a corner. I hadn't given my own life's story the gentle kiss of a butterfly's wings. I'd forced myself down a path of a gusting hurricane without an escape. Grandma was showing me it was time to change that.

CHAPTER TWENTY-ONE

"*H*ey! Emily!" The sound of a woman's voice pulled me into the moment. I turned to see Sienna jogging toward me.

Her ponytail swung in the breeze. Despite her quick pace she wasn't even slightly breathless when she reached me. "You're an early riser, too, huh?"

"I guess. More like I stayed up all night reading and decided that if I tried to sleep now, I would be wrecked for the rest of the day."

"Oh, my God, me too! The book hangover is real. That's why I'm out for a run. It's better than coffee for curing the post-reading blues." She shifted from side to side, I assumed to keep her body in motion while we talked. "Must have been a good book. I'm always on the hunt for recommendations, if you want to share?"

"*I Capture the Castle* by Dodie Smith. I read it years ago, and it holds up well." A pod of pale pelicans skimmed the waves, flying in formation as they searched the surf for food.

"I love that book." Sienna practically swooned. She threw her head back and clutched her heart with both hands. "I mean, that scene where they inherit a closet full of their aunt's furs. No joke, I begged my mom to let me get a fur coat after I read that, and I'm a vegetarian. I have been since I was ten years old." She laughed as she shook her head at the thought.

Granted she was in jogging attire, but her style, the loose ponytail, no makeup, and her effusive reaction to books made me wonder if she was a better match for Cameron than Martine.

Stop it, Emily. I blinked twice and refocused on what Sienna was saying.

"That book changed me," Sienna continued. "So good! I haven't read that since college. I'll have to see if the library has it."

"You're welcome to borrow Gertrude's copy. Her entire estate is basically a library. Come over anytime."

"Really?" Sienna lifted a well-toned arm behind her neck and stretched. "I have heard so many rumors about the estate. I would love to come take a look."

"Please do. I'd love the company and we could seriously talk books all day."

"Let's do it. I'll bring the wine." She stretched again and glanced at her watch. "I should probably keep going, but before I do, would it be really weird if I ask you a question?"

"Uh, what?" I braced myself for what she was going to ask.

She gave me a sheepish grin. "What do you know about Cameron? How has it been to work with him? I know we've only been on one date, but I'm kind of into him. He's not like anyone else I've dated. Probably because he's such a reader, too. That's the dream, right? A man who loves a book has my heart immediately. I mean, come on, no guy I've met in the last ten years has ever even heard of *The Great Brain* or *Babar the Elephant.* Cameron not only knows them, but he's read them, actually read them." She rambled on about their mutual admiration of classic authors. "Did you know that his mom is a librarian? I mean, come on. How great is that?"

"Pretty great." I tried to put on a happy face, but I had no idea how to respond. Was it my responsibility to tell her that Cameron was married? By her outpouring of emotion and blushing cheeks, it didn't take a super sleuth to figure out that

Cameron had likely failed to mention that minor detail. Or had he?

She danced from foot to foot, unable to hold still. I had thought that her constant motion was due to trying to keep her body from cooling down mid-run. Now I was starting to wonder if it was because of Cameron. "We're supposed to meet tonight. It's a book date. Can you believe that—a book date? He's pairing a bottle of wine with a book he thinks is going to be my new favorite. I feel super silly. I've been trying to run off the anticipation." Her cheeks brightened as she spoke. "I know it's stupid, but I haven't felt like this since middle school when I had a crush on a guy two lockers down from mine, who was the star of the football team, but secretly used to sneak into the library to read at lunch. He asked me to the after-school social and I remember being all aflutter, like something straight out of the pages of *Emma* for days. I seriously haven't felt like this in years. I've dated plenty of guys, but that spark is always missing, you know?"

I swallowed hard and nodded.

"I'm trying not to get my hopes up, but I think Cameron could be the one."

I doubted she would think that once she learned that he was married.

"Am I making you uncomfortable? I'm so sorry. I don't know what's gotten into me. I'm acting like a hormonal teenager. You don't want to hear this about your real estate agent. Please forgive me." She tapped her watch, resuming her workout tracking. "Can't wait to come by Gertrude's. I promise I'll bring wine."

She ran off in the opposite direction, leaving me staring after her and wondering if I had done the right thing. It wasn't my job to tell her that Cameron was married. Was it? If only I had left the forsaken manuscripts alone, I wouldn't be in this position. Cameron and Sienna never would have met. They would have gone their separate ways on the beach, and I wouldn't be in the middle of any of this.

Then again, Cascata was small. If Sienna had recently

purchased Letter Press, odds were good that her and Cameron's paths would have crossed sooner or later. I was probably giving my edits more credit than they deserved. Or at least, that's the way I could spin it for the short term.

My phone rang. Dad's face flashed on the screen.

I placed my hand on my stomach and breathed in deep to center myself before answering.

"Morning, Dad." I turned so the beach was to my back.

"You're up early, Em."

"Yeah, I couldn't sleep." In the distance I caught a whiff of bacon. Someone must be making breakfast in one of the brightly colored cottages that paralleled the coastline.

He frowned. "I'm worried about you."

"Dad, don't. Please. I can't do this with you now. I'm maxed out. I don't know what to do. I'm completely torn about staying here or going back to New York, and I need your help. You're my dad. I love you, but I'm starting to wonder if you really care about me." I could feel my courage building, or maybe it was anger, or sheer exhaustion. Either way, I couldn't believe the next words I uttered, even as I said them. "Why did you take us away, Dad? Why did we leave Cascata and never come back? I need to know. I need to know right now."

"Emily." His voice held a tone of warning.

"No! I'm done with the secrets." I paced in the damp sand, my tennis shoes sinking into the fine granules with each step. "I'm done tiptoeing around you, always worried that if I mention anything about Mom or the family, you'll shut down and not talk to me for days. Or end up pissed at me. That's not fair. It's not fair that you took me away from all of this. It's not fair that you and Danny can't figure your shit out. I'm remembering a lot of stuff, Dad, and it's not reflecting well on you." I had opened the flood-gates. Words spilled out of me like the waves rushing onto the shore. "Mom didn't want to leave, did she?"

He was silent.

"I knew it. Why? Why did you take us away?" I kicked a small, charred piece of driftwood that had washed ashore.

"Emily." His voice quivered. "This isn't the time."

"When is the time, Dad? Tell me that? I'm here in Cascata dealing with the fallout from *your* issues. This isn't on me. This is on you. You're going to have to fix this."

Again, he didn't respond. I paused for a minute, trying to think about what to say next. Memories of Mom and me on the beach rushed to the forefront as I followed a bank of clouds spilling toward me. Without hesitation I knew what I had to say to him.

"I know about Grandma, Dad. I know about her editing. It's happening to me, too."

"What?" he gasped.

"Dad, I'm serious. I want answers. You can either tell me now or when you get here, but I'm done with pretending like our past didn't happen."

He sucked in air. I thought I heard him whisper, okay, but I couldn't be sure.

"Did you say something?"

His voice almost quivered. "Okay." He paused. "It will be better to talk about this face-to-face. I'm coming. I promise. I'll be there in the next day or two. I just have to finish this job."

"Dad, you're going to have to do better than try." I started to hang up. I wasn't going to give him a minute more of my time until he told me the truth.

"Wait, Emily, promise me you'll stay out of it until I get there. Gertrude's clients. Those manuscripts. Don't get involved."

"Too late, Dad. Too late." I hung up.

CHAPTER TWENTY-TWO

I felt better after my blowup. It had been decades in the making, and I'd had enough. Tamir's impassioned speech had helped me see that. I didn't doubt that Dad loved me, but that didn't mean that he'd made the right choice. His job should have been to figure out what I had needed. He had failed me. And grief certainly didn't absolve him from his responsibility. Why had I tried to protect him? Not just with Danny and Keeshawna. I reflected on my teen years and early twenties, questioning so many things that I kept locked up inside because I knew if I asked, he would go mute. I never worried about him harming me, not in the physical sense, but I was beginning to realize his silence had left a lasting scar. His stoicism might have been his way of dealing with the grief of losing Mom, but it didn't work for me. I needed to own that. As soon as he arrived in Cascata, he and I were going to have a conversation that was long overdue.

I left the beach and headed into town. I found myself at Oceanic. This was becoming a habit.

Tamir was at the counter as usual, wrapping chocolate and lemon poppyseed muffins in parchment paper.

"Great speech yesterday," I said.

I wasn't sure if it was my imagination, but he looked like he was standing taller. His posture was upright with his shoulders squared and his angular chin tilted to the ceiling. His prominent mole and thick, bushy eyebrows gave him almost a regal appearance.

"Thanks. I don't know what came over me. It was like I was speaking in tongues or something. I can't say I regret it, though. It felt good. Really good." His head bobbed as if he were just realizing he actually believed what he was saying.

"Yeah, I can relate," I replied, my eyes lingering over a gooey cinnamon roll in the pastry case.

"I think there are a few people who would have appreciated it if I had kept my mouth shut." He smoothed a strand of dark hair back into place.

"I'm guessing you mean Kenzie? I can understand that she might be pissed, but I have to tell you that you moved me. You motivated me."

He gave me a half smile. "Thanks, but I think I pissed off more than Kenzie. A couple of my professors talked to me afterwards, and they might be placing me on probation. They feel like I violated the university's code of conduct. I think it has nothing to do with any code of conduct and everything to do with Kenzie. She blew up my phone and ranted all over social media. Did you know that she livestreamed it?"

I nodded. "Yeah, I thought that's what she was doing."

"I'm screwed. Her parents have donated a ton of money, and now they're on a mission to get me kicked out of school."

"But you don't think they'll actually succeed?" I protested.

"I haven't heard anything yet this morning, but I'm not sure what my academic standing is at this point. They've got money, so I'm guessing it's not going to be good."

I felt my shoulders slump. I wished I could go back in time. "Do you think they'll actually put you on probation?"

"No idea. I just hope I don't lose my scholarship." He sighed, placed the muffins in the case, and pointed to the specials board. "What can I get you this morning?"

"I'll take a latte." I considered ordering a cinnamon roll too, but my adrenaline was already pumping from my confrontation with Dad. An extra hit of sugar might put me over the edge.

Tamir put in my order. "So, I didn't know that Shay is your cousin."

"Yep."

"She's rad." He didn't make eye contact as he handed me the tablet to put in a tip and sign for the purchase.

"I agree."

"Do you know what her story is?" He leaned his elbow on the counter.

"Her story?"

"Is she single? Dating anyone?"

Why was I suddenly matchmaker today?

"Oh, I don't know, to tell you the truth. She hasn't mentioned anyone." His question made me realize how self-consumed I'd been. I hadn't asked Shay about her personal life. I would have to remedy that.

"It's cool. Don't worry about it." He handed me my credit card. "I'll bring you the latte."

"Thanks." I considered asking him if he wanted me to talk to her on his behalf, but I decided against it. I'd already done enough damage with my edits. My conversation with Sienna was still fresh in my head. Maybe the lesson of the forsaken manuscripts was *not* to get involved.

The plaza took on a radiant charm beneath the blue skies and puffy white clouds as I sipped the latte that Tamir delivered, and I watched from the window as students queued up at the bagel shop and a group of retirees practiced Tai Chi near the palm trees.

Keeshawna strolled past the window. I spotted her right away with her dancer-like posture. She caught my eye, waved, and came inside. "Emily, good to see you." She greeted me with a kiss on the cheek. "Do you mind if I sit?" She took off a navy pin-striped jacket and readjusted a pale yellow scarf.

"No, please." I motioned to the empty chair.

"I'm glad I saw you. You've been on my mind. How are you? I know it's been a lot, and I'm worried about you. I wanted to come by and check in, but I also wanted to be respectful of your space. I figured you might need some time with all of this." She held my gaze. Her eyes were filled with concern. Whether she was a great actress thanks to her time on the stage or whether it was genuine, I couldn't be sure.

"Thanks. I'm okay. My dad's coming."

She raised an eyebrow. "Stephen's coming to Cascata?"

"We talked this morning. He said he would."

"Wow. I never thought I would see the day. Maybe Gertrude knew what she was doing after all."

I leaned closer. "What does that mean, Keeshawna? I'm so confused. Danny won't say anything. He tells me that he swore on her deathbed, and I don't want to do anything that would jeopardize you guys losing the pub. But I don't even know what I'm supposed to be figuring out." I could hear the desperation in my voice.

"I know." She reached for my hand, placing hers over mine for a minute. Her touch was calming. "It's a terrible position for you. For him. For everyone. I know that Gertrude had her reasons, and if your dad really comes, then I have hope that she was right, but I feel for you. If you have questions, I'll try to answer what I can as long as it doesn't go against anything Gertrude spelled out in the will."

"Wait, what? You'll answer my questions?" Her words shocked me. "I thought Danny said that would jeopardize Grandma's specifications in the will." Why hadn't she been more forthcoming earlier?

"I'll try. Danny and I have gone over the will four times in the last few days. We both feel terrible that you're in this position. We've been trying to figure out a way to help. And after reading it again and again and trying to get past the legalese, I think we found a loophole. There's nothing that stipulates that I can't share *my* experiences with you." She gave me a crisp nod. "At least on a surface level."

It felt like all my nerves were firing at once. Was I really going to get some answers? "What do you know? My mom didn't want to leave, did she?"

Keeshawna ran a finger along her bottom lip. "I don't think so. I know that she wanted to be closer to her family, and of course there was the clinical trial, so I think that helped solidify her decision to go. It was such a sad time, though."

"Because they decided to leave or because she knew that her cancer was terminal?"

"Both, I think." She closed her eyes. A single tear slid down her cheek. "Your mom and Gertrude were so close. I can tell you that much. I always felt like an outsider. They had this connection around books that was impenetrable. Don't get me wrong, they both welcomed me to the family with open arms when Danny and I got married, but Gertrude and Jamie would spend hours dissecting books, analyzing them, debating alternative endings, and character development. I like to read, but I read for pleasure. I couldn't hold my own when it came to their book conversations."

She was confirming the memories that had resurfaced last night.

I hugged my arms around my chest, trying to shelter myself from the surge of emotions I wasn't sure I was ready to deal with.

"They were really alike. Danny used to tease your dad that he had married a younger version of their mom," Keeshawna continued. "Needless to say, your dad didn't think that was particularly funny. In the early years of our marriage the four of us were pretty inseparable. Your parents helped us get the pub up and running. They put in tons of sweat equity. You were young, of course, and we all adored you. Gertrude especially. You spent lots of time with her while we were tearing down old Sheetrock and painting.

You always had a book in your hand and two or three or twenty-seven in your book tote bag that you took everywhere with you."

A vision of a cream-colored tote bag with my name in rainbow letters and the words: Cool Kids Read flashed in front of me. My skin started to tingle. "I remember that. My memories have been so blurry."

"It's understandable." Keeshawna held my gaze. "It had to be so hard on you to lose your mom and then lose the rest of us."

I gulped hard. "If I remember right, I wore a hole in that book tote."

"You did." Keeshawna smiled. "Gertrude would take you to the library every Friday. You'd have a stack of books that you would devour over the weekend."

"She took me? I thought my mom did."

Her face shifted. "Well, she did before she got sick."

"What do you mean?" I clutched my locket as the tingling feeling spread to my stomach. Grandma didn't take me to the library. Not Grandma. Mom.

She blinked hard. Her chin quivered. "Emily, she was sick for a long time. It was so hard to watch and so hard to know how to support you."

"I'm not following. I thought the reason we left was because she got sick." My eyes darted around the room, searching desperately for any sort of talisman that might center me in the moment.

Keeshawna shook her head and brushed away tears. "No. No. That wasn't a secret. That was a known fact. Jamie was sick for years. You didn't know that?"

I clutched my jaw as tight as it would go to try and stop my chin from quivering. I couldn't meet Keeshawna's eyes, so I gave my head a quick shake.

"Oh, Hon. I'm so sorry." She placed her hand on her chest. "Jamie was diagnosed with cancer three months after you were born. The first couple of years were okay, but she went downhill pretty quickly. She and your dad spent a lot of time driving back and forth from the hospital for her surgeries, radiation, and chemo."

My breath stuck in my chest. She'd been sick for my entire life. "Wait, I don't understand."

"Gertrude basically raised you. Not because your parents didn't want to. They couldn't. The treatment was brutal. It was so hard on Jamie. She was a warrior. I can see her face. That gorgeous long hair and bright eyes. She was so determined not to let anyone see her pain." Keeshawna reached for a napkin and wiped her eyes. "Sorry, it's still hard to think about what she went through. It was unimaginable the pain that she had to bear. Physically. Emotionally."

A painful salty sting blurred my vision as Keeshawna tried to compose herself. She formed her hands in a steeple and continued. "It was even harder on your dad. He never missed a day. Jamie would tell him to stay home with you, but he refused. He was with her every minute. It was beautiful and heartbreaking to watch. For a short time, she went into remission. That's when we bought the pub. There was this feeling of relief and excitement. I was pregnant with Shay. Your mom was feeling better. It seemed like the treatment had worked, and then the cancer came back. The news wasn't good. There wasn't much hope."

I tried to stay in control of my body, but as Keeshawna kept talking, the room began to go fuzzy. Grandma had raised me? Were the memories that I held of Mom actually of Grandma?

"Your dad was distraught. We didn't blame him. Jamie had been through so much. Her poor body. He started doing his own research. That's how he found the Stanford clinical trial. Jamie didn't want to go. She'd had enough. I think she had come to terms with her mortality. She was worried about you, of course, but she knew that Gertrude would take care of you. She had already raised you, and then I think Jamie took comfort in knowing that we were here and that you'd have cousins and an extended family to care for you."

I thought I might throw up. "But then why did she go?"

"That's where it gets muddy for me. I think your dad convinced her to give it one more try. Stanford was doing cutting edge cancer research at the time, and the clinical trial needed participants. Her care would be free. It was a long shot, but it was their only hope. She had her family there, so as much as we were heartbroken to have them go, at least we knew you would all be surrounded by support."

"I don't get it. How did you all end up not talking? How did everyone desert me? None of you even came to her funeral."

Keeshawna's mouth hung open. "Yes, we did. We all came. Search your memory. You must remember that, don't you? It's etched in my memory. You wore a black and white striped dress, and your hair was tied in pigtails with matching black ribbons. Gertrude and I had been impressed that Stephen had taken the time to do your hair in the midst of losing Jamie." She choked up again. "Do you remember the gardens where he had the service? It was late May, and everything was in bloom. Roses, lilacs, and that archway that was dripping with fragrant jasmine. Jamie would have loved it. To this day whenever I smell jasmine, I think of her."

I blinked hard, trying to force away tears. I cradled my head in my hands and closed my eyes, remembering the dress and the sunlit garden. That image was quickly replaced by one of the living room in our mid-century ranch. I had curled up on the yellow couch with my copy of *Little Women* as strangers arrived with vases of flowers and casseroles. I remembered a knock on the door and Dad blocking my view, telling someone to leave, that they weren't welcome, before closing the door. The fuzzy memories that I'd been trying to bring into focus suddenly sharpened in my mind.

"Oh, my God, you were there, weren't you?" I said to Keeshawna, opening my eyes and trying to absorb the shock.

CHAPTER TWENTY-THREE

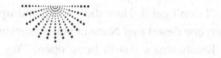

*W*as everything I had believed about my past a lie? Grandma had raised me, Mom had been diagnosed with terminal cancer shortly after I was born, and everyone had come to her funeral but had been turned away. Had anything that Dad told me over the years been true? Was this why I'd struggled against my memories for so many years?

"Keeshawna, I don't remember any of that. Well, now that you say it, there are some fuzzy memories, but I'm so confused." Pressure built in my chest; I had to force myself to keep inhaling.

She clutched my hand. "You were young, Emily. Gertrude didn't want to make a scene or make it worse for you. You had just lost your mom. She had lost her beloved daughter-in-law and her son and granddaughter at the same time. She really thought that Stephen would come around. She gave him time and space, thinking that once the rawness of grief wore off, they would be able to mend things, but the opposite ended up true. He retreated completely. We always guessed that his refusal to accept our help would change with time, when the agony of the loss softened, but it didn't. This is my perspective, though. I don't know the entire story."

"Then why didn't she try harder? For me?"

"Oh, she did, Emily." Keeshawna let out a hard sigh. She shook her head for a moment before continuing. "She wrote you letters. She called. She used to drive by your school and watch you on the playground from a distance. It broke her."

"She wrote to me?"

"Yes. Your dad never gave the letters to you, did he?" Realization spread across her face. "Oh, Emily, I'm so sorry."

The room tilted. Wavy lines zigzagged across my field of vision. Was I going to pass out?

"Emily, are you okay?" Keeshawna clutched my arm tighter. "Let me get you some water."

"No. I'm fine." I fought through the panic. "None of this makes sense. I never got a letter from Grandma. Why would Dad have kept them from me?" I thought back to Danny reaching out to me on social media after I'd graduated from college. I had shunned his attempts, believing that he and the rest of them had abandoned me when I was most in need. What if everything Dad had told me (or not told me in his silence) was a lie?

"I'm sorry, Emily." Her gaze drifted to the window for a moment. "I'm simply telling you what I know and observed from my end. I honestly have no idea what sort of interactions—if any —your dad and Gertrude had before her death. I just think it's so important for you to know that you were and are loved. That's why I got irritated with Arty the other night. You're right. This isn't fair and it shouldn't fall on your shoulders. We were the adults. We should have done better. Danny and I are committed to trying to find some common ground with your dad. I can promise you that much. I understand it's not enough. And I understand your frustration and anger with us. I would feel the same." Her voice caught. "I'm not absolved here, Emily. I could have done more. I should have done more. That's been keeping me up at night lately. That and a barrage of hormones making me drench through my pajamas and sheets."

Her joke fell flat.

"I think I need some time to sit with this." My mouth felt gummy.

"Of course." She cleared her throat. "Is there anything else I can do or say that might help?"

"No." I forced a smile. "But thank you for this. It means a lot."

"Okay. I'll let you be, but let's chat again soon. All of us— Danny, Shay, Arty. If we can have a collective plan before your dad arrives, it might help." She stood, put on her coat, and tucked her scarf inside the zipper.

"Yes, thank you." I smiled.

"If you're up to it, come to my show tonight. I'll leave your name at the door." Keeshawna started to move to hug me but stopped herself. She gave her head the slightest shake, offered me a pained smile, and walked away.

I waited until she crossed the plaza and was out of sight before getting up. Our conversation should have made me feel better. It was more information than I'd gotten about my family and past in twenty years, but it made me feel worse. Why would Dad have refused to let Grandma see me? Why had he banished them from Mom's funeral?

Keeshawna's perspective made Dad the villain in our family's story. I searched my memory. Vague images of a woman in a white mini van parked next to the playground at my elementary school came to mind. I remembered the smell of cedar bark chips and the sound of my classmates screaming with delight as they chased each other around the play structure, pretending that the bark dust was hot lava. I had taken my usual spot on a grassy patch near the swings and had opened my butterfly journal, a gift from Dad after the funeral, to write a story about a friendly witch who drove from schoolyard to schoolyard with her van filled with jelly candies and caramels. Like the book I had re-written, *The Candy Witch*. Then another image flashed in my mind, a teacher ushering the witch away.

Had Gertrude been the witch? Had she tried to come find me? Had she watched me grow up from afar?

I massaged my temples. My brain hurt from forcing long-forgotten memories that I wasn't sure could be trusted. Sitting at the coffee shop ruminating wasn't going to do me any good, so I took my coffee cup to the front and headed outside.

The question was, what now?

I was beginning to understand why Dad had tried to stop me from coming. What I was beginning to realize was that he didn't want me to learn the truth. He didn't want to have to face his own truth.

I meandered along the cobblestone pathway, barely noticing any of the activity around me. Morning was in full swing in Cascata, people happily going about their day. I wondered if they could see through me. Was my internal angst visible on my skin?

I had learned at Columbia that the gift of good writing, good storytelling, was allowing readers to temporarily inhabit someone else's soul. It's the only time in our lives when we actually live and breathe through another person's lens. Crack open the pages of any book and suddenly we're transported to a different world. My perspective had been expanded and altered thanks to the many, many pages of historical fiction and poetry that I had devoured. Stories had helped shape me, written by authors who had vastly different experiences than mine. Yet these writers welcomed me into their worlds and allowed me to glimpse (even briefly) what life was like through their perspective. Books had shifted my understanding, offered me an opportunity to see myself in a different light. From Keeshawna's description, it sounded like I had Grandma to thank for that.

I tried not to fume. I wanted to call Dad back and unleash on him. However, after years of trying to analyze his moods, I was certain that would backfire. We needed a face-to-face as soon as he arrived.

I shot him a text with trembling fingers asking him for a definitive arrival time. I wasn't going to let him ditch his responsibility this time. That was another strategy he had often employed. Promising one thing and relying on the fact that I might forget or not bring it up. Like when I would ask him to take me to Mom's gravesite on her birthday.

"Yeah, Em, I think we can make that happen," he would say. Then the day would come and go. I would note the occasion by swimming in my grandparents' pool, submerging myself in the deep end until my fingers and toes were wrinkled, and my skin tingled with salt, and then reading my favorite book and toasting her memory alone in my bedroom with a dark chocolate bar and a grainy picture of us on the beach.

My thirtieth birthday was only a few months away and suddenly I felt like I was shedding the thirteen year old inside of me. Had grief stunted my emotional growth, or was Dad responsible for that, too?

Trauma. That's what my therapist had labeled it. She had promised me that it was a normal coping mechanism. My brain's way of dealing with the enormous loss of a parent. It was like time had stopped when I was thirteen and I'd never quite found a way to keep the dials on the clock spinning.

I rubbed my shoulders, not from the crisp sea-soaked air, but because I hadn't expected that coming to Cascata would call into question everything I believed.

You need to stop, Emily, I told myself as I turned onto Grammar Street. Spinning endlessly on what ifs wasn't going to be productive.

Once I got back to the house, I called Cameron. I needed action. I needed a plan. I needed to do something—anything.

"Where are we at with the listing?"

He sounded a bit taken aback by my abruptness. "Uh, we're good. We should be all set. I feel confident about our pricing. We can go ahead and have you sign the contract and at least have everything lined up and ready to go, as soon as you can legally list the property. Is there a time that works for you to sign the paperwork?"

"Actually I want to talk about your proposal. Your idea about turning The Ballad into a guest house."

"You do? Wow. Yeah, great. I'm kind of surprised, to tell you the truth, but I think it's a brilliant idea."

"Can you send over the proposal? I want to take a good look at it as soon as possible."

"Of course. I'm not at my desk. Give me thirty minutes and you'll have it in your inbox."

We hung up. It felt good to take control. I ventured upstairs to Grandma's bedroom while I waited for Cameron's email. Her room was on the third floor with west-facing windows looking out to the ocean. Thus far I had avoided her personal quarters. Intruding in her professional life was one thing, but going through her underwear drawer was another.

Not surprisingly, Grandma's room mirrored the book theme in the rest of the house. It reminded me of the Hogwarts library with its extravagant fireplace and four poster bed. Stacks of books sat unread on the bedside table along with an aromatherapy mister and bottles of lemon and rosemary essential oils, a pressed flower petal bookmark, reading glasses, and a small rose-scented candle. Like the other rooms in the estate, everything was neat and tidy. I peeked into the closet to see flowing skirts and dresses in various shades of teal and purple. Her wardrobe had a bohemian meets Saks 5th Avenue vibe. Rows of ankle-high boots and sandals lined the bottom of the closet. Pretty hat boxes took over the top shelves.

I removed one of the boxes which was deep navy with pink flamingos. The box was shaped in an octagon and tied with a silky navy ribbon. Inside was a navy 1920s flapper hat with velvet white and yellow flowers around the base and a yellow lace veil. I remembered the hat from her Gatsby party. She had let me try it on, fastening it to my hair with bobby pins. How many costume parties had she hosted in the garden? How many had I attended? I racked my brain for any memory of Mom or Dad at the Gatsby bash, but I couldn't picture either of them in her glowing garden. Had Mom been getting treatment?

More memories rushed forward of sleeping in this bed, of

giggling under the covers as we read Amelia Bedelia's misadventures and drank hot chocolate with melty mini marshmallows. I must have mistaken Mom for her. Grandma had read aloud to me at night. It had been Grandma who encouraged me to find my own endings for stories when I was sad.

I put the hat back in the box and moved on to her dresser. There were soft flannel pajamas, fleece sweatshirts, rolled up pairs of jeans, and cabin socks. Aside from the books there was nothing personal in Grandma's room. Not a diary or journal. Not a family picture. It struck me as odd. The same was true for most of the house. Grandma had kept each room designed like a museum, but nothing looked lived in. Was that intentional? Or had she purged the estate of family heirlooms and reminders of me and my family when everything fell apart?

A sadness invaded. Instead of feeling bitter, I felt a melancholy for the grandmother I hadn't known. My thoughts went to Shay. Her description of her relationship with Grandma paralleled these memories. I had been cheated on every level. Mom dying young, a challenging relationship with Dad, and never having the chance to connect with my extended family.

I needed to shift my thinking. Instead of wallowing in the past and choices that I had had no control over, I was ready to start figuring out what I could control. Thinking differently about The Ballad was one of them. I had been happy here once. I could be happy here again. Dad had made a mistake that had colored every choice and decision. I wasn't going to follow those same patterns. Even if it meant that he and I never spoke again. It was time. I was ready.

CHAPTER TWENTY-FOUR

That night I finally took Keeshawna up on her offer to come to her show. I let my hair fall loose on my shoulders and put on the only dress I'd packed, a cute halter top sundress that I had scored at a vintage shop in Santa Clara a couple summers ago. The green fabric and flirty cut of the dress paired with strappy sandals and dangling jasper earrings seemed fitting for a jazz club.

Shay and Danny were seated at a table in the front row when I arrived. The Whale's Note jazz club was dark and moody with a small stage, a lounge, a bar, and a scattering of intimate tables. A mix of New Orleans-style artwork and beach prints hung on the walls. A massive whale carved out of driftwood hung from the ceiling. There was a large crowd—not an empty seat in the house —and the eager energy of an audience waiting for live music in the air.

"Emily!" Shay stood and waved me over to them. "You look amazing." She kissed my cheek. "Totally hot!"

"Thanks." I grinned. "You look great, too."

Tonight, her boho style included flared bell bottoms, a crop top, and gold hoop earrings that were practically bigger than my hands.

Danny stood to greet me with a hug. "Hey, Keeshawna told me about your talk. I'm glad you guys had a chance to get together."

"Me too." I meant it with my whole heart. "Is Arty coming?"

"Nope." Shay sat down and handed me a menu. "He's working at the pub. We all try to make as many of Mom's shows as we can, or rotate, but she mentioned that she invited you, so Dad and I snuck out early to get the best seats in the house on the chance that you showed up—and you did."

"Would you like a drink?" Danny asked. "They make a mean gin and tonic if you're a fan."

"That sounds perfect."

Keeshawna came on shortly. She wore a silver sequined dress that caught the overhead lights and reflected dazzling sparkles like bursting fireworks. She owned the stage with her sultry sound, the way she moved to the beat of her accompanying musicians and didn't simply sing the lyrics but embodied them.

"She's amazing," I said to Shay between sets.

"I know. She's the ultimate Goddess."

The evening wore late. I stayed for a second set and a second gin and tonic, laughing with my cousin and uncle and mesmerized by my aunt's performance like the rest of the crowd.

Walking back home I felt warm and fuzzy. Maybe some of that was due to a slight buzz, but I had the feeling most of it was due to the Bryant family.

After the concert, I cocooned myself in The Ballad for two days going room by room, figuring out what changes (if any) needed to be made to transform the estate into a modern-day bookish getaway. The more I lingered with the idea, the more excited I became. The Ballad was already a book lover's paradise. Short of picking specific author themes for the second and third floor rooms, there wasn't that much work that would need to be done. I daydreamed of hiding secret packages in the cubbies in the walls for guests, just like Grandma had done. I imagined craft paper tied with twine and inspirational notes left on pillows. Large brunches around the dining table, and outdoor words and wine nights in the garden under a canopy of stars. Was it possible? Was this dream within my grasp?

Hiding out in the mansion for a couple days had another upside, the fact that it had been days since I'd witnessed any strange scenes connected to the forsaken manuscripts. When Martine called to invite me to lunch on Friday in exchange for sharing my perspective and insight into Santa Clara, I felt like it was the least I could do after my major screwup with her and Cameron's narrative. Plus, I wanted to see if there was any chance she and Cameron were going off script too.

I dragged myself to the Italian bistro, wishing I had made up an excuse to get out of our lunch date. Having a reprieve from the forsaken manuscripts had been nice, but I knew sooner or later they were going to show up again. The minute I sat down across from her, I knew I wasn't wrong about that. Martine's eyes were bloodshot and puffed up like marshmallows over a campfire. She had obviously been crying—a lot.

"How's it going?" I asked, bracing myself for her response, as I slid into the red leather booth.

"It's been better. I told Cameron that we need to split up."

"You did?" I bit the side of my cheek. So much for a discussion about neighborhoods in Santa Clara. Martine obviously had other issues on her mind.

I studied her face, feeling underdressed in my jeans and sweatshirt. Martine was dressed in an impeccable white pantsuit. Her brushed silver jewelry matched the shade of her eyeshadow and her shimmering lipstick. Yet no amount of expensive makeup could conceal the bags under her eyes.

"It was the worst night of my life. I came home early to surprise him because I had toured some properties and found a perfect condo for us. I could see it on his face instantly. He wasn't excited. He didn't even want to look at any of the places I found. He only wanted to talk about The Ballad. You should have seen how thrilled he was when he was talking about possibilities of turning your estate into a book-lover's paradise." Her cheeks splotched with red marks.

"Maybe it's just the lure of a new project," I offered, fiddling with my napkin.

Martine cracked her knuckles. "No. I don't think so. I don't think it's going to work with us. He was pretty clear about what he wants and what he wants is to stay here in Cascata."

So Cam had gone off script too.

She pressed one hand on the table. "I've cried more than I have in my entire life, but now I'm done. It's out of my system." She shook her arms as if to prove her point. "The thing is, I knew we were both unhappy. We have been for a while. That's why I thought a move would give us a fresh start, but I realized Cam doesn't want a fresh start. He's happy here. I can't ask him to give that up, can I? But I also can't keep putting my dreams on hold." She paused momentarily when a waitress came by to take our order. "I'll take a large glass of Chianti and your Caprese salad."

I hadn't had a chance to study the menu. After giving it a quick scan, I opted for a chicken and pesto panini and iced tea.

"Do you think I'm making a mistake?" Martine asked after the waitress was gone. "Have you ever felt like you know what you *need* to do but you don't *want* to do it?

"Yeah. For sure."

The blotchy spots on her face evaporated. "It would be so much easier if I hated him. I don't." She pressed her lips outlined in dark burgundy lipstick together tightly. Her nails, which were polished with a pale glossy varnish, tapped on the table in a rhythmic motion, like she was playing an imaginary piano. "But I can't keep living in limbo like this. I don't want to commute. I want to take this job. I can't ask him to give up his dream, just so I can pursue mine."

I could tell from the sadness behind her delicate brown eyes that she was genuinely torn.

She swallowed hard, then pinched her lips together again. "Maybe splitting up is the catalyst we both need."

The waitress delivered our drinks. Martine downed sips of wine like a runner trying to rehydrate after a marathon.

"Have you noticed how apathetic he is about real estate?"

I sipped my iced tea and shook my head.

"He got his license for me."

"What do you mean?"

"He wanted to help find a way for me not to have to commute. Getting his real estate license brought in more money, but I kept telling him it wasn't even about the money. There's no future for me here. Cascata is hardly a beacon of industry. The work I want to do is in the Bay Area. No amount of money is going to change that."

Our lunch arrived.

"What happened with the job interview?" I asked, taking a bite of my panini oozing with mozzarella cheese.

"I got the job." She chugged more wine.

"Congratulations."

"It's some consolation knowing that I'll have something else to focus on for a while."

"When do you start?"

"Next week. I'm packing my things this weekend." She stabbed her Caprese salad. "That's not the only thing I'm taking with me. I'm taking half my client list at my old agency. My bosses are going to lose their shit when they figure it out. I can't wait. I guess the theme of getting screwed works both ways."

"How so?"

She poked her fork into the top of thick-cut tomatoes drizzled with balsamic vinegar. "That was part of the deal. I had to convince my clients to follow me to the new agency. It was surprisingly easy."

"Is that legal?" My career in high tech had taught me how protective most firms were when it came to clients and assets.

She shrugged. "Who cares? My bosses are such relics that they'll never be able to find the NDA that I signed years ago. They still trade in paper. Paper memos on my desk. Sticky notes. Interoffice files. Paper. Paper. Paper. I found my original contract and shredded it, so good luck to them trying to prove that it ever existed."

I left it alone. "Is there anything I can help with? You had mentioned you wanted some insight into neighborhoods."

Martine's second glass of wine was nearly empty. "I think I found a place. How do you feel about the area by Ortega Park? It's in walking distance to everything and seems pretty safe. I found a new condo in a complex with plenty of amenities—an outdoor pool, weight room, and a rooftop garden."

"That's a great area."

"Good. Because I already put in an offer."

"Wow, you really aren't wasting time."

She gave me a hard stare. "Have you ever had a moment where you realized you can't spend another second wasting your time? I'm done. I have to pursue my dream. If I don't do it now, I know without a doubt that I never will. This situation with Cameron has showed me that. Life is too short to put your dreams on hold for someone else's vision of your future."

Her words left a mark. Our conversation wasn't about me, so I merely agreed with a nod. But the truth was that, yes, I felt her dilemma in every cell in my body. Yes, working in publishing was my dream, but the longer I was here, the more I was realizing that didn't mean it had to be in New York.

"I'm sorry if I've been a downer. Let me at least pay for lunch." Martine set her credit card on the table.

"No, you don't have to do that."

"I insist." She smiled. "Good luck with whatever you decide to do about the estate. I can tell you with certainty that if you decide to partner with Cam on making The Ballad into a bookish escape, he will put every piece of his soul into it. As sad as I am about our marriage ending, no one should give up on their dreams. No one."

Her warning echoed as I left the restaurant. With each passing day I was meeting parts of myself like old friends I had lost touch with.

It took me a minute to adjust to the daylight outside in the plaza after being in the dark lounge-like restaurant. I walked past the bagel shop toward the far end of town, thinking about Martine's story. The theme of giving up on your dreams ran strong. Is that what I had done?

CHAPTER TWENTY-FIVE

"*E*mily!" I heard a woman's voice call and saw Sienna waving from Letter Press. "I thought that was you. Come here! I'm dying to show you what just came in."

Had she just seen Martine, too? Was I being pranked?

"Uh," I hesitated.

"Come in, come in." She motioned with both hands. "I got in a new order of pencils this morning that you absolutely need in your life."

She wasn't going to take no for an answer, so I went inside.

Sienna was dressed in a pair of maroon leggings, an oversized thin beige sweater, and a pair of sandals. Unless she was a master of subtlety, I didn't think she had an ounce of makeup on her face. "Hang on one sec, I have to get to the back to show you what just came in."

"How's it going with Cameron, by the way?" I followed her through the store.

Her eyes widened and she ran her pinkie along her bottom lip. "It started out great. I was crushing like a teenager. We had a blast together. It's going to sound super cheesy, but we hung out and talked books all night. It was amazing. He's amazing, but." She stopped herself and stared out onto the plaza for a minute. "Then it got really complicated."

"Complicated?"

She leaned in closer and lowered her voice. "Did you know that he's married? I mean they're in the middle of splitting up, but it's really sad."

I felt heat creeping up my cheeks. I couldn't lie to her.

Fortunately she continued before I had a chance to choose my words carefully. "I feel terrible for him. It sounds like they grew apart and want different things. Our book chat quickly turned into a sob session for him. He's pretty broken up about it."

I waited for her to say more.

She straightened a postcard in a rack near the door. "It's the story of my life. I meet a good guy at the wrong time, but that's okay. I told him, I'm here if he needs a listening ear and we can totally be bookish friends." She waved her hands like she was trying to force herself not to say more. "Look, sorry. I shouldn't bother you with my non-existent love life."

"It's fine."

"No, really. There's not much to tell." Sienna moved behind the counter. "Do you want to see the pencils that just arrived?"

"Sure." I wanted to keep talking about Cameron, but I could tell she was uncomfortable so I followed her to the cash register, which had been constructed by placing two large card catalogs together. An oversized piece of plywood connected them. More bunting had been draped in three strings across the front. Potted succulents and apothecary candles lined the wall behind the unusual desk.

Sienna unpacked one of many boxes waiting to be sorted and its contents distributed throughout the store. "Here they are," she said after digging through the first box. She handed me a thin narrow black and red box with white lettering. "They are editor pencils. How cool is that?"

I took the box from her. The editor pencils were billed as pigmented vermilion colored on one end with firm graphite on the other. According to the packaging it was a "must have" for any professional editor. The set of six half red, half black pencils came with a twenty-dollar price tag.

"You need these. Am I right, or am I right?" Sienna encouraged me to keep them when I tried to give them back to her. "No, please, consider them a welcome to Cascata gift. Everyone, including your grandma, was so welcoming when I moved here, I want to pay it forward."

"That's okay. You don't have to give them to me." That was thoughtful of her.

"Really, keep them. I'll feel good knowing that a real editor is using them." She refused my money when I reached into my jacket for my debit card.

Before I could protest further, Kenzie came into the store, followed by the woman in aviator sunglasses from Crafts & Drafts the other day. I was surprised that she was still in town. Kenzie marched straight to Sienna.

"I have an order waiting for me, and I'm kind of in a hurry for it." She reached into her intentionally ripped jeans and pulled out her phone in a bejeweled case.

"You ordered the Italian leather journals, right?" Sienna asked.

"Yeah, five of them. They're swag for some very important guests coming on my show. I called yesterday and was told that the shipment had been delayed, so I really hope they've arrived." She scrolled through her phone, not bothering to make eye contact with Sienna.

"That was me you spoke with," Sienna replied, turning back toward the stack of delivery boxes. "Let me check. I'm hopeful they're in one of these. UPS just came so your timing is good."

Kenzie ran her fake nails, painted with fluffy clouds and unicorns, on her phone while she waited. The woman in the sunglasses perused the shelves with an equal amount of disinterest. She picked up a wax seal kit, studied it for a minute, let out a long sigh, and discarded it as if it were tainted.

"Ah, I think we have success." Sienna held up a gorgeous

Italian leather journal with a mosaic bookmark. "These are the ones, right?"

"Yep." Kenzie looked up briefly before returning her attention to her phone. "How much?"

"They're fifty each, so for five that's two hundred and fifty."

"Victoria, I need some cash!" Kenzie called to the woman.

The woman sauntered over to us, visibly irritated. "Kenzie, knock it off. I've told you not to call me Victoria. I don't care what your Women's Studies professor says, I'm your mom."

"Gawd, you're so archaic sometimes, *Mother*." Kenzie scrolled through her phone as she spoke.

"How much, Kenz?" She opened a cream purse with gold trim.

"Two hundred and fifty, Victoria. Oh, sorry, Mother."

Victoria let out a sigh as she unlatched a matching wallet. "Kenz, did you take my cash? I had a stack of hundreds. They're gone."

"I didn't take your cash, Mom."

"You must have. It's not here." She unfolded the wallet. "I had at least a thousand dollars. I know you like to take my cash whenever I come for a visit."

"Mom, I didn't take your cash." Kenzie snarled. "Like stop accusing me of everything. You're totally embarrassing. You're being like totally paranoid, okay?"

Victoria glanced at Sienna and me for the first time as if we had appeared out of thin air. "Apologies, ladies, but it seems that someone has stolen my cash." She removed a platinum credit card and handed it to Sienna. "Kenzie, I need you to be honest, because if you didn't take my cash, that means that as soon as we're done here, I need to go straight to the hotel and lodge a formal complaint. The housekeeping staff must have gone through my wallet."

"Mom, for the last time, I didn't take your cash."

Sienna rang up her order. I stood in a frozen panic, knowing full well what had happened to her cash. She had dropped it in Lindi's tip jar.

"This is so disturbing. I almost locked my purse in the hotel safe." Victoria searched her purse. "I should have known a small, hippy college town would be untrustworthy. I still don't understand why you had to choose this sad spot for school, Kenz. You need to come home and go to UC Santa Barbara or somewhere less remote."

Sienna wrapped each of the journals in tissue paper and placed them in a bag.

I hesitated, not sure what to say. I couldn't let the housekeeping staff at the hotel take the blame for her lost cash, though. "Did you happen to be at Crafts & Drafts the other day?" I asked without thinking.

"Me?" Victoria sounded put off that I had dared speak directly to her. She shared the same petite frame and expensive blonde highlights as Kenzie. Close up her age was apparent in the wrinkles buried beneath expertly applied makeup, but from a distance they could have passed as sisters.

"I recognize you. I was meeting my real estate agent for lunch the other day."

She studied me for a minute, like she was trying to place my face. "I don't remember. I may have stopped in, why?"

I didn't want to get Lindi in trouble, but at the same time I couldn't let an innocent staff member at the hotel take the fallout.

"It's just that I was sitting at the bar, and I remember you putting some money in the tip jar."

She gasped. "I did. That's right. I did. I got a phone call from my agent and had to leave before I got my drink."

Kenzie started toward the door.

"Thank you," her mom addressed me. "I'm going to head that way this moment and get to the bottom of my stolen cash."

"Well, it wouldn't be stolen if you left it as a tip," I noted.

"Who leaves a thousand-dollar tip?" She stroked her neck. "Whoever pocketed that cash is going to be fired."

"But you told her to keep it." I couldn't stay silent.

"I certainly did no such thing." She swung her hair over her shoulder, turned, and traipsed out the door.

I felt sick. Had I done the right thing, or had I just screwed Lindi?

CHAPTER TWENTY-SIX

"Wow, they are a pair," Sienna commented as Kenzie hurried to catch up with her mom. "They're straight out of an episode of the *Real Housewives*. I wonder how they picked Cascata for college? It seems like an odd choice."

"Yeah, good question." I hesitated for a moment but needed someone else's input. "Here's the deal. I saw her put the money in the tip jar. The bartender tried to tell her about it, and Victoria totally blew her off and left. What should I do? I had to say something because I didn't want her to demand that the hotel fire the housekeeper responsible for cleaning her room, but now it sounds like she's going to get the waitress fired, which isn't fair either. Plus, that was a couple days ago. She can't expect to get her tip back now."

"No way," Sienna agreed. "Maybe you should go over there and give them your side of the story. It sounds like you were an eyewitness."

"That's exactly what I was thinking." I couldn't believe that at every turn I ended up more and more enmeshed with the plot lines in the forsaken manuscripts. That couldn't be the reason I was supposed to edit them, could it?

"Let me know what happens," Sienna said as I left. "That woman strikes me as the kind of person used to getting her way."

"Yeah, that's what I'm afraid of." I tucked the editor pencils in my coat. "Thanks again for these."

"I'm sure you'll put them to good use." Sienna waved.

I didn't share her enthusiasm. I was dreading getting in the middle of yet another confrontation, but it was my fault. I owed Lindi that much.

I crossed through the plaza toward the art pub. Not surprisingly Kenzie's mom—aka Victoria—had beaten me there. When I pushed open the door, the bar was nearly empty except for a couple of tables that had been pushed together in the back. Two groups were building a LEGO cityscape and downing baskets of chips. Victoria stood near the tap handles berating Lindi. Her skinny index finger stabbed at Lindi's face as Victoria demanded her money back.

My stomach dropped as I shut the door behind me and moved toward the bar.

"Listen, there is no way you thought that I had left you a thousand-dollar tip. That's ludicrous. And it's theft. I want to speak to your manager immediately!"

Lindi inched away from the spew of Victoria's anger. Kenzie wasn't anywhere to be seen.

"My manager isn't here yet. He's picking up kegs in Sacramento. He'll be back tomorrow." Lindi kept her head tilted toward the floor. Her voice sounded shaky.

"That's unacceptable. I want you to call him now, or else I call the police. You choose how this is going to go down."

Lindi's hands quaked. "I don't know what to tell you. You're the one who left the tip. I tried to tell you that you'd left that much money, but you blew me off and went outside and never came back."

"Okay. Let's think about this, why don't we?" Victoria's tone was condescending as if she were speaking to a toddler who'd snuck a piece of candy. "Why is it that you are so hesitant to involve your manager? I have a solid guess. I understand how the restaurant business works. My husband and I happen to own a number of restaurants. You don't take all the tips. They're shared amongst the staff—the kitchen staff, the wait staff. Did you share that cash or did you keep it for yourself?" she challenged.

Lindi's face turned ashen.

I knew from the color draining from her cheeks that she had kept the money for herself.

"I'm right, aren't I? That's why you're not picking up the phone and calling your manager. You saw an opportunity and snatched it. Where's my money?"

"I don't have it." Lindi's voice was barely audible.

"Let me guess, you went on a spending spree. Excellent." She mocked Lindi by clapping twice. "Here's what's going to happen. I'm going to call the police. You're going to call your manager. I'm sure there's video footage that will reveal you taking the money. That's option one. I press charges, and we involve your boss, who I'm sure will show you the door."

Lindi gulped.

"There's a second option and that is that you return the cash in full by the end of the day tomorrow and we call it good. A simple mistake. But that means every single cent is returned to my hotel room in full, understood?"

"But I don't have it."

"Well, I suggest you find it. I'll be back tomorrow when your manager arrives." She tapped a diamond-studded watch on her wrist. "You can let me know what you've decided then." She spun around in my direction and stopped. "Oh, you."

"Listen, I came over to back Lindi up. I was there when it happened, and she's right. She did try to tell you that you'd left too much cash."

"That's water under the bridge now." Victoria looped her purse over her shoulder and clicked away on her three-inch heels. She shot Lindi one last challenging glance before slamming the door.

Lindi and I stood in silence for a minute. I wondered if she, like me, were trying to process what had just happened.

"What am I going to do?" Lindi massaged her jaw.

"Can you get the money back?"

She shook her head. "No. It's gone."

"It's gone?" I wondered if my fear had come true. Had she taken the cash and gone straight to the casino?

Lindi's eyes held a vacant look. She stared off behind me. "Yeah, I used it to pay rent and medical bills for my kid. I can't get it back and when my boss hears that I kept the tip money to myself, he's going to fire me for sure. She said she's going to press charges. I already have a record. I can't go back to jail again. I can't do that to my kid."

I wished I had the money to loan her. "I'm sure we can work something out. Maybe a payment plan? I'll back you up. I was here. I saw you try and get her attention. She was so distracted with her phone call that she didn't even bother to listen to you. That's her mistake, not yours."

"Yeah, but she's right about the restaurant policy. We're supposed to split all the tips. I didn't. I pocketed her cash and shared everything from the rest of my shift with the team. I'm going to get fired for that. I know it. It's fair. I knew it was wrong, but I did it anyway." She hung her head and looked at the floor again. "I'm repeating the same mistakes. I thought I had changed. I thought I had learned from the past, but I guess I haven't. Now it's all going away again. I was just starting to build trust with my son."

"You don't know that. I'm sure we can find a solution. Tell your boss the truth. Maybe he'll understand. He might surprise you." A thought invaded my pep talk. "You used the money for a worthy cause—rent and medical bills."

She gave me a half nod but didn't meet my eyes. I wasn't sure she was telling the truth. "Maybe. But I doubt it. He was pretty clear when he hired me. He knew about my past. He already gave me a shot by taking a chance on me. I've let him down. I've let everyone down."

I felt terrible for her and irritated with myself. I should have kept my mouth shut. Why had I said anything to Victoria?

I had to find a way to fix this. Lindi didn't deserve to be fired and lose out on a chance to rebuild her life. Victoria hardly seemed strapped for cash, either. It had taken her days to realize that the money was missing. She didn't need it. She wanted to belittle Lindi. She wanted to exert her power and flaunt her privilege.

Maybe if I talked to Lindi's boss he would listen to me. I wasn't sure if it would help, but I had to try.

CHAPTER TWENTY-SEVEN

J promised Lindi I would come back tomorrow and tell her boss what I had witnessed. *So much for Shay's theory of continuing to edit the forsaken manuscripts*, I thought as I cut through the center of the plaza past the leafy palms and turned onto Grammar Street. My second round of edits appeared to have the same effect as the first—sending every character into more of a tailspin. But I tried to remember Grandma's advice, picturing the butterfly note in my head. I'd only given each of these characters a nudge. The rest was in their hands, right? Is that what she had wanted to teach me in requiring me to edit the forsaken stack?

Shay was waiting for me on the front porch in one of the rocking chairs when I returned to The Ballad.

"Hey, you're here." She stood up from the rocker. "I was wondering if you were ever coming back. In fact, I had this terrible feeling that maybe you took off without saying goodbye. You wouldn't do that, would you?"

"Never!" I grinned. "Did I forget that we were supposed to meet?"

"I stopped by because I have some big news. Big!" She tagged after me.

"What's your news?" I unlocked the front door.

"You're not going to believe it." She rocked on her toes, reminding me of a ballerina warming up, except instead of ballet slippers and a leotard Shay wore a pair of black and white Chuck Taylors and skinny jeans. Her eyes were bright with enthusiasm. "I want you to think about what I'm going to tell you because it's hard evidence—*proof*—that your edits have helped."

"I hope so. I could really use that because I'm feeling like I've just made even more of a mess." I dropped my keys on the small table in the foyer and walked toward the kitchen. After witnessing Victoria and Lindi's exchange I needed a drink of water, or maybe something stronger.

"Why? Wait up." She followed me down the hall. "Uh-oh. Did something happen again?"

"Yeah." I told her about Kenzie's mom and the tip money as I found a glass in the cupboard and filled it from the tap. "I'm not sure if our second attempt worked for Lindi. Victoria, who, get this, is Kenzie's mom, is out for blood for no reason. I don't know why, because I doubt that a thousand dollars is more than pocket change for her, but she wants to eviscerate Lindi."

"Shocker. The apple doesn't fall far from the tree. Kenzie must get her winning personality from her mom." Shay helped herself to a handful of M & Ms in a canister on the counter. "That's terrible about Lindi. We have to do something."

"I know, but what?" I reached for a couple pieces of the chocolate candies. "I told her I would stop by tomorrow and back her up in front of her boss, but he doesn't know me. He could think she put me up to it."

"What about Cameron? He was there too, right. I'm sure he'll help," Shay suggested, munching on the candy. "He's been part of this town for years."

"That's not a bad idea. Maybe we need to rally the town, but Cameron's gone off script too."

"How?" She tossed a red M&M in the air and caught it in her mouth.

"Well, Martine is leaving him. They're breaking up. She

decided she didn't want to waste any more time on not following her dreams and she doesn't want to hold Cameron back, either. She's packing up her things and moving to Silicon Valley, oh, and taking her client list with her, which by the way is completely unethical and perhaps also illegal."

"That sucks." Shay grimaced. "But they weren't happy, right?"

"No, you're right, they weren't. I keep reminding myself of that, and then I feel equally guilty."

"Don't. Don't do that to yourself. You don't need to beat yourself up. These are real people, Emily. They're making their own choices."

Relief flooded my body. "Thanks. I needed to hear that." I refilled my water glass. "Tell me your news."

"Okay." She danced back and forth on her toes. "It's about the podcast. Apparently there were a couple producers in the audience who were here to meet with one of the professors. Anyway, it's a long story but it turns out they're interested in doing a professional podcast with Tamir and me as the hosts. They're going to do a demo and potentially partner with us on distributing it on the major channels. It's not a done deal, but it's a pretty big in." Shay couldn't contain the grin spreading across her face. "The best part is they want me to do the writing for it. I didn't see myself telling stories in this way, but it's kind of perfect, you know? It will give me experience, and maybe one day I'll finally be a storyteller too."

"What? Are you kidding me? That's incredible news." I reached out to hug her. "And you're absolutely going to find a way to share your stories. I'm sure of that."

Her face glowed with a happy sheen. "Who would have thought this would be the outcome? I mean, think about it, Emily, if you hadn't changed that one scene with Tamir and Kenzie this never would have happened."

"I can't believe it. I'm so happy for you." I squeezed her hand.

"It's not going to be so shabby having to spend time with

Tamir either. Professionally speaking, of course." Her eyes brightened.

It took me a second to catch her meaning. My mouth opened as I laughed and sucked in a quick breath. "Strictly professionally speaking."

Tamir. Of course Tamir had been the guy she was into. Clearly I had been way too self-consumed with my own issues when I'd gotten here. I hoped that with shedding some of the unwanted and untruthful layers of my past, that was changing. I was changing.

"Hey, on that note, I have an idea I want to run by you."

"Hit me." Shay waved her hands toward her.

"What do you think about throwing a party in Grandma's honor. Here. This weekend?"

"Um, you had me at party."

"No, I'm serious. I've learned so much about her and our family and myself since being here. And everywhere I go in town people talk about her. I thought it might be nice to do something to honor that."

"Yes, I'm all in!" Shay ran over to the breakfast nook which was flooded with light. "We can go through her cookbooks, come up with some of her favorite and our favorite bookish recipes. You are thinking book themed, yeah?"

I finished my water and placed the glass in the sink. "One of the strongest memories I've had since returning to Cascata was of her Great Gatsby party. You were probably too young to remember it, but I can't get it out of my mind. I was thinking we could invite the town, ask people to come dressed as their favorite literary character. Maybe your mom would be willing to sing?"

"Oh, yeah, you can count on that." Shay pulled a handful of cookbooks off the shelves. "I don't remember the Gatsby party specifically but Grandma had costume book parties every summer. We didn't do one this summer because she was sick, so this is perfect. I know my parents will help and I know the entire

town will show up, so we had better start thinking food and libations now."

She offered me some of the cookbooks.

We spent the next few hours brainstorming and mapping out
plans for a book bash in Gertrude Bryant's honor. It felt good to
do something joyful, positive, like Grandma was here in the
kitchen with us gently blowing suggestions in our ears.

CHAPTER TWENTY-EIGHT

*T*he next day as I walked through the plaza, I realized how much my circle had expanded in the last two weeks. People waved and said hello as I passed by. I knew nearly every shopfront by name. I had met most of the owners and shop-keepers. It had taken coming to the remote Lost Coast to an off-the-beaten-path town, sequestered behind the mystical Redwood Curtain, to stretch my world view.

While I appreciated my newfound community, I couldn't stop spinning on whether I'd made things much, much worse for Lindi.

When I arrived at Crafts & Drafts, there was a handwritten sign posted on the door that the pub would be closed for a "staff meeting" and opening late.

The door was unlocked so I slipped inside and waited for a chance to defend Lindi.

A man, whom I assumed must be Lindi's boss, was trying to hear both sides of their stories but they kept talking over one another and interrupting. It was like a bad wrestling match.

"She stole a thousand dollars from me," Victoria spewed spit as she spoke. She twisted the cashmere scarf around her neck tighter and narrowed her eyes. "I gave her a chance to return the money, but since she's refusing, I am going to involve the authorities."

"Wait, slow down." He held out his hands to try and calm her. The man looked to be about my age with a well-trimmed beard. His flannel shirt, jeans, and boots made me wonder if he spent time foraging for rare mushrooms in the redwoods when he wasn't tending bar at Crafts & Drafts. "Lindi, why don't you tell me what happened?"

"She pocketed cash, clearly not intended for her," Victoria shrieked. "She's trying to play innocent, but come on! Who in their right mind would think that someone left them a thousand dollar tip for a ten dollar drink? That is absolutely ludicrous. I own a number of restaurants in Southern California and no one ever leaves that kind of cash. She knew exactly what she was doing. She intentionally took my money and made sure that no one knew about it. If she was so innocent, why did she cover it up? Why didn't she tell you?"

"Lindi, go ahead," her boss focused his attention on her.

Lindi wrung her hands together and stared at her feet. "I should have told you about the tip. But I swear I didn't steal it. She put the money in the tip jar and left. I flagged her down and told her she'd put a lot of cash in there, but she just dismissed me." She paused and noticed me standing near the doorway. "She'll tell you. She was here." Lindi pointed to me.

Everyone turned to me.

My cheeks flushed with warmth as I approached the bar. I was not about to let this woman ruin Lindi's chance at happiness. "It's true. I saw it happen. Lindi's telling the truth."

Victoria shot daggers at me. "They're probably in it together. Split the cash, huh, girls?"

I wasn't exactly a girl. Nor was Lindi.

Her boss motioned for me to come forward. Upon closer inspection, a little flutter erupted in my chest. His kind, warm chocolate eyes drew me in. "And who might you be?"

"I'm Emily Bryant. I was here with Cameron, whom I think

you know. We were going over some real estate paperwork and we both saw the exchange. Lindi *is* telling the truth." I paused and met Victoria's piercing gaze with equal confidence. "I'm not saying that it wasn't a mistake that you left the cash, I'm just saying that Lindi did try to tell you and you wouldn't listen. I wasn't the only one who heard her try to give it back to you, either."

She huffed.

"Thanks for coming forward." Lindi's boss smiled at me. "I'm Aaron. I own the pub, and it's important that we get a clear picture of what happened. That's good to know that other people witnessed the scene, too. Hopefully, that will help."

"I'm sure he'll be willing to tell you what he saw," I replied. Why was my heart speeding up? Aaron was handsome in a rugged, non-traditional way. I tried to shake off the feeling and concentrate on the problem at hand, but I kept stealing glances at his strong jawline and kind eyes.

"Okay, I think this is a misunderstanding, and our best bet is to pour a round of pints, go take a seat, and see what kind of solution we can come up with that will feel beneficial for everyone." Aaron addressed Victoria. "What kind of beer can I get you?"

"I don't drink beer. It's way too fattening." She placed her hand on her tiny waist. Her tailored skirt and well-cut jacket highlighted her narrow figure.

"What else can I get you, then?" Aaron didn't sound impressed.

"I'm not thirsty, and I know exactly what you're trying to do."

"Yeah." Aaron nodded. "I just told you what I want to do. I want us to go sit down like mature adults and figure out a solution that's fair for everyone." He met my eyes. "What about you?"

"Me? Uh, sure. I'd love to." Did I sound as unsure as I felt? It was like my mouth had forgotten how to form sentences. Love to? God, Emily, you sound like a teenager.

He nodded. "I think having another voice of reason would be helpful. If you're game."

"Uh, I guess."

He held an empty pint glass. "What can I get you?"

"I'll take a pint of the amber."

Aaron poured drinks, including a white wine spritzer for Victoria. His forearms were muscular, I guessed from slinging drinks and carrying trays of frothy pints around the bar. He ushered us to one of the drafting tables and passed around drinks.

Victoria huffed again as Aaron tried to mediate the conversation. "Lindi, as you know, we have a strict staff policy about sharing tips."

Lindi couldn't meet his eyes. She stared at her beer and nodded. When she spoke her voice was barely audible. "I know. I shouldn't have kept it for myself. It was a stupid mistake and I'm sorry."

"Please." Victoria feigned interest in the zipper on her purse, zipping it partway open and then shut. "Lay off the sob story. You knew exactly what you were doing. You need to fire her and I want my money back—all of it," she said to Aaron in a forceful tone.

"Well, I'm not sure how that stands up in terms of legality." Aaron made eye contact with me. "Emily here is a credible witness who saw you leave the tip and ignore Lindi's attempts to let you know about your mistake. It's doubtful that the police will have any interest in getting involved in this."

"What about cameras?" She scanned the ceiling as if expecting to see cameras mounted on the exposed beams. "You must have cameras which will be proof of her guilt."

"I don't. It's not my thing. We're in Cascata. I don't need security cameras, and I don't think it's an issue of guilt. It's more of a misunderstanding. You didn't intend to leave such a large tip, and my staff member followed protocol in alerting you to your mistake. Where's the guilt in that?" Aaron kept his cool. He was calm and relaxed in his approach, which just seemed to make Victoria that much more irate.

"But she kept the money!" Her voice developed a piercing

nasal quality. "She admitted that herself. Are you telling me that if at the end of the night when you were doing the books and you learned that a customer had left a thousand dollar tip, that wouldn't have raised a red flag?"

"No. We probably would have celebrated." Aaron raised his pint glass. "You read about this kind of stuff in the paper all the time. A rich patron pays things forward by leaving the waitstaff a big tip. That's front page news. Such a great human interest story." He snapped, a smile spreading across his beard. "That's it. That's how we can spin this situation."

I knew exactly what he was thinking. Our eyes met across the table. I coughed on my beer. *Nice, Emily. Classy.*

"You okay?" Aaron sounded concerned.

"Just swallowed wrong." I coughed twice, feeling flames lapping at my neck and cheeks.

"What in the world are you talking about?" Victoria remained rigid, her arms barricading her petite frame, and holding her purse with a death grip as if she expected Lindi to reach across the table, steal it, and run off.

"Here's an idea." The gleam on his face broadened. "What if that tip that you left Lindi was in a show of kindness and generosity? You stopped by the pub for an afternoon drink and while you were enjoying your cocktail…"

Victoria cut him off. "I didn't even drink my cocktail."

He lifted one hand. "Hear me out on this. While you were enjoying your afternoon refresher, you happened to strike up a conversation with the bartender, who you learned had been dealt a tough hand. She shared that she was working diligently to provide for her young son and to rebuild her life. You were so touched by her story that on your way out the door, you slipped a thousand dollars into her tip jar. You intended to become her secret benefactor, but Emily here saw the entire thing, and tracked you down. This story has media darling written all over it, and I went to school with a reporter for the *San Francisco Chronicle*. I can make a call right now. I'm sure he'd love to write a feature story about such an incredible gesture of generosity during these times of disconnection. It seems to me like the kind of feature that ends up getting picked up by the AP wire and before you know it, you're a guest on *The Today Show*. Think of the publicity. That's worth way more than the thousand dollars you gifted Lindi, am I right?"

Victoria appraised Aaron with newfound respect.

I could tell his pitch was hitting the right notes and stroking her ego.

Lindi remained silent. She laced her fingers together, unclasped them, then repeated the move over and over again.

"I'd be happy to help. I've written hundreds of press releases," I offered.

Aaron shot me a look of thanks before turning to Victoria. "What do you say? I think it's a win/win for all of us. Crafts & Drafts gets our name mentioned, and you get to take the credit for playing the role of personal fairy godmother to a woman in need who is working twelve-hour shifts to pay for her son's care and to get her feet back on the ground after a string of unfortunate circumstances."

Was Lindi actually working twelve-hour shifts? That had to be exhausting. I also noticed that Aaron steered clear of discussing the fact that Lindi had done jail time, wisely opting to laser in on her quest to rebuild her life and skimming over the gritty details.

"You can't pay for this kind of publicity. Everyone loves a feel-good story. It's a classic fairytale." Aaron held her gaze. Had she met her match?

Victoria nodded slowly, taking her time to respond. "I'll consider it."

"What's there to consider?" Aaron pushed her for an answer. "Press coverage like this is a no brainer. I'm convinced this story will get great traction. The PR you'll receive would cost you thousands of dollars and there would be no guarantee that whatever angle your expensive publicist attempted to pitch to the media would even get covered. This is a sure thing and well worth a thousand bucks."

She sighed. "All right. It might be good for Kenzie's podcast. We can work that into the story. You have press contacts who you can distribute the story to?"

"Yep." He looked to me. Was it just my imagination or did his eyes sparkle with flecks of gold? "You're game to help."

"I'd be happy to."

"Awesome. It's settled then." Aaron reached across the table to shake hands with Victoria. He smiled with genuine enthusiasm. "I love getting to spread good news."

Victoria offered him her hand as if she were a royal princess and he should bow and kiss it. She couldn't resist giving Lindi a parting sneer as she left.

We sat in silence for a moment, letting the tornado of negative energy evaporate. Once Victoria was long gone, Lindi spoke first. She looked to Aaron with tears.

"Thanks, I didn't deserve that." Lindi forced a smile. "I'll pack up my things and get out of here."

"Why would you do that?" Aaron scowled and shook his head.

"Because I kept the money. I broke the rules, and I'm guessing you're going to fire me anyway so I figured I would save you the trouble." Her voice was monotone, like she knew she had already sealed her fate.

"Hang on. Hang on." Aaron held up a muscular arm. "You're part of this press spin. We can't very well pitch the media a feel-good story only to have one of the key players absent. You have to stay. Am I disappointed that you kept the cash, yeah, but I can tell that you feel worse about it than I do. I'm not going to say another word about it and I'm not going to let you quit. That woman is a complete narcissist, but this is seriously good press for the pub. I owe you."

Lindi wiped her nose on the back of her sleeve. "Thank you. It won't happen again."

"I know it won't." His voice was gentle. "Why don't you take off? I've got the bar covered, and Emily has graciously agreed to help me with this press release."

Lindi thanked him again.

"That was really kind of you," I said after she left. "I think she's trying to make changes."

"I know she is. That's why I hired her. I can always tell based on the eyes. Honest eyes don't lie. You've got them too." He held my gaze for a minute, then gathered the empty glasses. "So, you want to write a press release?"

"Yeah." I followed him behind the bar to his office, feeling a spark of excitement that was entirely unsettling, but definitely not unwelcome.

CHAPTER TWENTY-NINE

"*I*t's cool of you to help," Aaron said, showing me into his office, which was packed with beer memorabilia and funky artwork. "Lindi mentioned that you're a book editor visiting from New York. Are you buying a summer beach house out this way?"

"No." I chuckled. "I wish, but editors don't make that kind of money. Unfortunately I'm here because my grandmother died. Gertrude Bryant. Did you know her?"

"Oh! You're Gertrude's granddaughter?" He pushed aside a stack of receipts and bar catalogues. His eyes were the color of cinnamon with tiny flecks of gold. The way he ran his eyes over me for a brief second sent tiny goosebumps up my arms. "I see the resemblance. Of course. Your grandmother was one of a kind. I was so sad to hear that she died."

There was no denying that he was attractive, although he wasn't my type. Was that even fair to say? I didn't exactly have a "type." Most of the men I had dated were developers who wore the same uniform—khaki pants, white button-down shirts, and Chuck Taylors. None of them were into literature but would and usually did talk my ear off for the entire, painful dinner date about their latest coding conquests. I hadn't had a chance to meet anyone in New York, but I was holding out hope that I would find my modern version of Mr. Darcy at a swanky cocktail party for my celebrity author's debut launch party.

My romantic fantasies were fashioned upon decades of page-turners. Brooding heroes who had no idea how smoldering hot they were and who knew how to capture a woman's attention with unsettling charm and wit. They were always well-read, dashing, and knew nothing of swiping right. Shudder—banish the thought.

"Did you know that Gertrude used to host writing workshops here? They were a blast. The minute I would list a new one—every spot would fill within minutes. Her philosophy was to *tap into* the old school method of writing. Get it?" He paused and winked. "Sorry, I can't resist a good pun. Anyway, Gertrude's philosophy was to loosen everyone's creative energy up with a drink or two and then send them off with her clever writing prompts to let them make magic." He smiled at the memory. "She asked me to come up with a special menu for the workshops. I would make cocktails for whatever writer she was going to spotlight for the evening. She found this great book, *Tequila Mockingbird,* and we paired up to put together Romeo and Juleps—a mint julep with a splash of rose water. And my personal favorite, Vermouth the Bell Tolls—a shot of vermouth with a twist of lemon. Gertrude would read a passage from the author. She designed writing exercises for the group based on those passages. It was so much fun. Maybe we could revive them. I'm sure the writers who attended faithfully would love to have you take the lead."

Partnering with Aaron was tempting. "I'm not sure what my plans are yet, but my cousin Shay and I are planning an impromptu party this weekend in Gertrude's honor. Would you want to make a special drink or two for that?"

"Count on it!"

"Great." I felt another wave of heat trickling up my neck. It was great that Aaron was willing to help and I certainly wouldn't mind having an excuse to hang out with him again soon.

He made a note of the date on his desk calendar, then leaned forward, resting his chin on his hands. "What do you need from me to write the release?"

"More details." I looked around for something to write with.

As if reading my mind he opened his desk drawer and handed me a pen and notebook. "Hit me with your questions."

"Can you give me more background on Lindi? If not, I can talk to her."

"No, no, I can tell you a lot about her." He proceeded to launch into their history. "We went to high school together. Lindi was two years older than me, but Cascata was small so we ended up running in some of the same circles. Lindi's dad was a raging alcoholic. The bad kind. He eventually died of cirrhosis of the liver, but not before leaving lasting damage." He paused and met my eyes. I could see real sadness in his face. "He was an abusive drunk who beat her mother to the point of hospitalization. Lindi's mom suffered multiple concussions, broken bones, and bruises. Lindi escaped with school at first. She was a good student, naturally bright, but she didn't have much of a chance. Family patterns like that are hard to break." Aaron sighed and shook his head.

I wasn't sure I wanted to write any of this down, but I held the pencil anyway, waiting for him to go on.

"Lindi started dating a guy who everyone knew was an asshole. He perpetuated the same kind of brutal violence on her that her mother had experienced at her father's hand. She began drinking. I don't know for sure, but I suspect there may have been drugs involved as well. After graduation she couldn't keep a job. She drifted around town. Things changed when she found out she was pregnant. She left her boyfriend—it feels wrong to call him that—the definition of boyfriend in my book doesn't involve physically harming someone you love."

"That's so sad." I felt even more empathy for Lindi.

"It was sad. People were worried she and the baby would end up dead. A few women in town rallied around her and got her help. Gertrude may have been involved in that, I'm not sure, but anyway, they were able to place her in a woman's shelter in Eureka where she had the baby. She stayed away from Cascata, I'm sure because she was worried that her boyfriend would find her. Turns out she didn't have to worry. He plowed into a tree on the Redwood Highway, high on meth, and died on impact. It's not going to sound very nice, but it kind of seems like karma to me."

"I don't understand, it sounds like Lindi was on the path of recovery."

"She was, but things got worse. Her dad murdered her mom. He shot her while she was sleeping."

I set the pencil down. Thus far I had yet to write a single word. "That's horrible." My struggles with my memories, Grandma, Dad, the manuscripts seemed tiny in comparison. I had been loved. I had lost some of that love, but that was very different than never being loved.

"It set Lindi back. She started drinking again. Couldn't hold a job. Her aunt took over raising her son. She racked up a lot of debt gambling and got arrested for breaking into a house on the cliffs and stealing a bunch of money. I think she was set up by the crowd she was hanging around with. I always felt sorry for her. She couldn't catch a break. I don't know how to explain it other than the eyes and that I knew her when she was more together. Once she finished her time in prison, she needed a job. I didn't hesitate. It takes some kind of crazy resiliency to go through what she's been through and come out the other side still standing—even if slightly messed up."

"Yeah." I couldn't think of anything else to say. I tried to blink back the tears welling in my eyes, but it was no use. Lindi's history pierced my heart. Dad had cut himself off from the world after losing Mom. Their love had been that deep. Lindi's experience had been the opposite. She'd had to watch her father beat her mother and eventually murder her? Tears spilled, rolling down my cheeks. I brushed them away with the back of my hand.

Aaron handed me a tissue. "It's the worst, isn't it? Anyway, that's why I want to help her. I don't care about the money. I know she's trying to rebuild her life. Honestly, if she had told me about the tip, I would have told her to keep it."

Not only was he crazy handsome, but he obviously had a kind, caring heart.

"Victoria was out for a fight from the minute she walked in. Her disdain for this town is palpable. Everything I said out there is true. Lindi really did try to do the right thing." I made a couple of notes, not sure what pieces, if any, of Lindi's background would be included in the press release.

"I know. That's why we're going to make sure we help her solve this. Re-writing her story, if you will."

My throat tightened. Did he know?

"As an editor you must be used to re-writing happy endings."

I gulped. "Uh, yeah."

I shifted the topic to Crafts & Drafts, asking him some questions about how long he'd owned the pub and the concept of an art bar. The press release needed background on the bar, but I was already feeling out of sorts since my stomach fluttered every time I glanced down at his muscular forearms. Him bringing up re-writing endings sent a new round of nervous energy pulsing through my veins. Part of me wanted to confess that I had re-written Lindi's story. His connection with Grandma had been solid. Was there any way he could know the truth? But how in the hell would I go about asking that?

CHAPTER THIRTY

I took enough notes to put together the press release and went home. How strange that ten days ago I had been a foreigner in these halls and now they felt like a part of me.

I went straight to work on the press release. It didn't take long to type up a one-page document, but it was painful to have to spin Victoria as a benevolent, empathetic hero. I tried to tell myself I was writing a work of fiction to get through it. As much as it went against my inclination to want to call out her terrible behavior, Aaron was right. The press would love the angle of a big city socialite rescuing a down-on-her-luck single mom. I had learned enough about PR in my time in high tech to know that securing a feature was all about the pitch. If Aaron's friend agreed to cover the story, I could see it getting national play. And I had gotten Lindi into this. I would do whatever it took to get her out of it.

I emailed the release to Aaron and went to the parlor to try and unwind. I had missed a text from Dad while I was at Crafts & Drafts, and I could barely believe the words in the little blue bubble.

COMING SUNDAY. WILL LET YOU KNOW WHEN I'M ON THE ROAD.

He was coming to Cascata.

Finally.

That either meant we were going to make some forward progress and perhaps even find some closure about our shared past, or things were about to go nuclear. As much as I hoped that Dad's arrival would go smoothly, given the surreal events of the past week, I was leaning toward the latter. But it didn't matter anymore. I didn't know the ending of my own story, but I knew the direction my narrative was heading.

I lit a fire and found a book of Mary Oliver's poetry on the bookshelves. Her lyrical wisdom was the salve for my soul. I had first discovered her works in college, which had served as therapy in the form of a tightly bound book of individual poems. Poetry should be read aloud. It's like song in motion. Whenever I was feeling down, I would flip open one of the many collections of Mary's work that I owned and let the pages fall where they would. Whatever poem I landed on, I decided would be the message I needed to hear.

Tonight it landed on this:

"It doesn't have to be the blue iris, it could be weeds in a vacant lot, or a few small stones, just pay attention, then patch. A few words together, and don't try and make them elaborate. This isn't a contest, it's a doorway. Into thanks, and a silence in which another voice may speak."

I was familiar with the passage from her famous poem *Praying*. It was such a profoundly simple reminder that understanding comes in paying attention. Not in focusing on the bright and shiny objects glittering like treasured gems, but on the ordinary.

Had I been doing that?

Had I been so caught up in trying to steer a course to my future that I had missed what was right in front of me?

I lingered in the thought, allowing the earthy scent of woodsmoke to envelop me like the cashmere blanket wrapped around my legs. I must have drifted off because I woke later to a dark parlor backlit by the fire's dying embers. I stretched, then returned the poetry book to its spot on the bookcase. The fire had nearly burned out, but I removed the iron poker and stabbed the coals. After I had spread out the remaining charred pieces of wood, I returned the grate to the front of the fireplace. In doing so, a thick stack of paper bound with a rubber band caught my eye. It was tucked in next to a collection of Barbara Kingsolver hardcovers. I'd picked up a copy of *Unsheltered* the other day and never noticed anything next to it.

The stack of papers turned out to be another manuscript, bound with a rubber band like the forsaken pile in Gertrude's office. However, there was something very different about this manuscript. The title immediately sent a cold sensation piercing down my spine. It read: *Emily's Story*.

My knees buckled. The title couldn't be a coincidence. And there was more: unlike the other manuscripts I had edited, this one listed an author at the top—Gertrude Bryant.

Any tiredness that I had been feeling vanished. I removed the rubber band and began reading.

~

Emily's Story

She came into the world, pensive and knowing. Tiny eyes that held a lifetime of wisdom, a tender kindness. Eyes that would lock onto mine as I kissed her soft hair, rocked her in my arms, and soothed her to sleep. This miniature being captured my heart from the moment she was born, binding me to her with an invisible string. In those early days I could have never imagined that the tether might one day remain the only piece of her I had left.

Emily, I write this to you, my dearest granddaughter, whom I raised like a daughter, in hopes that these pages will find their way to you, when it's time and when you're ready. Words and stories were always our connection. From before you could walk, you were a reader. Your parents and I used to marvel at how most babies would gnaw on the cardboard edges of board books, working in their new teeth. Not you. Your pudgy fingers would crack open each page, absorbing the pictures and pointing to each word. "More, more," you would sign when the story ended. It's one of the reasons that this is almost too painful for me to write. When I thought of your future, I never envisioned that I wouldn't be a part of it.

And, yet as is so often true in fiction, it's the unexpected twists, those blindsiding shockers that make us want to turn the page. I wish I could have re-written a different ending. An ending that would have us seated in the breakfast nook with cups of my homemade hot chocolate, which was your favorite bedtime story accompaniment.

By the way, before I continue, I must tell you that it's important for you to know that the secret to incredible hot chocolate is a healthy dab of butter. Good chocolate, whole milk, and a splash of vanilla are essential too, but it's the butter that gives the hot chocolate a special rich creaminess that can't be achieved any other way. Trust me, I've tried. I have also never shared my secret ingredient with anyone, so the choice is yours whether to keep it for yourself (If I might be so bold to suggest, I have found over the years that keeping a few things close to the chest helps to add a spark of mystery and zest to life, especially when it comes to pouring the perfect cup of cocoa. You never know when you'll want to dazzle guests and leave them wanting more.) but as I say, the choice is yours. I'll harbor no harm or ill will if you decide that the secret is too sweet to share. Then again, if this story has found its way to your lap, it's most likely that I'm off to my next incarnation.

It won't seem like this is true, but I have watched every step of your growth and evolution, and I'm so very proud of you, Emily. Yes, my admiration has come from afar, but it doesn't change the deep, deep swell of emotions I have every time I think of you. I don't have many regrets. I've found with age that it's better to embrace the mistakes I've made as lessons, opportunities for self-reflection. Each moment in my life has built on the next. It's writing that's taught me that. My writing, other people's writing, reading, editing. An examined life is life lived through the pages of books.

If you're in Cascata and sitting in my parlor reading this, then you may be wondering about my gift. A gift I knew from the very first day I held you in the hospital room that you had inherited as well. It's not really a gift, Emily. It's a knowing. It's trusting your instinct—that internal compass—knowing that everyone has to not only write their own story but live right in the pages, word for word. Our gift isn't about taking a red editing pen to the page and excising the pieces we don't like. Our gift is guidance.

I left the forsaken manuscripts for you. You'll know what to do with each of them, even if it feels like you don't. The heroes in each of those stories just need a nudge. They don't need more direction. Your job is to help push them forward or off a cliff and they'll take it from there. This is something I learned through many failed attempts to force my broad strokes upon the page. It's the delicate changes that make the difference. You'll learn that soon, if you haven't already.

Don't fear your wisdom. Don't hide from it.

Think of why you're here now in this moment with these pages. Has it been divinely scripted, or did you just need a nudge to connect with the life that you somehow knew you were always missing? When we feel that tug on the invisible string, we can choose to ignore it or we can see where it leads.

I paused momentarily to brush a tear from my eye. Wet salty splotches landed on the manuscript. If I could call it that. It was more like a letter. Or maybe a guidebook? I couldn't be sure, but I felt her love pouring out of the page.

I read on.

Emily, I've spent years dissecting what I might have done differently. There are a million options, an infinite amount of choices I could have made. But I didn't. Not from the lack of wanting to, but from a place of understanding that no amount of editing can change someone else's story, even if that person is someone you love more than you love yourself.

You see, I've been a book therapist, or whatever you want to call it, for many, many years. After your grandfather died, I moved here to Cascata. This was his family home, did you know that? I was grieving his death, and your dad and Danny were both young at the time. I wasn't sure what to do, but I knew I needed a change. I couldn't stay in Los Angeles with two young sons in a house that was chock full of memories of the man I had loved and lost. Cascata felt like a fresh start, and so far away and remote. It was hard. I won't lie. Grief, as you well know, invades every cell in your body and if you let it, will consume you. I nearly let it, but this house saved me. Lost Coast Literary saved me.

I'll try to paint a picture for you. One night not long after we moved in and after a particularly hard cry, the guttural kind (you know, that leaves your abs quivering and your eyes like sand) there was a knock on the door. I had just put the boys to bed, and I didn't know many people in town yet. When I opened it, there was a manuscript sitting on the porch. Bound with a single rubber band. There was no author noted. No return address. Nothing.

I have to admit it was a distraction I needed. I found myself sucked into the story and without thinking, I began to make some edits. I'm sure it won't come as a surprise to you to learn that a day later when I dropped the boys off at school, the very edits I had made on the page happened right in front of my eyes. Does this sound familiar? Did you think you were going crazy? Did the changes you made seem like they were the right thing to do? Were they? Or did the story you wanted to write or imagined that you were helping to finish go completely off the rails? That's what happened to me at first. But then, as more manuscripts would arrive, I began to see a pattern. I began to learn that it wasn't my changes or suggestions that shifted the future, it was putting my pen to the page. My edits weren't the answer. They were the start —a launching point. That first movement that launches a character on their ultimate quest. That was my job.

No matter what edits I made, the story played out from there however it was meant to. Give yourself permission to accept that, truly and deeply at your core. Give yourself permission to let go of the outcome. If you can do that, I am confident that Cascata is where you're supposed to be.

~

I stopped reading when I realized that I had such a tight grip on the pages that the tips of my fingers had turned white. The woman who had written this letter bore a strong resemblance to the grandmother who had lived in my dreams. This was the final confirmation that I needed. I felt her in a way I never had before.

I closed my eyes and drank in the smell of her parlor and the power of her words before reading on.

~

Emily, I'm sure that you want to know about your parents. Your dad and Danny were embarrassed by my storytelling when they were teenagers. Word got round the town that I was a book doctor, or therapist, like I said. I'm pretty sure that's how the manuscripts appeared. I've never known for sure.

Did you know that in Verona, romantics leave letters to Juliet, asking for her guidance in finding love? Isn't that such a lovely thought? In a sixteenth-century courtyard surrounded by ancient brick walls, the forlorn can pay homage to Juliet's statue cast in bronze while casting for answers to their love life. A bright red mailbox receives letters from the love-sick throughout the world and the Secretaries of Juliet answer every letter by hand.

I saw the forsaken manuscripts the same way. People who felt like they had a different story burning inside them to tell, but not knowing how the first scene should be written. Lost Coast Literary became the landing spot for forsaken souls, ready to bring about great change in their lives. Was the change painless? Rarely. But why should it be? Resiliency, that strong muscle, builds from damaging it again and again. Healing it, with the remnants of scars and bruises.

The longer we were here, the more people would talk of my gift. That's one of the reasons I don't like to call it a gift. It embarrassed the boys, your dad the most. He never wanted me to talk about it and did everything he could to avoid being part of any conversation about my work. Let me be clear, the forsaken manuscripts weren't my primary work. I've been blessed with a long career as an editor. My clients have been varied and scattered around the country and globe.

I learned not to talk about the forsaken manuscripts in front of him. It was okay with me. It wasn't his burden. I understand that nearly everything a parent does is mortifying for the teenagers. And certainly re-writing the future had to rank high in the category of embarrassing things your parents do.

That changed when your mom got sick. Oh, Jamie. What a wonderful soul. What a love she and your dad had. Shakespeare couldn't have penned it better. They truly completed one another. Not in a way that they consumed each other, but in a way that lifted them up together.

Stephen came to me and begged me to fix it when the news came through that she was terminal. I explained to him that that wasn't the way it worked. My edits only worked on the forsaken stack, not on anything else any of my clients had ever written. Believe me, I tried to write my own stories, and of course none of my edits on those came to fruition either. That's not how it works.

Oh, how I wish it was. The forsaken manuscripts are different. They always have been. I suspect they always will be.

I didn't have any power to change her diagnosis, no matter how much I wanted to. He was furious with me. He wouldn't talk to me for days and weeks on end. I realize now this is likely when he made the decision to leave, but before he did, I found a manuscript (a short one) waiting on my office desk. He had written it along with a note pleading for me to work my magic, claiming I was the only person who could change Jamie's fate.

Emily, words can't relay how devastated I was, we all were. Your mom was like a daughter to me and seeing her beginning to succumb to the ravages of cancer was the worst thing I've ever had to witness. That and knowing that she wasn't going to be there to watch you grow. I would have done anything to change that, but I couldn't.

Your dad followed through on his promise. He never spoke to me again, and he took you away from me. As you'll see in the pages that follow, no amount of re-writing changed that fact. What I want you to know more than anything is how much I have and will always love you. That's why I'm giving you the house and Lost Coast Literary. I know without a shred of doubt that both will be safe in your hands.

Love,
Gertrude

CHAPTER THIRTY-ONE

*G*randma's words made her feel real, like she was sitting next to me, her hand on my shoulder, her gentle voice calming me. My hands trembled as I stared at the pages. I didn't know where to start in terms of what to take away from her letter. Suddenly it made sense why Dad had been so insistent that I take a practical job. Why he clammed up when I asked him about Grandma and what she'd done. He'd been heartbroken over losing Mom and turned to his own mom for help. He must have seen her explanation as a refusal. I felt terrible for both of them.

When I flipped through the remaining pages of the manuscript, I felt even worse. The first few pages were Dad's story. They ended with Mom's terminal diagnosis, but it was hard to decipher because Gertrude's handwriting covered each page. She had tried, again and again. Not just attempting to change Mom's fate, but ours too. There were passages from the funeral. Instead of her and Danny and Keeshawna, hiding in the back, there were scenes of reunions. Of our life rebuilt together. Of our returning to Cascata. Of her teaching me, passing on her editing pen. Of a contented connection with my extended family. Garden parties, bonfires on the beaches, her holding me as we cried together on the anniversary of Mom's death each year. Marking the bitterness and the beauty of missing her with bagels with slug slime and Mom's favorite almond cake.

Nothing she edited or tried to re-write had come true. The pages were muddled with her many attempts, obviously over years. Different colored pens filled the margins. Entire sections of the manuscript had been crossed out and written again.

Why hadn't she told Dad?

Or had she?

Would it have mattered?

I bundled the tear-stained pages together again and secured them with the rubber band. It was a lot to digest, but there was one thing I felt solid about and that was that the minute that Dad arrived, I was going to force him to read my story. Mom and Grandma were both dead. I had lived too long without a female force to guide me. In her words, Grandma had brought them both back. Neither woman was a mystical, half-sketched fictional character that I had constantly been trying to color in any longer. They were both a part of me. No one could take that away and more importantly, I could carry them forward with me.

I went to bed ruminating on that knowledge and wondering if Grandma's final words could be true—could I be happy here?

The next morning I woke with a lightness that I hadn't felt in years. Shay and I agreed to meet at Oceanic at nine. When I got to the coffee shop, she and Tamir were laughing at the counter. I snuck up behind her and tapped her on the shoulder. I had stopped to pick up a bundle of fresh sunflowers at the corner kiosk on my walk over. "These are for you." I handed her the flowers when she turned around.

"Emily, that's so sweet. You didn't need to." She wrapped me in a hug.

"You deserve congratulatory flowers," Tamir said, beaming at Shay. "On that note, coffee is on me this morning."

"Thanks." Shay gave him a fist bump and dragged me to a

table. She set the flowers down and stared at me. "You look different this morning."

"How?"

"I don't know. Softer?"

"I'll take that." I rubbed the base of my neck. "I found a letter from Grandma last night."

"A letter?" She leaned closer. "Where?"

I told her about finding the manuscript, and how it had confirmed everything I had come to understand about our grandmother.

"Damn, Emily," Shay sniffed through her tears. Her eyes were dewy. "That's beautiful, and so sad."

I reached for her hand and squeezed it tight. "You were right all along. Grandma brought us together." My voice caught in my throat. "To the Bryant cousins."

She squeezed mine back. "We're going to do amazing things and make her proud."

Tamir came by with coffees for us. "These are my signature confetti lattes." He placed the drinks in front of us.

"Dare I ask what's in a confetti latte?" I asked.

"It's your classic latte with confetti sprinkles for future podcast stars." He shared a look with Shay that made me fairly confident he wasn't upset about spending time with her either, before heading back to his post.

Shay cradled her mug after Tamir left. "That's not fair that your dad wouldn't listen."

"Yeah, I agree, and I also have a new sense of his role after reading the manuscript. I think it's what was supposed to play out. Maybe for both of us."

"What now?"

"Well, he's coming on Sunday so things are either going to get better or a whole lot worse."

"I guess we really need a bash on Saturday, huh?"

We spent the next hour reviewing our guest list, food, and costume ideas. I wanted to invite everyone whose story I had touched. It felt like the thing I needed to do. For closure for myself and for them. And I wanted to honor Grandma's memory in the best way I knew how. A Lost Coast Literary party, complete with bookish bites, fairy lights, and music. My grandmother might be dead, but for the first time in my life, I finally felt like I knew her.

CHAPTER THIRTY-TWO

$\mathcal{S}$hay and I spent the next two days running around town, getting everything we needed for the party. The Ballad didn't need much to make it magical, but strings of golden lights and outdoor tables draped with white tablecloths and center-pieces with purple hydrangeas did the trick. Keeshawna had agreed to perform a set of Grandma's favorite songs. The three of us had been cooking for hours to create a seed cake from *Jane Eyre*, pickled limes from *Little Women*, roasted chicken from Heming-way's *A Moveable Feast*, even a potato peel pie from one of Shay's and my more recent favorites, *The Guernsey Literary and Potato Peel Society*. I had recruited Aaron to set up a bar with literary-themed cocktails.

When the night of the party finally arrived, we appraised our costumes in the garden. We decided to dress up like Elizabeth and Jane Bennet in matching empire waist dresses with dainty flowers in our hair. Wispy layers of cream organza embellished with elegant silver beads gave Shay an ethereal glow.

"I'm an actual Goddess tonight." She spun in a circle, her open-toed sandals leaving imprints in the grass. "Sige is glowing up right now."

To be honest, I felt a bit like a goddess, too. We had discovered the vintage dresses on a sale rack in one of the antique shops on the plaza. Mine was pale blue with whispers of moss green embroidery along the waist and sleeves. I had tied my hair up with a ribbon, allowing tendrils to fall loosely along the side of my cheeks.

When Tamir arrived in a Shakespeare costume, complete with tights and a feathered cap, Shay clapped and kissed my cheek. "That's my cue. You don't mind if I ditch you, do you?"

"I would be seriously offended if you didn't." I waved to Tamir, who tipped his felt cap to me as Shay raced up to him and embraced him in a giant hug.

Danny came as Bilbo Baggins with Hobbit ears and a red velvet coat. Arty showed up, not in costume but rather in a trim suit that gave him a debonair air as if he belonged on the pages of an Ian Fleming novel.

I pulled him aside as the rest of the guests began to arrive. "Can we please call a truce?"

He shrugged. "That depends on what you're going to do about this place."

"Honestly, I don't know yet." I fiddled with a single silver bracelet, reflecting on how much had changed in such a short time. "Arty, here's the thing. I've learned a lot about Grandma, and I think I understand where you're coming from. I really do, although I don't think that completely absolves you from being pretty terrible to me."

"Trust me. Mom's been all over me about that." He hung his head. "It's been hard, though, losing her and then feeling like we're going to lose The Ballad, too."

"You're not." I was surprised by how quickly the words escaped my lips. "Look, I'm hoping tonight can be the beginning of a fresh start. I want to give it some time before I make any final decisions." I paused for a moment, wanting to make sure I said the right thing. "I want to give us some time, I guess, is what I'm trying to say. Maybe we can start over. Get to know each other better. I have some brainstorms about The Ballad that I think we should talk about if you're up for it?" I tried to convey my willingness to compromise with a timid smile.

"Yeah." He nodded and fixed his gaze on the porch where a group of partygoers was sipping cocktails. "I'm up for it, and for what it's worth, I'm sorry."

My chest felt lighter. It was almost like my need to hold tight to my past struggles had finally loosened its grip. "I get why this place is special to you. Being here has changed me. I feel her here, too."

He smiled genuinely for the first time. It transformed his face. "Grandma always told me that I was one of the rare people in the world who feel the energy of a place. She knew how attached I was to this house. That's why this has been hard for me."

I rubbed my arms as the cool evening breeze fluttered through the strands of twinkle lights. "It's been hard for me, too, but I think your dad was right. I think Grandma knew that if I came, we'd all find a way forward."

"Probably. That sounds like her." He grinned genuinely. Then his tone turned nostalgic. "I loved her, you know. I guess it's just been hard to wrap my head around you. You've been gone. You didn't have a relationship with her like Shay and me. I guess it's not fair to any of us. Mom has been reminding me of how lucky I was to have had Grandma for my whole life."

"Yeah, that's fair." I could see the pain on his face. Grief etched its permanent mark, like a tattoo. It was a look I knew all too well. "Let's sit down over coffee tomorrow. I think there's a future for The Ballad that could be good for all of us."

"Coffee, tomorrow, okay."

He gave me a fist bump, and then he headed for the food table. It wasn't exactly one of the tear-jerking reunions that Grandma had tried to write, but it was a start, which was all I needed.

Cameron arrived as Sherlock. He had tucked his hair beneath a plaid deerstalker cap. A pipe rested between his teeth.

"Nice party. Gertrude would be proud."

"Thanks." I glanced around the garden, which glowed in

dreamy, golden light. Music fluttered overhead, and a symphony of delicious aromas wafted from the food tables. "I felt like I needed to do this for her, but also for me, you know?"

"I do." He tapped his pipe to his teeth. "Have you made any decisions yet?"

"No. I've got some stuff to deal with first, but I think I want to take a bit more time to think about things."

"Smart. Watson would approve." Cameron smiled.

Danny interrupted us. He handed me a cocktail. "Great party, Emily. You and Shay have outdone yourselves." With that, he raised his drink in a toast. "To you."

"To Grandma." I clinked my glass to his.

His eyes widened in surprise. "To Mom."

Cameron joined in. "To Cascata." He swirled the burgundy wine in his glass.

"Hey, about that, have you two been plotting together?" I looked from Danny to Cameron. It was strange to think that they had both been strangers to me a short time ago. Now they felt like old friends.

"How so?" Danny's forehead wrinkled with worry.

"Come on. Cameron practically begged me not to sell. What real estate agent does that? Then you came up with such a cool idea for the property, and it was almost like you guys had thought it out in advance." I paused and took a sip of my cocktail. "And, Cameron, was it a ploy to get me to go to Ferndale, or did you have grander visions for this place all along?"

Cameron shot Danny a sheepish grin.

"Not plotting, but when Cameron told me about the property in Ferndale, I may have suggested he take you to see it, that's all," Danny admitted in a pacifying tone. "Think of it more like buying time. Mom wanted you here while you were editing the manuscripts. I figured you and Cameron would be fast friends with your mutual love of books. You needed to be able to experience Cascata and immerse yourself in our world in order to make the right decision for you. And we needed to be able to get to know you and help you see that we really do want to build a relationship. Like I've said from the beginning, you're a Bryant. You're stuck with us, whether you like it or not, sweet niece."

I leaned in to give him a half hug, and he planted a kiss on the top of my head.

Cameron got swept into another conversation. I noticed that he and Sienna, who came as Nancy Drew, locked eyes a few times but otherwise kept their distance. I suspected that nothing would come of their beach meet-cute for a while. But, as sad as both he and Martine had been about the dissolution of their marriage, Grandma's letter made me realize that maybe his meet-up with Sienna had been what they'd both needed to push themselves forward. The words had taken care of it without me.

Danny drifted over to listen to Keeshawna's first set.

I bumped into Lindi, who had opted for a pair of jeans, boots, and a soft pale purple hoodie. "Sorry. I'm not really a costume kind of person, but Brayden was excited to dress up." Her son, who was dressed as a train conductor, grasped her hand tightly as she introduced him to me. "Brayden, this is my friend, Emily." She caught my eye and gave me a look of thanks.

I knelt to shake Brayden's hand. "Nice to meet you, Mr. Conductor."

Brayden gave me a shy smile. "I'm Thomas, the tank engine."

"You are. Sorry, I should have said nice to meet you, *Thomas*."

"He loves the Thomas the Train books," Lindi said to me. "We've read the same book at least twenty times."

"That's my kind of reader. You can never read a book too many times, in my opinion." I winked at Brayden.

He dropped Lindi's hand and went to join some kids to play with the bubble wands and chalk that Shay had wisely suggested we put out.

"How is everything going? Any more run-ins with Kenzie's mom?" I studied her face. Her eyes looked a bit brighter, and her cheeks less sunken.

She glanced at Aaron pouring drinks behind the makeshift bar. "Did you hear?"

"Hear what?"

"Aaron was right. The media picked up the story. It already ran in a few smaller papers. Now it's going to be on the front of the living section in the *San Francisco Chronicle* tomorrow, and someone set up a GoFundMe page for us. It already has close to ten thousand dollars in it. I'm going to be able to pay for half of the year's rent and all his medical bills. I can't believe it."

"That's great news. You deserve it."

"I don't know about that, but I know I'm going to use the money for good." Her jaw was set, and her face was filled with determination.

"I'm sure you will." I placed my hand on her arm. "If there's anything else I can do, please let me know."

Movement caught my eye. I gasped and threw my hand over my mouth as I glanced to see Dad coming toward me. He was dressed in a casual pair of jeans and a fleece. I recognized his slow and measured stride as he cut through the crowd. His face refused to betray a single emotion.

A prickling sensation spread along the back of my neck. He was here. He was really here.

"Sorry, I have to go," I said to Lindi and walked to greet him, barely noticing my feet making contact with the ground. The sinking sun cast a halo around his body like he was an apparition.

I ignored the urge to pinch myself or flee.

"Dad," I whispered.

"Em." He wrapped me in a hug and held on tight. I let my body collapse in his firm grasp, drinking in the smell of dirt and sunscreen.

"I, I thought you were coming tomorrow. Why didn't you tell me you were on your way?"

"Sorry, I was worried that I was going to chicken out." He released me, scraping his hand through his hair. "I didn't know you were throwing a party." He raised his eyebrows above his glasses as he surveyed the festive scene.

"Dad, listen, we have to talk." I glanced around. Everyone appeared to be enjoying themselves. The hum of happy laughter and Keeshawna's soulful voice filled the garden. People danced in front of the gazebo. Brayden and the other kids darted between guests, squealing with delight as they played tag on the dewy grass. "Uh, let's go inside."

He didn't answer but followed after me with a nod, continuing his long, slow pace as if we were part of a procession.

Emotions threatened to overtake me, like the waves crashing on the shore nearby. He was here in Cascata, after all these years. This was it, the face-to-face I'd been waiting for, and yet suddenly, I found myself at a loss for words.

When I opened the front door to The Ballad and stepped inside, he let out an audible sigh. I watched as his mouth opened and closed. He gave his head a quick shake like he didn't believe this was happening either.

"Should we sit in the parlor?" I asked, noticing that his hands were trembling.

His lips pressed together in a grimace like he was trying to hold back a swell of emotions, too. I reached for his hand. It was cold and clammy. A feeling of confidence washed over me—I needed to take control. This was my narrative. "Come with me, Dad. Let's talk."

His eyes drifted to the ceiling as we entered the parlor, his hand clutched tightly in mine. "She changed some things in here. Danny and I used to call this the brown room."

"The brown room?" My pulse pounded in my throat. I could feel my cheeks beginning to warm. I needed to show him Grandma's story. I needed to help him understand how much she had tried. How much she had loved him.

"Everything was brown." He let out a strangled-sounding laugh. "The walls were brown, the bookshelves were brown, the floor was brown, and the ceiling was brown. It was dark and depressing." He dropped my hand.

"It's not now. It's beautiful, don't you think?" I ran my fingers over the wallpaper, keeping my voice soft.

"Emily, I'm so sorry that I got you into this." He pinched the bridge of his nose where his glasses rested and closed his eyes. "I've been thinking a lot the past couple of weeks, and this is my fault. I should have warned you that nothing but unhappiness comes from my family."

"Dad, I don't think that's true." I sat down on the couch and motioned for him to do the same. A calmness had taken over. It felt like Gertrude was guiding me, and I was happy to let her lead. "Do you know that I have Grandma's gift?"

His gaze flittered around the room, never settling on any one thing for long. He clutched the edge of the couch when his eyes finally landed on me. "What do you mean?"

"You know what I mean, Dad." The conviction in my voice surprised me. Something had shifted.

He sighed, then ran his hands over the top of his jeans. "Em, it doesn't work. It just leads to more unhappiness." He trailed off.

"There's something you need to read, okay? I think it will explain a lot." I stood and went to get the manuscript. "Before you say anything else, read this. In its entirety. Then we'll talk, okay?"

He frowned, but he took the manuscript. I studied his rugged jaw, and the lines etched around his eyes. It was impossible not to notice how his hands quivered as he read the story that both of us had been missing for the better part of our lives.

I held my breath, hoping that Gertrude's words might crack through his emotional armor. It finally came when he got to the last pages. He looked from the paper to me and back again. "She tried to change Mom's story?" His voice was thick with disbelief.

"Dad, she tried." My voice sounded far away like it wasn't coming from me. "She tried for her entire life. Look at how many sections have been crossed out and re-written. The thing I don't understand is why she never told you."

"What do you mean?" He tightened his grip on the pages. Then he rubbed his chest as if his heart physically hurt.

"I mean, if she lost us and tried this hard to fix it, why didn't she ever tell you? Why didn't she reach out and try to tell you in person, not just in words?"

He hung his head. "She did. I wouldn't listen."

Years of grief forced his shoulders to collapse as tears ran down his weathered cheeks. I hadn't seen him cry since Mom's funeral, but the floodgates had been opened, and the tears poured out. His neck crumpled as he sobbed.

My vision tunneled. A lump that had been forming in my throat broke free with a wave of salty tears. I didn't try to hold them in.

Shockingly, neither did he.

"Em, I couldn't forgive her." He wiped his nose on the back of his sleeve. "I tried. I really did. There were dozens of times when I picked up the phone and started to dial her number, but then I chickened out and hung up. I've probably written her at least fifty letters over the years that I never sent over the years. I wish I had a better answer for you, but I just couldn't face Cascata, not without your mom." He shook his head as more guttural sobs erupted, shaking his entire body and the couch.

Watching him crack open made me cry harder. My nose dripped like a sieve. Heat rushed to my cheeks. It was hard to breathe, but I felt strangely comforted. This is what I needed. This is what I had been waiting for.

He closed his eyes and took a long, slow breath. "I couldn't face Mom, Danny, any of them. Every room in this house holds a memory of your mom. Every place in the plaza, the beach, the redwoods contains a little piece of Jamie. This place is alive with my memories of her. It was too much for me. I couldn't handle it. I couldn't face this house or this town that remains here without her. She was strong. Not me. She would have hated what I've become. She would have hated that I kept you from here."

I clasped his hand. He squeezed mine in return so tightly that I thought he might crack my pinkie in half. I didn't care. His hands were rough. His fingernails held a smidge of dirt. His gripping touch was the only thing I needed at this moment.

We sat knee to knee on the sofa, crying together. I wasn't sure whether I was crying for me, for him, for Mom, or Grandma. Maybe for all of us.

Everything around us vanished like in a dream. The sound of laughter and music in the garden and the aromas of food and salty sea air disappeared. I couldn't believe how long we'd both allowed our grief to become like a myth—a singular plotline. As tears continued to flow, I watched how vulnerable his face had become. Our roles had reversed. He was my parent, but I could see how desperately he needed parenting.

Time felt fuzzy. I wasn't sure how long we'd been sitting in our own sorrows when he finally broke the silence.

"Em, I'm so sorry." His voice was shaky. "I don't know what happened. I guess I blamed Mom. She was easy to blame because she accepted it. She bore my grief and sadness for me. How terrible is that? I let her carry my pain for me. I stopped being angry at her years ago, but I couldn't bring myself to make it right. I knew that to do that, I would have to come here, and I couldn't do it. I couldn't make that drive up the 101 and not see your mom's face grinning at me as she named each elk we would pass or hear her giggle when she would tease me about being her own personal Mr. Darcy. She was right, you know? The only difference was that I never evolved like Darcy. I stayed stuck, and you paid the price."

My thoughts went to my conversation with Arty. His words about his attachment to the house thudded in my head. He and Dad were alike. Maybe that was another Bryant family trait. "I get it, Dad." For the first time, that was true. I leaned into him. He smelled of Ivory soap, mint toothpaste, and dirt.

His grip on my shoulder was firm and steady like he was doing his best to try and hold us both upright. "I was so angry that she was sick. Why? Why did it have to be her? There are so many horrible, awful people in the world. Why her? She was kind, caring, loving to everyone she met. She was my soul. She was everything. Why?" His sad eyes held mine. "She loved you more than anything. You know that, right?"

I pressed my hand to my chest. "I know."

"I couldn't begin to replace her. I didn't know how, so I just didn't." He sighed, inhaling deeply to try to regain control of his emotions. "That's why I took you to Santa Clara. Some of it was selfish. I couldn't face staying in Cascata without her, but I thought you would be better off with her family. I thought that would provide you with a lifeline to her. In hindsight, I see that was wrong."

I let my head fall onto his shoulder as he wrapped his arm around me tighter like a solid fortress.

We stayed in our two-person huddle for a while, his hand massaging my head, our tears spilling out in rhythm.

"I'm sorry, Em. I'm so sorry." His voice was tender.

"Me too, Dad." I sat up and pulled away from him. "The thing is, Dad, I'm pretty sure it's random. Mom. Cancer. The good stuff. The bad stuff. It's random. It's out of our control. That's what the manuscripts have been trying to teach me. That's what Grandma wanted me to learn by coming here. That we make our own destiny. Maybe sometimes we need a little nudge, but the rest is up to us."

"If only I could go back." His chin trembled. "If I had known about this." His eyes drifted to the pages.

"Dad, don't." I grabbed his hand and helped him stand. "That's the thing. I think we're supposed to go forward."

He kissed the top of my head. "How did you get so wise?"

I grinned and nodded to the wall of bookshelves. "Books."

A smile tugged at his cheeks. "Just like your mom and your grandma."

"Exactly."

With that, I led him outside to the garden, where I knew Danny, Keeshawna, Arty, and Shay were waiting. I knew this definitely wasn't the end of my story, but I had learned one thing for sure. I was okay with not knowing—with not scripting—what came next. The forsaken manuscripts had taught me that. This was the first step. The first sentence on a page that would launch an entirely new story.

We'd spent too much time looking behind us. I was ready to turn the page to my next chapter.

EPILOGUE

$\mathcal{I}$ sat at my desk, my fingers numb from making suggestions in the margins of the first book that I had acquired. Sunlight streamed through the bay windows. The repetitive sound of the waves lapping on the coastline brought a smile to my face and an ongoing calm to my body. I glanced at the new sign Arty was installing on the spacious front lawn: LITERARY LIBATIONS & LODGINGS. Was it too much alliteration? Maybe, but then again, it perfectly captured The Ballad's new mission.

I finished some brief line edits and then reviewed my editorial letter. My feedback to the author began with three paragraphs of pure gushing.

"I loved this book. I adored this book, and I know that readers will, too."

Were there small things that the author could consider to make it stronger?

Absolutely.

It was my job to point those out. To give the author a sense of what was working and areas they might consider revising or places where they could step deeper into the character's world.

I chuckled as I read my sentiments. Phrases like "you might consider" and "unfortunately, I don't have the answer for you, perhaps it lies somewhere in the love triangle you've created, but I'll leave it to you to decide."

My words sounded so familiar. Grandma's influence was evident in my broad strokes. What a gift I had inherited, and I wasn't talking about The Ballad. Before coming to Cascata, I never would have considered the weight and responsibility of my editing pen. The forsaken manuscripts had taught me not to take my ability to transform stories lightly. These notes on the page, these scribbled marks, came from somewhere within me and outside of me. Once I sent my suggestions into the world, it was up to the author, the characters, and ultimately readers to write the rest of their stories.

This story represented the next chapter in my life. I tucked my editorial letter in front of the edited manuscript and wrapped the pages together with a pale purple rubber band. Then I added a handwritten note to the author on a creamy notecard stamped with a picture of The Ballad.

"Thank you for the opportunity to read *I Find You Tolerable* and for letting me be a part of sharing Jane's revised story. As a long-time Austen fan, I firmly believe that this novel gives readers the ending we've all been wishing for. I loved watching Jane transform on the page as she learns who she really is and takes the scary leap from writing about fictional love to finding lasting love.

I can't wait to see this on bookshelves, and I'm so excited that you're our first Lost Coast Literary title. I hope that you're ready for a book bash here. All of Cascata is excited to celebrate with you.

Congratulations and happy editing,

Emily Bryant

Editor, Lost Coast Literary"

ACKNOWLEDGMENTS

Lost Coast Literary is the first book that's ever come to me in a dream. I woke up on a warm summer July morning in 2020. That's right, 2020. I had been having vivid pandemic dreams, but this was different. Emily and her entire story felt like they'd been downloaded to my brain overnight. So I made a strong pot of coffee and went straight to work outlining the story and everything I could remember from the dream before it vanished.

Even though I've written dozens of books, the process of bringing Emily's story to life was so unique. It felt like I was venturing into unknown territory. It was exhilarating and terrifying. And, yet through every draft and re-write, her voice was clear in my head, like she was my personal editor, nudging me onward.

I'm deeply grateful that I've had a community of friends, readers, and writers who have helped strengthen Emily's narrative and cheered me on along the way. To Erin Cox, Kelly Sacks, and my dad (who brought his red editing pen out of retirement) for reading very early drafts and recognizing the threads of the story amongst everything that needed to be fixed. To Kim Stein for her insight into living on California's Lost Coast. To Shalini Gopal for her initial readthrough that really sparked the heart of the story and set me on Emily's path of self-discovery.

To the beta reading team at Quiet House Editing—Stacey, Katherine, and Christina—for providing early thoughts and suggestions, which gave me hope that Emily's story was beginning to take shape.

I can't say enough about Lily Choi. Her editing lens made me wonder if Gertrude is actually real. Working with Lily was like the best book therapy session ever. Her light touch paired with innate wisdom was the nudge I needed to make Emily's story my own.

My creative writing professor in college once told me that I needed to become intimately acquainted with the comma, a skill I have yet to acquire. Fortunately, Raina Glazener's copyedit ensured that all those pesky commas and grammatical errors were tied up before publication.

When I visited the Lost Coast for the first time, I was utterly captivated by the stunning Victorian architecture set against the rugged coastline. Jennifer Anne Nelson was able to take my vision for The Ballad and transform it into magical watercolor cover art. Every time I see the cover, I imagine Emily curled up in front of the fire with a book in hand.

Living with a writer isn't always easy, especially when the writer spends her days escaping to fictional worlds and tends to linger there long past the time she's shut down her computer and left her office. This book wouldn't have been possible without Gordy and Luke, who trekked to California with me on research trips, listened to endless plot ideas, and fell in love with Emily's story, too. I'm endlessly grateful for both of you.

On that note of gratitude, books and my bookish community have been my safe harbor during times of such disconnection. A special shoutout to my Tuesday night crew for all the fun, tears, and laughter. Books brought us together at a time when everything else in the world felt wrong. I'm forever indebted to you for being a point of light and joy in the darkness.

And to you for picking up this book and joining Emily on her journey to find the story that lives within her. May you find yours.

With love,

Ellie

DISCUSSION QUESTIONS

When we first meet Emily, she's consumed by books. Do you think books have helped or hindered her personal growth?

What do you think of Emily's habit of rewriting endings to books that have made her sad? Have you ever wanted to rewrite the ending of a book?

What would you do if you had Emily's ability to edit stories and impact real people's lives?

Books play a significant role in Emily's story. Have you read any of the books referenced in *Lost Coast Literary*, and if so, did they resonate with you?

Where do you think the forsaken manuscripts have come from? Do you believe that these stories were resolved once Emily gave them a nudge instead of a complete rewrite?

Even though Gertrude is dead, how do you feel like Emily's relationship with her grandmother evolved through the book?

How do you feel about the rest of Emily's family? What's their role in Emily's journey?

Cascata is a fictional world. If it were real, would you want to visit?

What do you think happens next? The ending of the book is open to interpretation. Do you think there's a reason for this?

If you had a chance to edit your own narrative, would you?

ABOUT THE AUTHOR

Ellie Alexander is a voracious storyteller and a lover of words and all things bookish. She believes that stories have the ability to transport and transform us. With over twenty-six published novels and counting, her goal is to tell stories that provide points of connection, escape, and understanding.

facebook.com/elliealexanderauthor

twitter.com/ellielovesbooks

instagram.com/ellie_alexander

youtube.com/elliealexanderauthor

tiktok.com/@elliealexanderauthor

pinterest.com/elliealexanderauthor

goodreads.com/elliealexanderauthor

bookbub.com/authors/ellie-alexander

amazon.com/author/elliealexander

ALSO BY ELLIE ALEXANDER

THE BAKESHOP MYSTERIES

Meet Your Baker

A Batter of Life and Death

On Thin Icing

Caught Bread Handed

Fudge and Jury

A Crime of Passion Fruit

Another One Bites the Crust

Till Death Do Us Tart

Live and Let Pie

A Cup of Holiday Fear

Nothing Bundt Trouble

Chilled to the Cone

Mocha, She Wrote

Bake, Borrow, and Steal

Donut Disturb

THE SLOAN KRAUSE MYSTERIES

Death On Tap

The Pint of No Return

Beyond a Reasonable Stout

Without a Brew

The Cure for What Ales You

Hold on for Beer Life

CPSIA information can be obtained
at www.ICGtesting.com
Printed in the USA
BVHW080758130423
662286BV00017B/1103